TRIUMPH OF BLOOD!

Against Conan, three Picts had no more chance than three goats against a lion. None of them ran, so they died all the more swiftly. Conan threw a spear that impaled one Pict through the back of the neck, until the spearhead burst the head in a shower of blood and teeth. He threw a stone that caught the second Pict just above his loincloth. The Pict tumbled and ran into a tree hard enough to knock himself senseless.

This left the last Pict alone, with nothing to do but fight. He did this with a warrior's courage, but the descending sweep of Aquilonian steel sheared through shoulder and ribs into the man's belly.

Conan put his foot on the last Pict's ribs and jerked his sword free. His grin was a leopard's.

"Now I'm beginning to feel better!"

Conan Adventures by Tor Books

CONAN

AT THE
DEMON'S GATE

BY
ROLAND
GREEN

A TOM DOHERTY ASSOCIATES BOOK
NEW YORK

This is a work of fiction. All the characters and events portrayed in this book are fictitious, and any resemblance to real people or events is purely coincidental.

CONAN AT THE DEMON'S GATE

Copyright © 1994 by Conan Properties, Inc.

Cover art by Keegan
Maps by Chazaud

A Tor Book
Published by Tom Doherty Associates, Inc.
175 Fifth Avenue
New York, NY 10010

Tor Books on the World Wide Web:
http://www.tor.com

Tor® is a registered trademark of Tom Doherty Associates, Inc.

ISBN: 0-812-52491-8

First mass market edition: August 1996

Printed in the United States of America

0 9 8 7 6 5 4 3 2 1

"It is said that in another continuum:

". . . mighty Conan bold is Sergeant of United States Marines."

So this tale of his adventures is dedicated to the Sergeants of the United States Marine Corps.

Prologue

The Pictish Wilderness, in the reign of Conan the Second, known as Conn:

My name is Nidaros, son of one who did not care to acknowledge me. Likely enough he was a noble with a full purse and influence at Court, both of which he used for my advancement. Otherwise I might be in the ranks of the Tenth Black River Guards instead of commanding a company.

On the edge of the Pictish Wilderness, the patrols beyond the outpost line wait for spring. The Picts in their native forests are no easy prey even when one does not have to fight the snow and cold as well.

In the sixth year of the reign of Conn, son of Conan, King of Aquilonia, Great Count of Poitain, Protector of Bossonia, and bearer of too many other titles to burden you with here, spring came early. It was decided (I do not know by whom, and it hardly matters anyway) that we should begin our patrols at once.

I looked from the sky to the face of the messenger (an officer of the elite Black Dragons, the royal bodyguards) and back to the sky.

"At once?"

"At once."

"The ground is not yet dry enough to let a soldier put one foot in front of another."

"That does not seem to stop the Picts. They have already raided farms along Silver Creek."

I wished, not aloud, that demons fly away with Silver Creek and all its Poitainian colonists. I cannot believe that any part of Poitain is so crowded that folk with their wits about them would flee to a land where a Pict can spit in their soup kettles any evening.

The messenger seemed to read my thoughts. He tapped the seal on the parchment. I did not suspect forgery, only the wits of whoever penned the command.

"As it is ordered, so it shall be done," I said. "But the wet ground is a fact that all the generals of ten realms cannot alter. A barefoot Pict can skip lightly where a booted and battle-ready soldier will sink."

"The orders do not say how the patrols shall be equipped," the man said. "Or how far they shall go."

I must have gaped. A Black Dragon with his wits about him was a marvel, like a two-headed calf, or a babe with one arm a bird's wing. The man replied with a grin and a shrug.

"I have kin who fought the Picts when Conan the Great commanded on the border," he said. Those kin told many tales around the fireside, and I have not forgotten all I heard then."

"Nor have I forgotten what became of friends who

sought dry ground and ran into a Pictish ambush," I said. I added a few details, half-expecting the man to turn pale and excuse himself. Since the wars of Conan's early reign, the Black Dragons have mostly stayed close to the palace. Few of this man's apparent years (ten less than my forty) were battle-seasoned.

Instead, he nodded. "I never thought my kin lied, but hearing and seeing are not the same." He frowned. "The next fort is my last duty. If you have not led out your men when I return, may I come with you?"

"If you are your own master—" I began.

"I am," he said.

I could hardly put into words my suspicion that he was a spy for one of rank, perhaps even for one at Court. Nor in truth did I feel any great desire to do so. I trusted my men (half Bossonians, half the best sort of Gunderman mercenaries) and my sergeants as I did myself.

Barring ill luck, no bad reports would return to this fellow's master. If ill luck did come, nothing and no one would return from the wilderness at all.

Moreover, this man looked to be a worthy addition to our ranks. I judged he might have had Gunderman, or even Cimmerian, blood himself, from his height and breadth of shoulder. I could not see his hair under a rain-sodden hood, nor his eyes clearly in the dim lamp-light of my hut.

The mail I glimpsed at his wrists seemed well-wrought, though, the sword and dagger on his belt were both for use rather than show, and his riding clothes had seen long journeys if not hard fighting. None of these would keep a Pictish arrow from his gizzard if his luck was not in, but they showed he did not trust alto-gether to luck. Such a man knew the first lesson of bor-der warfare, and so might live to learn others.

"You will be welcome. Make haste, though. If we march swiftly enough, we may catch some of the woodsrunners' hunting parties. No Pict is ever easy prey, but one with an empty belly gives honest men a fighting chance."

As a toast to his safe journey and good hunting afterward, we drank the last wine fit to offer a guest. My second sergeant saw him to his horse while the first and third turned out the men.

Battlements of thundercloud rose to the west the morning we at last found the Picts, or they found us.

They found us at a disadvantage, because we were a watering party of twenty. I led, because it was my turn, and Sarabos of the Black Dragons came because he wished it. I did not wish to have two leaders away from the camp at the same time, but one could argue that Sarabos had no real rank.

The men obeyed him readily enough, however, when the Picts struck. This was just after we had picked our next campsite, a stretch of open ground at the foot of a frowning rocky hill.

They came out of the woods howling fit to waken the dead and put the living in their tombs, behind a shower of arrows and throwing-spears. Knowing that our bows had the range of theirs, they waited until the lay of the ground and the pattern of the trees let them slip close, all in that silence that none except cats and Picts on the hunt can maintain.

Our archers had time for but one flight before five times their number of Picts let loose. The Picts still favor flint for their arrowheads, but try telling a man struck deep by one that it is a child's weapon. That we suffered little was due more to the stoutness of our armor than the weakness of the Picts' weapons.

The Picts were of two different clans, and as is often the case, one attacked a trifle before the other. So we had warning and escaped being surrounded, although by the margin of the thinnest hair in the mane of a new-born foal. We turned and ran for the best place at hand for defense, that open ground at the foot of the outcrop.

Our archery took some of the heart out of the first clan, not to mention leaving two-score warriors kicking or still among the ferns and rotted logs. We covered some hundreds of paces through tangled second growth with only one man dead, his comrades able to carry him, and no one else hurt past fighting.

Then the second clan attacked, without the warning of an arrow shower but instead charging from cover to reach close quarters almost at once. As with most Picts, they wore feathers and tattoos, breechclouts and war paint, and precious little else. But more of them than I cared to see had swords and knives of metal, sometimes their own bronze or copper, sometimes captured steel.

I do not know how long the fight lasted. I had my broadsword, a short-handled mace, and good Aquilonian mail with a helm of Zingaran style standing between me and the Picts. All did good service, too. I know I slew a fair hand'sworth and more, and took only two grazes in return.

Others were less fortunate. Six of us died or were hurt past fighting in that brawl at close quarters. It ended in our favor because, as was most often the case, the two clans' war parties had leapt into battle without any common plan. Most Pictish chiefs would sooner serve up their sons in a stew than take orders from another chief.

So there was no one to tell the first clan to hold their arrows until the second had drawn away from us. The first clan began shooting again, and their arrows rained down alike on friend and foe. Foes mostly bore armor, although a Gunderman died with an arrow in the eye. Friends were mostly naked, and another score of Picts died howling or moaning with Pictish arrows through their gizzards.

Sarabos leapt into the midst of this fratricidal slaughter with a broadsword in one hand and a long dagger in the other. I saw him behead one Pict, geld a second, chop the arm from a third, and break the leg of a fourth with a kick like a mule's, all in one continuous flow of movement. A circle grew around him, inhabited only by the dead or those about to die.

At last he sheathed his weapons, hoisted the fallen Gunderman over one shoulder like a miller hoisting a sack of grain, and pointed toward the rocks.

"I thought I heard you bid us withdraw that way," he said to me. "I see at least one cave in that ravine to the south." With a long arm covered in other men's blood, he pointed.

His eyes were keener than mine, and his ears had heard no such orders, but I thanked him with a nod for saving my authority over my surviving men. I put myself with the rearguard while Sarabos and his burden led, and we tramped up the slope.

It was my plan, formed in my mind as we moved, to climb to the crest of the rocks and light our smoke torches. That would tell the camp where we were, and they would be up with us long before the surviving Picts could muster numbers or courage to come at us on the high ground.

Conan the Great had a favorite saying: "A man can think out a battle beforehand as much as he pleases, but Fate will still spit in the beer." (Although he did not say "spit.") He never called it his own invention, and I much doubt that it was. Kull of Atlantis could have coined it in his wars against the Snakemen of Valusia.

What spat in our particular tankard that day was the thunderstorm. The clouds swept over the rocks before we could reach the heights. As Sarabos laid the dead Gunderman down, the first drops of rain fell.

Thunder crashed overhead. I looked up to see a thunderbolt sear the ridge. I spat from an all-but-dry mouth. If we climbed to that crest in our armor and the lightning went on playing, more than torches might be set alight.

I looked downslope to judge the closeness of our pursuers. To my surprise, I saw them running off as if we had turned into a band of demons and were on *their* heels. They were even leaving the weapons of the dead, and it takes great fear to make a Pict do that.

It struck me that whatever so daunted Picts might also be something Aquilonians could justly fear. I saw the same thought on faces around me, but—and all honor to my men and their kin—no one said a craven word.

We did keep our formation as we searched the slope for that cave. It was well that it was not far, for in about the time it takes to change the guard, the rain was coming down in a deluge. We might have been standing under a waterfall, and neither good leather nor oiled wool nor any armor ever forged could keep us from being sodden to the skin.

We covered the final paces to the cave with more haste than dignity, and with small regard for a proper formation. Once inside, with the rain no longer battering on our helmets until it addled our wits, I quickly arrayed the men. Sentries at the mouth of the cave, sentries toward the rear, the driest and cleanest place for the wounded, and those neither standing sentry nor tending the wounded allowed to strip and dry their weapons, armor, and clothes.

I set myself to counting our resources in the matter of food and water. Each of us had come out with two days' salt meat and hard bread, and a full water-bottle besides the ones we were to fill. If the Picts did not cut us off from the streams, the rills would be swollen full by the rain, and there might be water toward the rear of the cave, which seemed to lead far into the rocks. Such rocks in Pictland were usually honeycombed with underground springs and—

"Captain! To the rear!"

It was one of the rear sentries, a clear-headed Bossonian who would not have let confusion or fear show in his voice without good cause. I ordered all to their feet and all weapons readied, and went to stand beside the sentry.

At the edge of the torchlight, I saw worked stone. It was far too fine to be Pictish work, and far too fresh to have come down from the time of the old Hyborian invasions. I thought I could make out lintels, doorways, benches of living rock, and unwholesomely sinuous figures.

I lit another torch and remembered that this had best be the last I used, or we might not be able to signal the camp when the rain ceased. The spread of the light extended. I saw that the sinuousity of the figures was no fancy; the worship of Set had once found a home in this cave. I recognized Stygian hieroglyphs and even more arcane signs, of which I neither knew nor wished to know the meaning.

I strode farther to the rear, saw that the cave made a bend, and moved on until I could look beyond the bend into what appeared to be a chamber. Something tall and upright loomed at the outer edge of the light. I took two more steps—

"Crom!"

It was not an image of the Great Serpent, as I had feared. It was the life-sized image of a warrior of gigantic stature, in a strange mix of weapons and garb, half-Pictish and half-Black Coast, with a stout Hyborian broadsword at his waist.

Nor was it hard to put a name to that warrior. On three different campaigns I had seen the same face, older, weathered, the square-cut mane of hair gray, the face adorned with a mustache and in time, a beard, but none other than the one I beheld on the image.

The soft, swift tread of a hunting-panther sounded behind me, and I turned to see Sabaros. He had removed his hood and undone his hair, and I saw in the torchlight that it was jet black. Nor was there any more doubt about the hue of his eyes. They were blue, the same blue as the ice I had once seen in a cave in Gunderland, and fixed on the image with an intensity that seemed to make them glow with an inner light.

It struck me that I had not been wrong to invoke the chief god of Cimmeria and patron of our late king. It likewise struck me that Sabaros of the Black Dragons could doubtless, far more easily than I, put a name to his father.

None of this told me, however, what an image of Conan was doing here in a cave where no civilized man had ever set foot. Stygian sorcerers were civilized only by courtesy, and rumor named some of them not quite wholly men.

Suddenly the cave seemed less a refuge, and the rain—and even the Picts outside—less a peril.

One

The Black Coast, many years earlier:

The man passed through the shadows beneath the great trees by the Umfangu as silently as a lion on the hunt. Indeed, there was much of the lion in his soft-footed tread, the mane of black hair that swept to wide, bronzed shoulders, and the eyes that searched endlessly about him for either prey or rival.

Those eyes, however, had never graced a lion's face, nor that of a man in the Black Kingdoms. They were chill-blue northern eyes, with an intensity in their gaze that might have made a real lion cautious. Certainly they had done so with more than a few men, and those who had not learned caution from the ice-blue gaze had mostly died before they'd had time for a second lesson.

Now the man's steps took him away from the riverbank and the stout trees there. He approached a small clearing, where a forest giant had toppled years ago, bearing to the ground all in its path. The robust life of the jungle already had saplings and vines mounting the dead tree, but through the gap overhead, sunlight still reached the jungle floor more freely than elsewhere.

The man was only a spear's length from the edge of the sunlight when he halted, studying a patch of ferns. With the woods-wisdom gained by many hard lessons, some few not easily survived, he knew that he must watch from some other place today. The ferns would hold traces of his presence far too long.

Left or right? Left, he decided. That would take him away from the trail that entered the clearing on the far side. Never had he seen more than a handful of the natives—nor any animal he could not face bare-handed—come down that trail. Never, likewise, did the jungle cease to hold deadly surprises for the unwary.

Now he moved even more silently than before, and more cautiously. His steps took him from a root that would bear little trace of his passing to dry ground that could be brushed clean of footprints, and from there on to a swinging vine that kept him entirely clear of the ground for six good paces. The vine sagged under his massive weight, but neither broke nor left other traces of his passing.

At last the man reached his goal. The blue eyes narrowed as he studied the clearing, finding no changes and no movement. He settled into the roots of another giant tree, so completely still that his massive limbs might have been part of the roots themselves.

The eyes would have revealed life to anyone drawing close enough. That revelation would have come too late for any foe, however. A broadsword lay across the cal-loused knees, a stout dagger hung from the thong of a rawhide breechclout, and two handmade spears leaned against one of the roots. Any or all of these weapons would have drunk a foe's lifeblood before the man recognized danger.

In this also, the man was like a lion. Indeed, his name in these lands was "Amra"—the lion. Fairly earned in battle, too, although he did not care to let his thoughts dwell long on those battles.

His birth-name, though, matched those eyes of northern ice. He was called Conan, and his native land was bleak Cimmeria.

Kubwande, son of D'beno, bore a headdress as well as a loinguard of zebra-hide. These marked him as an *iqako*—a Bamula title best translated as "lesser war chief."

He also bore a stout boar-hide shield, two spears with sharp bog-iron points, and a war club carved with signs against witchcraft. He wore anklets of feathers dyed with berries and roots known best to the Bamulas' wizards. He expected that before this day's sunset, he might need all of these weapons and protections.

Not only was this hunting party on the trail of wild boar—nearly as cunning and well-armed as the great cats for leaving empty places in the huts of the Bamulas—but also Kubwande was hunting under the leadership of *qamu* (greater war chief) Idosso.

The *qamu* was not Kubwande's mortal enemy, because even Idosso knew that a man must sleep sometime. While he sleeps, it is as well if those who wish his death are too few to overcome those who guard him. It was no secret between the two warriors that Idosso wished to be the next war chief of the Bamulas and that Kubwande wished someone else would be so honored. But this did not make for blood-feud between them, as yet. Indeed, Kubwande was ready to see Idosso honored by gods and men alike . . . if he would but give ear to Kubwande's advice.

Kubwande still thought it was somehow fitting to hunt boar in Idosso's company. The man was larger than all but a handful among the Bamulas, as strong as he was large, fierce of temper, but not without some cunning. A dangerous man to judge lightly, as two hand'sworth of the bleached skulls of enemies outside Idosso's huts made plain to all but fools.

Being no fool, Kubwande intended that his skull should remain upon his shoulders. This meant giving Idosso no cause for a chiefs' bout unless there was a chance of victory.

Or perhaps that the battle not be to the death? Kubwande knew that Idosso had enemies among the kin of those he had slain. Those kin might not fight Idossa themselves, but some of them had the ear of greater chiefs. Kubwande was no mealie-bearer girl but a seasoned warrior more useful to the Bamulas alive than dead.

It would all be as the gods wished, of course, but Kubwande was one to go about his life as *he* wished until the gods told him otherwise. Today he wished a good hunt, with a fine boar at the end of it, and a feast of roast pork whose flavor not even Idosso's presence would be able to spoil.

Kubwande licked his lips at that thought, aimed an imaginary spear at an imaginary boar some fifty paces off to the right, and sank the spear deep between the shoulder blades. The boar took two steps, then went to its knees, rolled over on its side, and died kicking in the dead ferns—

"Kubwande!" Idosso called. "Are we at peace with the Fish-Eaters?"

Kubwande did not start, but knew shame, and more-over, that the shame was just. His attention had not been where it belonged.

"The Fish-Eaters are no great peril even when they are enemies," Kubwande said. "Nor do I think they have much stomach to be so, after our last battle with them."

Idosso grinned, showing front teeth bearing the ritual carvings of one who had slain a lion with a spear. It was Idosso who had led the last Bamula war party against the Fish-Eaters, and slain with his own hands six of their warriors.

Kubwande thought that any man who could be so easily turned by flattery was not a good choice for war chief, but the vice had its uses. Keeping peace among the hunters today was not the least of them.

It was time to watch behind. Kubwande and six other warriors halted, turned to face back down the trail, and raised spears. One blew a bone whistle. Its eerie call drew equally eerie replies from birds, but none from humans or spirits.

To finish the ritual, Kubwande raised his war club, whirled it three times around his head, and flung it down the trail. It struck a tree so hard that the club bounced back and fell almost at his feet.

The signs were all good. Nothing they need fear was on their trail. While hunting boar, that was just as well.

Conan the Cimmerian could sleep as readily as any cat, but he remained wakeful as he lay among the tree roots, watching the clearing. He was not in one of his regular hiding places, each chosen carefully, then set about with snares and traps that none could pass through without waking him.

He was half a day from the nearest of those refuges, in land claimed by the tribe called the Fish-Eaters. The

Fish-Eaters could hardly have been a menace even if they wished to be, but fear can make weaklings deadly.

Also, the Bamulas had taken to wandering in the Fish-Eaters' land as if it were their own. No one on the Black Coast despised the Bamulas. Conan knew of them only by what their enemies said, but there had been several warriors from tribes hostile to the Bamulas aboard *Tigress*. The Bamulas had offered a good price for those warriors, or so Belit had said, but she refused.

"I will sell no one to the Bamulas," she added. "If I deal with them at all, I will *buy*—and at the same price I pay the Stygians."

Blood and steel, death and fear, were the coin Belit used against the Stygians, until her own end. Now the clean seas held her ashes and those of *Tigress*; the jungles along the Zarkheba River held the bones of her crew, Conan's erstwhile comrades; and the Cimmerian's mind held . . . what?

Memories of sharing more than he had ever dreamed he could share with a woman, far more than a shared bed—although those memories alone would have given many men wakeful nights. Memories that made her . . . call her a cherished comrade and one would not be far off the mark.

Nor, the Cimmerian thought, would Belit's spirit disdain the name. Anymore than her body had disdained his embraces, or her warriors Conan's leadership. . . .

It had been a good time, and now it was past. No son of Cimmeria spent much time mourning what was gone forever—the harsh northern land allowed few luxuries, and that one least of all. Moreover, Conan had sent Belit home to the ocean aboard the ship in which she took such pride, and of which she had made so fearful a name along the Stygian shores.

The slate was clean. But he had known when he put

the torch to *Tigress* that it would be a good long while
before he set foot aboard ship again. With his memories
and weapons, his knowledge of the Black Coast gained
from his comrades aboard *Tigress*, and a sailor's kitbag
slung over one shoulder, he had plunged inland.

A footfall that none but a hunter, human or animal,
could have heard ended Conan's brief reverie. He moved
only his head, having contrived his position so that he
need move nothing else to study the whole clearing.

The footfalls continued, light, sure, and drawing
closer. The Cimmerian raised a finger to test the scant
breeze. The finger said again what his ears had already
told him, that the visitors were coming down the path.

Now he could count their number by ear. More than
one, all but certainly. Not enough to fear, even if they
were not Fish-Eaters.

Conan waited. If the Bamulas were thrusting their
hunting parties this deep into Fish-Eater land, it was
worth knowing. It was not worth a fight; only in tales to
amuse children did a single hero defeat a whole tribe.
But peaceful oblivion in the depths of the jungles of the
Black Coast would be as much past as Belit, and—

Three women stepped into the clearing. Each carried
a jug on her head and a basket on one hip, slung from
the opposite shoulder. The sling thong was all the
women wore above the waist, and below it they wore
only cloths wrapped from hips to knees. Nor did any of
them look the worse for being thus revealed. A well-
formed woman never hurt a man's eye, no matter what
hue her skin might be.

The women set down their jugs, unslung their baskets, and placed all of them in a rough circle in the middle of the clearing. Then they knelt and prostrated
themselves seven times toward the offerings. An earring

of raw gold dangled from each woman's left ear, and one of them had a ring of ivory and gold in her nose.

They rose, breasts bobbing in a manner that would have made a stone statue stare wide-eyed, and looked about them. Conan wondered what they were expecting, awaiting, or perhaps hoping for.

He decided that it was probably not him leaping from his hiding place. He had yet to meet a woman who warmed readily to a man who began by scaring her out of her wits.

The vigil lasted, as did the silence. Conan had just noticed that the girl with the nose ring also had blue feathers woven into her tightly curled hair, when his instincts warned him of something else.

The silence had lasted too long and grown too complete. The normal din of the jungle had ceased, and it did that only at the appearance of something unknown or hostile.

Neither Conan nor the girls had provoked the jungle life. This said little about the new presence, but what it did say made Conan slide from his watching place, lifting a spear as he moved. A snake might have envied the smoothness and silence of his movement; certainly it drew no response from the women.

Then something unheard even by the Cimmerian made all three of them whirl. A moment later they had vanished up the path, with only the last flicker of the last woman's skirt lingering briefly in Conan's vision.

If it had not been for the jugs and baskets in the clearing, he might have thought the women had been a dream, risen from bad wine or an empty belly.

There was no wine in this jungle, although the native beer was robust enough to satisfy a drinking man's thirst. But an empty belly was another matter. Conan's stomach chose that moment to rumble, reminding him to check his snares on the road homeward. In this steaming forest, snared animals died quickly, and more quickly still became unfit to eat.

The thought of beer turned Conan's eyes back to the jugs. It could do no harm to see what the women had left behind, and if it looked doubtful, there were plenty of apes to test it for poison.

Conan's eyes roamed ceaselessly around the clearing as he crossed it to the offerings. His long arms barely bent twigs or disturbed leaves as he reached in for baskets and jugs. With one of each in either hand, he withdrew into the shadows, walking backward as if each step was made on a carpet of spiderweb stretched over a bottomless pit.

Invisible in the shadows again, he drew the bark stopper from the jug. Its contents smelled like beer, surely enough, and felt like it on the back of his hand. Moreover, when he cautiously licked that hand—

It was then that the Cimmerian noticed the sign on both the jugs and the baskets. It was the Fish-Eaters' sign of an offering to an unknown spirit. The tribe had five chief gods, each with his own sign, and a sixth sign for spirits, good or evil, who came from none of the five.

Beer and mealie-bread, fruit and dried fish, would be a welcome addition to his diet. They would also be stolen from something as near a god as made no difference.

No lover of priests or believer in their babble, the Cimmerian doubted the gods cared much for what men did or left undone. He had also spoken truly to Belit when he said of the gods, "I would not tread on their shadow," and who could say how hard he was treading on whose shadow with this little theft?

There were wise thieves and foolish thieves, and Conan walked the forests of the Black Coast only be-

cause years ago in Zingara, he had learned the difference. He would be a wise thief and return the offerings
from whence they had come.

He had just risen to take the first return step when a
woman's scream sounded from well down the trail.
Then Conan heard war cries—some of them Bamula,
some in no tongue he recognized—fierce gruntings, and
another scream.

As he snatched for weapons, Conan let the offerings
fall from his hand; let the spirits pick them up if they so
wished. A single leap took him over the other offerings
and the tree trunk. Vines looped serpent-like around his
legs but he pulled free, without sound and almost without slowing.

He had a spear in his left hand and the broadsword
blazing in his right as he plunged to the trail.

Kubwande and the warriors watching the rear
whirled at the sudden din, raising spears and shields,
waiting for the jungle to sprout enemies, or at least answers. Curiosity might eat at them, but it was the honor
of a Bamula warrior to watch only where he had sworn
to watch and not let his eyes wander like a woman's.

Only when Idosso shouted, "All men to the fore!" was
the rearguard released from its oath. Then curiosity lent
wings to Kubwande's feet as he led his men forward to
Idosso's aid.

It was not at once clear what aid the senior chief
might need. He gripped one Fish-Eater woman by her
nose ring and the waist of her skirt, while another warrior was kneeling on the back of a second woman.

The second woman was entirely naked, save for the
rawhide thongs now being swiftly looped about her
wrists. A hobble hung from the warrior's loinguard,
ready to encircle the woman's ankles.

"Idosso, it will be a sad day for the Bamulas when a warrior such as you needs help with two Fish-Eater women!" Kubwande said. He hoped the flattery would take the edge off the statement.

Idosso's woman kicked sharply backward, landing a bare foot in the big warrior's groin hard enough to make him grunt. His hands tightened, ready to twist and tear.

Kubwande's breath caught. He had heard of what Idosso could do to captive women if angered. He did not wish to see it, and indeed wished that it not happen at all, if he could contrive this without a challenge to Idosso.

"There were three women," Idosso said. "All had been making offerings to the unknown spirit. Then something frightened them. They will not tell me what."

"If it is peril for them as well as for us, they will tell without torture. If it is peril only for us, they will die before they warn us."

"That may take a while," Idosso growled.

"Too long, if one has escaped and even now runs to warn her folk," Kubwande said. "True, they are only Fish-Eaters—"

The woman on the ground made a foul suggestion about what Kubwande could do with his manhood. The woman in Idosso's grip looked ready to spit in someone's face. Kubwande hoped she would not.

"—and one Bamula is worth ten of them. But we are so deep in Fish-Eater land that they may come ten times ten for each of us. Then all we will have is a praise-song over our bones instead of an answer."

"True. Also, bones enjoy no woman's flesh." Idosso let go of the nose ring, shifting his grip to the woman's arm. In spite of her kicks, he gripped both wrists in one gigantic hand.

"Now, girl, you earn our being kind to you. What brought you here, and what frightened you?"

Kubwande saw the play of hatred, doubt, and fear on the woman's face, and at last her decision to speak, before Idosso had done more than twist her wrists lightly. That showed wisdom, facing Idosso, or indeed, many Bamulas.

"We . . . we came to offer to the unknown spirit, who has taken a man's form," the woman said.

"A man's form? When? And what kind of man?" Kubwande's questions leapt like spears before Idosso could open his mouth.

Idosso looked a savage curse at the lesser chief, but ere he could gather wits or words for more, a crashing of trampled jungle foliage made everyone snatch weapons. Then the curtain of leaves to the right flew apart, and a thin brown-skinned man clad only in a dirty white loincloth leapt onto the trail. Kubwande saw blood on the man's arms and thighs.

He also saw blood on the tusks of the colossal boar that followed the man into view a moment later. Even Bamula warriors needed a moment to gather courage and wits to face a creature that size, high as Idosso's waist at the shoulders and grizzled with age that brought cunning without taking away strength.

Another man who ran from the shadows down the trail had no such hesitation. His spear flew as swiftly and as truly as if his eye had commanded his arm without the need for thought.

Only a shifting of the boar's feet kept the spear from striking a mortal blow. It pierced deep into the beast's flank, but did not reach his life.

Instead, it drew his attention to the newcomer. The boar whirled with a squeal of rage and pain. Then it lowered its head and lunged for the spearman.

Kubwande raised his own spear, but found that he could not throw without risk of hitting either a comrade or the man. As the man flung a second spear, aimed to gouge the boar's back, Kubwande had a clear look at him for the first time.

No warrior of this band save Idosso could have looked the man in the eye. His hair was as dark as any jungle dweller's, but long and straight, and the Black Kingdoms had never given birth to such a pale skin. No land that Kubwande knew had ever produced those fierce blue eyes, like a lion's in all but color.

It seemed to the Bamula warrior that they now knew what form the unknown spirit had taken.

Two

Conan had just time to notice something odd about the wounded man, the boar's first victim. Then he had to give all his attention to the beast, lest he become its next one.

An ordinary broadsword was not the best weapon against a boar perhaps slowed, perhaps weakened, but yet with tusks and muscle enough to be deadly if it reached close quarters. That was the problem with the broadsword: only by chance could it keep the boar at arm's length.

By chance, or by a single swift cut.

The boar whuffled. Conan shifted to a two-handed grip, although the sword's hilt barely had room for both his broad hands.

The boar's hooves churned earth as it charged. Conan crouched, swung, and leapt aside in a single flow of movement as swift and smooth as the strike of a viper.

The sword sheared through the boar's forelegs. Sheer momentum carried the beast forward, to ram its snout into a tree. There it thrashed and scrabbled frantically with bloody stumps of forelegs and intact hindlegs.

Then the Cimmerian's sword came down like an executioner's axe, on the back of the bristly neck. Flesh and bone parted, a final bellow ended in silence, and the boar lay still.

Conan studied the blade for nicks, then wiped it quickly on the boar's hide. The jungle was as hard as the sea on a good weapon. The broadsword was not his whole arsenal, but it would be his weapon of choice as long as rust did not eat it like a crocodile gulping down a baby.

Only when he was satisfied at the condition of his weapon did the Cimmerian rise from a crouch to face the watching men. He recognized them as Bamulas from their headdresses and tattoos, and as alert and wary from their stances and lifted spears. It seemed best to make a gesture of peace toward them, lest some of those spears fly because of some witling's fear.

Conan thrust the broadsword into its scabbard and crossed both arms on his chest. "I am Conan the Cimmerian. I am here in peace. I make you a gift of this boar."

Most of the spear-points and shields dipped a trifle. The Bamulas seemed to understand him. Now would they believe him? He hoped the pirates' cant he had learned aboard *Tigress* would be enough. The crew had been of a score of different tribes, and their common tongue was a stew of words from all, flavored with Shemitish and even Stygian words for good measure.

Before Conan could speak again, a woman broke

away from the grip of the tallest Bamula and ran toward the Cimmerian. At this, one of the Bamulas flung a spear, and Conan's sword leapt from its scabbard with the speed of thought.

The spear fell harmlessly to the ground, cloven in two as neatly as any butcher ever divided a sausage, and the woman flung herself at Conan's feet. She babbled and wept at the same time, speaking too quickly for him to follow more than one word in five. It seemed likely that she was asking for his protection, and it seemed certain that the Bamulas would be displeased if he granted it.

Nonetheless, no woman had ever called on the Cimmerian for protection without receiving at least some measure of it. He put his foot lightly on the back of her neck, a gesture he had seen Belit make in claiming lordship over certain prisoners.

The tall Bamula who had been holding her frowned. "Is this your woman?" he asked.

"I could ask you the same," Conan said. "I take no man's woman, but I wonder what a Bamula does here with a Fish-Eater girl."

"I am Idosso, a *qamu* of the Bamulas, lords of this land," the man said. "The girl is my prize."

"The last I heard, this was the land of the Fish-Eaters," Conan said mildly.

"The Fish-Eaters have only what the Bamulas allow them," Idosso said. This drew a glare from a second woman Conan now saw for the first time, lying bound and entirely bare on the ground among the other warriors. The woman at Conan's feet raised her head. He gently pushed it back down. Idosso seemed a man with a long tongue and a short temper, the sort best not angered without need, in any land.

"Pardon, *qamus* Idosso and Conan," a Bamula warrior said. "But I think we need to take thought for this man." He pointed at the boar's victim, now sitting with his back to a tree, his eyes closed. "He babbles in no tongue I have ever heard."

Conan saw Idosso frown at the Cimmerian being given the honorific title, and he recognized a cunning trap. The warrior who spoke was no giant like Idosso, who had nearly Conan's own height and thews, but his eyes told of sharp wits that he made useful in place of sheer strength.

"Why do you ask me—?" Conan said.

"Kubwande, son of D'beno, *iqako* of the Bamulas as was D'Beno before me, is he who speaks," the warrior said, making several gestures of obvious formality whose exact nature Conan did not recognize.

He did recognize, though, the wisdom of taking every chance for politeness when he faced odds of twenty to one, and the twenty all stout fighting men. Judging by his first sight of Bamulas, they were living up to their reputation.

Kubwande was hardly as fair to the eyes as Belit, but he seemed as ready to give Conan a friendly welcome among strangers.

"Kubwande, I will help this wounded man if you will tell me why you think I know his speech. I will also take nothing that any Bamula claims as his, nor shed the blood of any who does not seek mine. By Crom and Mitra, I swear it."

Those last names some warriors clearly recognized; Conan saw gestures of aversion. The two women stared wide-eyed at him.

"The women say you are the flesh of the Fish-Eaters' unknown spirit," Kubwande said. "They were on their way from offering to you when we met them."

"They have part of the truth, anyway," Conan said. "I

am flesh, and need food. But not as badly as this poor wretch needs help.".

Conan knelt beside the wounded man. No, dying—he had the look the Cimmerian had seen too often, on many battlefields. The boar had struck deep enough to reach the man's life, which would flee his body no matter if three kings' doctors did their best for him.

Conan's best was not that good, but he had survived enough wounds of his own and tended more than a few wounded comrades. His hands were firm but light as he bound the man's wounds, listening all the while for some words that would explain the mystery of his appearance here.

For it was a mystery. By garb and appearance, the man was a Vendhyan, and Vendhya was half a year's hard journey from the Black Coast! Perhaps he had fled slavery in Stygia, where folk of every race on earth, and (so it was whispered) some not of earth, toiled under the lash of Stygian slavemasters.

But Stygia was also a good long journey from this jungle trail, and the man showed no marks of either a journey or slavery. He was slim but well-fleshed under the brown skin, his hands showed no callouses from years of brutal labor, and his back showed no wounds save those from thorns and the boar.

Then the man began to babble in his dying delirium, calling for his mother, and the mystery deepened. Certainly the man was a Vendhyan; Conan had spent enough time in that land to do more than separate a few jewels from its rich lords. He had warred, wenched, and learned the tongue the dying man was now speaking.

But he was not speaking to much purpose, as was only to be expected of the dying. Conan knew that no shaking or shouting would bring the man to his senses, and held his peace. What the gods wanted the man to say, he would. Otherwise he would take his secret with him—and Conan did not find it in him to blame the man, dying as he was, alone and far from home.

Suddenly the man's eyes widened and he sat up with a shriek of indescribable terror. He flung one arm up so violently that Conan's dressing of his wounds tore free and blood flowed again. The Cimmerian turned to look where the bloody hand was pointing, but saw only air and jungle before it.

"The gate!" the man cried out. "The demon's gate! It opens again. The demon calls. Beware, beware, be—"

Blood gurgled in the Vendhyan's throat and trickled from the corner of his mouth. His arm fell back limp, and although his eyes remained open, they saw nothing.

Conan was reaching to close those staring eyes when he felt something prod his back. He turned his head, to see a young Bamula warrior holding a spear with two hands, neither of them entirely steady.

Slowly, Conan rose to his full height. Just as slowly, he turned around. The warrior raised the spear until its point touched Conan's chest.

Then two massive arms swung like bludgeons. The first rammed into the pit of the warrior's stomach, doubling and lifting him at the same time to meet the second fist on his jaw. He flew backward through a gap in the Bamula ranks and fetched up in a tangle of vine.

Conan waited to see that the warrior was still breathing, then picked up the fallen spear. Without apparent effort, he snapped the stout shaft in two.

"The next man who prods me, I will feed his own spear," the Cimmerian said. "The Bamulas have no name for being fools, so what ate his wits?"

Kubwande met Conan's eyes without flinching. "He thought you were a demon, for knowing the speech of the stranger."

A demon, and the Vendhyan had spoken of a demon's gate. It seemed that the man had left behind him an even deeper mystery!

Conan looked at the fallen warrior, who was struggling to rise. "I am no more a demon than you are," he growled. He strode to the dead boar and drew his own spears from the carcass. "Have you ever heard of Amra, the pale-skinned warrior, companion to Belit of *Tigress*?"

Even this far inland, that was a name to conjure with in the Black Kingdoms. The fallen man nodded as two comrades helped him to his feet.

To speak the truth did not avoid peril if the Bamulas had received injury at Belit's hands or at those of one who followed her. Conan knew of no such incident, and he and Belit had sailed, loved, and fought together for so long that he doubted she'd had many secrets from him. But it was always the one secret a man did not learn that doomed him, and if so, Conan would soon follow the Vendhyan.

At least then he could ask the man what his dying babblings had meant.

But no hostility showed in the chiseled black faces or watchful dark eyes around Conan. Then Kubwande spoke, in accents of surprise and pleasure.

"You are he?"

"The very man. No need to worry about my being a Fish-Eater spirit or a demon."

"Eh," Idosso said. "We heard that Belit was dead and *Tigress* no more. Also her warriors."

"You heard the truth," Conan said. He kept his voice level. "She fell afoul of the ugliest sort of magick and died of it, with most of her men. I avenged the dead, sent the living home, and gave Belit and her ship to the sea."

His tongue grew more nimble as he spoke of *Tigress*'s last voyage, and his eyes no longer saw the Bamulas around him. When he finished speaking, it seemed that they too no longer saw what lay around them, but instead, the burning ship carrying the Queen of the Black Coast to her ocean grave.

"Were there any Bamulas among those who lived?" Kubwande asked after a long silence.

"None who called themselves so," Conan said. "Also, some of those who lived were of a mind to seize another ship and go on bedeviling the Stygians. I was not. I had a sign from the gods to go inland and find new friends there."

In truth, he had lacked the heart to look again at the sea, the shroud of a beloved battle-comrade. But he had given the Bamulas all the truth they deserved, and if they still doubted him, they could send him to join Belit!

Whether Conan's tale or what they saw in his eyes and in the calloused hands gripping the spears won over the Bamulas, he saw them lowering spears and unslinging shields. Two of them bent to lift the dead Vendhyan. Others improvised a litter of spears, to bear the dead boar.

"Will you follow us, Amra?" Kubwande asked when the warriors were ready to depart.

Conan shook his head, then handed Kubwande one of the spears. "Take this as a pledge of my friendship for the Bamulas, but do not ask me to come with you. My vision said I must stay apart from all men yet a while longer."

"But the Fish-Eaters—?" asked the young warrior who'd paid for his spear-prodding with a sore jaw and belly.

Conan laughed at the youth's concern. "I am as good

a man as any Bamula, and which of *you* would fear Fish-Eaters?"

The two women's sharp looks and Idosso's raised hand reminded Conan of a last matter. "I wish that these women decide freely whose they shall be. This also my vision has told me to ask."

The two women stared at each other, then at Idosso, and finally at Conan. The one with the nose ornament pointed at Idosso.

Conan had long since understood that women had no more sense than men, but these women's decision seemed altogether foolish.

"May I ask why?"

"You are god-touched, Amra. We cannot be to you as women to a man. Idosso is only a warrior—" at which words the man grunted very like the boar "—and not . . . not . . ."

"A speaker of demons' tongues?"

The women looked bleak as Idosso howled with laughter. Conan bit back curses on the women and sharp replies to the big chief.

"So be it. But I owe the women this much for their offerings. If they are ill-treated, I will learn of it, and those who ill-treat them will answer to me."

Idosso's stance said how little he cared about that, and Conan wondered if he should press his claim more vigorously in spite of the women's fancies. Idosso seemed likely to be a harsh master, but also likely to be in a fury over losing the women. Not because they were so rare among the Black Kingdoms, but out of a surfeit of pride.

The Cimmerian had seen rather more such men than he cared to remember, and killed a good many of them. Too swiftly adding Idosso to their number, however, might not win friends among the Bamulas. And unlike the Fish-Eaters, the Bamulas knew who he was, where he was, and how to send enough warriors to drive him into desperate flight, or an equally desperate last battle.

"Let it be so," Idosso grunted. Then he spoke sharply, too fast for Conan to follow his words. The warriors had no such trouble, however; they were formed up in a few heartbeats and hurrying down the trail in a few more.

Conan looked at the bloodstains where the boar had fallen and where the Vendhyan had died, then slung his spears over one shoulder and drew his sword. He returned up the trail as he had come down it, sword in hand, but at a more leisurely pace.

He also had no hesitation about making a meal of the offerings, although when he was done, he knew at least one bread-maker among the Fish-Eaters who should be thrashed!

Three

Far to the north, a sorcerer named Lysenius sat in a cave whose rock he had shaped into the likeness of a Stygian temple, and cursed in a scarlet fury.

No one in the Black Kingdoms heard his curses, nor would they have understood them if they had. Indeed, no one at all heard most of them save his daughter Scyra, who had heard them far too often for them to have any power to either amuse or anger her.

Some Picts heard a few of the curses, borne on the night wind. *They* made signs of aversion, telling one another that this time the anger of the white shaman was so great that surely it would lead him to make war on the very gods themselves.

If that were to come about, they wished to be a long way from the battlefield.

* * *

Conan spent little time after his meeting with the Bamulas wondering if they saw him as friend or foe, man or mage. He commonly left that sort of thing to scholars and scribes with no real work to fill their days.

Here in the Black Kingdoms, Conan was beyond the reach of scribes and scholars. The days settled into an endless flow, with a rhythm of eating, sleeping, hunting, bathing in streams, and tending his weapons and snares. The Fish-Eaters brought no more offerings, but there was ripe fruit and fat game aplenty; only a fool could starve in the Black Kingdoms.

Being no fool, the Cimmerian fed well. Being no fool, he also grew eyes in the back of his head and ears in his elbows and knees whenever he left his refuges. The Fish-Eaters might someday be moved to do more than refuse him offerings, brooding over those wenches whose fancies had led them to go with Idosso. Not likely, and hardly soon, in a land where a single spearman's share of loot from *Tigress* would buy a harem fit to make Iranistani noblemen jealous, but still, it was a danger to be considered.

A danger, also, that like leopards, crocodiles, wild bees, and poisoned vines, was likely to strike only those who did not consider it at all.

Among the warriors of the Bamulas, some talked of the white man the Fish-Eaters thought was a god. They did not talk of him by the name of "Amra," for that name was a secret kept among Idosso's band, who had bound themselves to its secrecy by fearful oaths. Both Idosso and Kubwande had also bound the women by similar oaths, likewise by threats of dire and lingering punishment, and in Kubwande's case, by the promise of gold and a servant of his own from among Idosso's women.

Idosso seemed to think that promising rewards to the women, instead of merely threatening them with punishment, was a madman's whim. It was, however, one that he seemed prepared to allow.

He was likewise curious over Idosso's insistence that Conan's perhaps being the notorious Amra should be kept a secret. So curious, indeed, that he asked Idosso about it, in tones that would brook no silence.

"As simple as a Fish-Eater," Kubwande said, then asked pardon for the insult of calling Idosso by that name.

"One day you will ask pardon for your tongue's nimbleness and I will reply by pinning it to the roof of your mouth with my spear," Idosso said. "I am not a tame ape, to be made to perform until you can sell me to the Stygians. You sell me to anyone, Kubwande, and you will go there with me."

Kubwande assured the chief that buying and selling anyone except a few more women was as far from his mind as the Mountains of the Moon were from the hut where they sat and drank beer served by the Fish-Eater women. Idosso grunted what might have been assent.

The lesser chief took it as such. "Do we know that *Tigress* and her mistress are gone? Has anyone seen their bones?"

"If Amra tells the truth, he went to some trouble to be sure that no one would."

"*If.* Or he might be spying on us for her, while she finds new men and readies ships to come upriver."

"We will fill her new men and her old alike with spears if she does that," Idosso said around a mouthful of mealies. "Her, too, if she is as brazen about leading her fighters as the tales have it."

"Should we do that before we know what she wishes in these lands?" Kubwande asked. "Remember, a dozen

tribes have given warriors to her crew. Hardly a single
tribe has any feud with her, or she with them. And we
are no better friends to the Stygians than she was. Since
either of us were warriors, has a year gone by when
their slave-raiders have not needed to be chased back
into their own lands, with spears prodding the laggards?"

Idosso laughed at the picture, not least because he
had led such war parties more than once, and made
much of his reputation thereby. "So. You think maybe
Amra is spying for one who might be a friend of his?"

"I do not *know* otherwise. Until I do, this man is like
a dagger hidden in one's loinguard. Do not bring it out
before the right time, when it will strike a single deadly
blow."

Kubwande could see Idosso's wits struggling to grasp
what the other truly meant. He waited in patience. Better if the man understood it without aid.

"*He!*" Idosso exclaimed at last, and tossed the beer
gourd so high it stuck in the grass of the hut's roof. "We
keep Amra's secret, and he may talk to us alone among
the Bamulas. If his mistress has friendship to sell, then
she will sell it to us. Whoever brings the Queen of the
Black Coast to friendship with the Bamulas—"

He did not finish. There was no need. Kept a secret,
Amra would be a dagger to thrust into the bellies of ri-
vals for the ivory stool of the war chief. Thinking that,
Idosso was content to let his ambition rule him. And
Kubwande, well aware of that ambition, knew that he
might rule Idosso.

At least for as long as necessary. One could not keep
the peace with such a man forever, even if one pretended friendship for him. He was too quick to anger
and too slow to think.

But the blood-feud might be like the concealed dagger

or Amra, something to be brought out only at the proper time.

Conan knew nothing of the intrigues among the chiefs of the Bamulas. Had he known, he would have cared much less than Kubwande hoped, at least until someone insulted Belit's memory.

Then doubtless his temper would have got the better of him and it would have been a red day in the history of the Bamulas before the Cimmerian went down under the sheer weight of spears, if indeed he went down at all. Foes as formidable as the Bamulas had in the past thought long odds meant a dead Cimmerian, and had ended as food for the vultures before they could learn greater wisdom.

Conan intended to leave the Bamulas in peace; he hoped they would do the same and not give him any cause to change his mind by mistreating the women. If they were thus amenable, they could fight all their neighbors, none of their neighbors, themselves, demons, or the very gods, without troubling his dreams.

He was more wary of the Fish-Eaters. Doubtless they would learn the truth about the women's disappearance. Doubtless also, they would in time consider avenging themselves on a foe they could overcome, which would not be the Bamulas. Conan added more snares to the paths around his refuges, which began to look like lairs, slept lightly, and kept weapons to hand every moment, waking or sleeping.

He also set fish-traps in certain streams. *Tigress* had carried away more loot than gold and jewels from her prey—weapons, ship's gear, and food among them. The food had often failed between one prize and another, however, and during those long days, nets and lines went over the side. The catch went into the bellies of

Belit's sea-wolves, either at once or after some while in
barrels of salt brine.

Belit had always jested about fish being food for lov-
ers and insisted that Conan eat his fill to be a fit consort
for her. On the whole, he did not think that anything
short of starvation could kill a man's interest in a
woman like Belit. But while he held her, he held his
peace . . . and grew accustomed to fish.

So when he found a stream that ran deep but no more
than two lance-length's wide, and abounded in strange
but succulent fish, he turned his hand to catching some
of the bounty. Saplings and reeds, with thongs of grass
and vine coated with plant sap to keep them from rot-
ting, were enough for his purpose.

He soon had three traps set, close enough together
that he could visit all of them once at dawn and once at
twilight. He had them placed where he thought that
both he and they were safe from prying eyes and greedy
hands.

He was right, at least about human eyes and hands.

On a still night, Conan awakened to the roll of thunder. But his near-animal keenness of instinct found
something wrong with the thunder.

It had come not only without rain, but without wind.
He would not say that it had come without clouds, for
here one could not see the sky without climbing trees
taller than the towering pines of the Border Kingdom.

He listened, ears searching the darkness for the slightest sound that might tell him more. He heard nothing
but the common night birds and insects of the jungle,
with their rasps and shrieks, their whines and chirrs, as
they sought food or mates.

The Cimmerian slipped from the hammock that was
one of the few comforts he had taken from *Tigress* be-

fore she sailed on her last voyage. His feet made no more sound than that of a leopard's, and his hands, guided by night-keen eyes, moved surely as he girded on his weapons.

After the thunderclap, the silence had lasted too long. Natural thunder did not come in single claps.

Something not of nature, or at least not of the jungle, was abroad tonight. Conan did not know whether he could fight it, or even if it would be worth his while to do so. But he knew that it was always better to be the hunter than the hunted.

He stalked rather than strode as he swung in a wide circle around his lair, a circle that took him toward the principal stream in the area. He disturbed ferns and grass, branches and vines, hardly more than one of the great cats would have done, prowling the jungle in search of prey.

Now he searched the night with every sense alert, one hand on sword-hilt, spear in the other hand, dagger on belt, and two more spears slung over his back. Even a leopard plummeting from above would have found the Cimmerian no easy prey, for besides bearing ample steel, he looked upward with every few breaths.

Halfway around the circle, Conan had found nothing amiss. He had begun to think that his ears, or the jungle, had deceived him, drawing him out into the night on a fool's errand.

He kept on, however. As long as he walked·this path, it would do no harm to pass by his fish-traps, saving himself the journey in the morning. Also, he knew that the jungles of the Black Kingdoms held much that he did not know of. He had come a long way from the young thief in Zamora, more boy than man, only less clumsy than an ox and so ignorant he did not even know that he *was* ignorant.

At first, Conan thought the growls ahead did come from one of the great cats, mating or feeding, perhaps wrathful at being disturbed. Then he heard a deepness in the growls that spoke of a beast larger than any of the cats—or indeed, of any other creature of the jungle.

The hippopotamus and elephant grew larger than the cats, to be sure, as did the crocodiles. None of them growled. Conan walked softly now, and his broadsword rode free in a weathered, scar-knuckled hand.

At the last moment, he swerved aside from his usual path to the stream and slipped through the undergrowth to a spot that he knew would let him see without being seen. If this was a natural creature, that is; he remembered the single thunderclap, and the Vendhyan who babbled of "the demon's gate."

It was a natural beast Conan saw from his hiding place, and indeed, one he had seen before. But nothing in nature had ever brought it here.

It was one of the great snowbears of the far north, beyond not only Cimmeria, but the lands of the Aesir and Vanir. The hardiest of northerners, men who could trade blows all day and hoist mead horns all night, walked softly in the presence of the snowbear. It was twice the height and five times the weight of a large man, swift as a ferret, with teeth a finger long, and claws like daggers in all four platter-sized feet.

It was also nothing that the Black Kingdoms had ever seen. Nor, as far as the Cimmerian knew, was there any land within half a year's travel that had seen them, or any mountains closer by to offer one a home of snow and ice.

The bear showed no signs of any long journey. Its thick white fur hung damply from flanks unsunken by hunger, and the gaze in the chill black eyes held no weariness. Conan had fought serpents whose gaze held more warmth than the snowbear's.

From what Conan remembered of northern tales of the snowbears, they were great eaters of fish. So it surprised him hardly at all when the bear ambled to the stream, thrust a paw in and came up with Conan's fish-trap and all the fish within it. The fish-trap slithered onto the bank, the fish twisting and flopping.

The bear's paw came down like an axe. Stout reeds and well-tied knots parted like rotten threads, and fish flew everywhere. One flew higher than the rest. The bear reared, opened its mouth, and plucked the fish out of the air with the ease of an Argossean youth playing street-ball.

In that moment, the bear's vitals lay open to a shrewd blow from spear or arrow. It was long range for a spear, but Conan wasted not a single breath regretting that he had no bow.

Propelled by a thick Cimmerian arm, the spear struck with the force of a shaft from the heaviest of Bossonian longbows. A hand'sbreadth left or right and the fight would have been over in the same moment it began.

Ill luck—some fault in Conan's aim, or perhaps a puff of breeze—sent the spear astray. It drove through fur and skin but struck a rib before doing any harm.

The bear reared again, its growl becoming a roar. One swipe of a vast paw plucked the spear from its chest. The shaft flew again, driving its point a finger'slength deep into a stout tree.

Then the bear charged at the Cimmerian, as unerringly as if more senses than natural guided it and as fiercely as any beast the Cimmerian had ever faced.

Conan flung a second spear, thanking Crom as he threw that he had brought three. The bear swerved as the spear left Conan's hand, and the spearhead only gouged fur and skin along one flank.

The Cimmerian thrust with his sword, not made for thrusting but longer than the bear's forelegs. The tales of the snowbears told him of more than their food. They made it plain that no man ever came alive out of reach of those paws.

The point sank in, and the bear twisted, roaring like all the fires of Set's dark abyss. Conan jerked his sword free, hope dawning as he made to thrust again. The beast shuffled forward and batted at the sword.

The blow all but numbed the Cimmerian's arm. A trifle more force to it and it would have swept the sword from his hand. He flung his third spear, aiming at the snowbear's eyes, and this time his aim was true.

The bear reared up, the spear dangling from the bloody ruins of one eye. Conan could have thrust again, but his awareness of the ground told him that this was folly. The bear had hemmed him in against several stout trees. If his thrust miscarried, he would have nowhere to flee to when the foe charged again.

So he darted to one side, slashing hard at a forepaw. His sword sheared claws from the right paw, making the bear roar again. It was shaking its wounded paw furiously as the Cimmerian leapt through the first gap in the trees large enough for his massive frame.

In among the trees, the bear's greater size would be more burden than blessing in its pursuit of the Cimmerian. He could go where it could not, and strike from hiding places its one remaining eye could not find in the darkness.

He could slay it without coming within reach of those forepaws, Mitra willing! There would be no peace for a man in this land with the snowbear hunting free, and

Conan did not think the Fish-Eaters were the folk to put an end to it.

The bear was willing enough to follow the Cimmerian's trail. Its wounds had enraged it; Conan doubted that it had any thought but to rend and tear what had hurt it.

The bear also seemed clumsier at this task than the Cimmerian had expected. Perhaps it had lost the scent of its prey among the unfamiliar odors of this new land. Perhaps, like many northern creatures, it had slept during the Time of Endless Night and so had poor night-sight.

Regardless, the Cimmerian soon found himself at his wits' end for a way to bring the beast into some trap where he could fight and it could not. After what seemed half the night and oaths sworn by all the lawful gods of every land he knew, he saw it evade his fifth (at least) attempt to bring it to bay.

"By Erlik's brass tool, I'll have that beast's hide for a new hammock yet!" he vowed. He gave more ground, and this time he stepped through a wall of vine onto a trail. Moreover, he stepped onto the trail in plain sight of a clearing where at least two-score Fish-Eaters were crouched with spears and war clubs.

Conan cursed again, but his loudest oaths were drowned out by the cries of the Fish-Eaters as they leapt to their feet and waved their weapons.

"The woman-stealer and demon-bringer Amra!"

"Kill the lion-man!"

"Wash the spears! Wash the spears! Wash the spears!"

For a folk commonly called peaceful, the Fish-Eaters seemed to be remarkably zealous for war against the Cimmerian.

Conan had no quarrel with the Fish-Eaters, and indeed wondered why they called *him* a demon-bringer. "Fear makes folly," was all he could think of.

"Ha!" he thundered. His bull's roar beat down the Fish-Eater's cries. Heads turned, but for the moment, no spears flew.

"I am no demon, but in those trees is something worse than any demon I ever saw. It could eat lions. It will eat you and your children if we do not slay it now!"

That was as far as Conan went before the Fish-Eaters started shouting again as they had before. The Cimmerian felt a mighty urge to leave those fools and the bear to amuse one another and make his own way to safety.

But he had insulted the Fish-Eaters to make peace with the Bamulas. He owed it to them not to add injury to insult.

In the next moment, the matter was taken out of Conan's hands. The bear lunged and crashed into view, streaming blood and roaring now like a volcano in full eruption. Its growls drowned out the Fish-Eaters and its charge turned their cries at Conan to howls of fear, then of agony.

Two Fish-Eaters died in that first charge. Others were wounded, either by lighter swipes of the paws or by their fleeing comrades knocking them down and trampling them. Spears flew, but few struck and none drove deep.

The bear whirled, striking with left and right paws in succession, like a human adept at the pankration. More bloody furrows opened in black skins, but there were some stout hearts under those skins. Conan saw one man—no, boy—run in with a long-tined fishing trident and thrust it deep into the bear's unhurt leg.

Then the lad died screaming as the creature whirled, bending like a bow to clamp its jaws across his belly. The screams ended as the fangs reached his vitals. The bear tossed its head, then flung the corpse away and turned to seek new victims.

Conan saw that the Fish-Eaters might fight with the courage of despair but had neither weapons nor craft to contend with the beast. Nor would it be easy for him to best it in the open, where it could whirl about in its own length to face and strike seemingly in every direction.

An icy chill ran down the Cimmerian's spine, even in the heat of the jungle night. Had the dying Vendhyan spoken the plain truth, that demons had a gate through which to send men and beasts where nature would not allow them?

Demon-sent or no, however, the bear was flesh and blood. It could be slain, and with the battle-fury upon him, Conan knew that if it was not, he would not see another sunrise.

The Fish-Eaters were making a wide circle around the bear, some braver than others darting in to drag away the bodies of their dead. The most courageous of all thrust their spears, but their courage only cost them their lives. The bear still had one eye, much vigor, and a hide too thick for the light spears of the Fish-Eaters.

Conan waited only long enough to be sure that the Fish-Eaters saw him. Whether they could tell him from the bear, he could not be sure. Whether they would check their throws even if they could was still more doubtful.

The one thing Conan did not doubt was that a warrior's honor demanded the creature's death.

Spears did fly as he plunged at the bear, but two missed and he plucked one out of the air. A fourth only grazed one shoulder blade. Then he was moving too fast for the Fish-Eaters to follow him as he closed with the bear, sword in one hand, spear raised high in the other.

He was also moving too fast for the bear. It was slow

to turn to face him, and Conan let out a roar of triumph. That roar seemed to finally put the beast in fear. It shook its head in confusion and pain, as if its wounds were finally besting its fighting spirit.

Conan dared to close. He flung the spear from just outside touching distance, and it pierced fur and hide. The bear turned, snapping with blood-dripping jaws at the shaft in its side. Doing so, it offered the Cimmerian the back of its neck.

Even a good broadsword driven by both of Conan's arms was unequal to slaying the bear at one blow, and from that, the Cimmerian nearly died. The bear forgot the spear, remembered his old foe, and spun, both paws striking at Conan, who was leaping backward after his sword-blow. One paw struck him, and fortunately it was the right paw, from which he had already sheared half the claws. Otherwise he would have been gutted like a sheep carcass and flung down upon the bodies of the dead Fish-Eaters.

That was the bear's last blow. Blood gushed from its neck wound, staining the already much-stained white fur. It lay down, then settled its head on its paws. It growled a final defiance as one Fish-Eater drew close, then rolled over on its side.

Conan saw the light go out of the bear's remaining eye, and he was all but tempted to sing a death-song for it, as for a vanquished human foe. Snatched from its own land and flung out here in the stifling jungle, it had done its best to live and had met death with a warrior's courage.

Then the Fish-Eaters were all around the bear, blocking Conan's view of it, thrusting with spears and hammering it with clubs . . . all except one man, older and slighter than most of his comrades, and wearing an elaborate feathered headdress taller than he was.

This one pointed a cunningly wrought stick at Conan and shouted: "The demons war among themselves! Kill Amra and we will be done with them! He has slain his rebellious servant. Now it is his turn to die!"

At least that was the sense that came to the Cimmerian. It took a while for it to reach the Fish-Eaters, deafened by rage, blood-lust, and triumph.

It took no time at all for Conan to realize that the Fish-Eaters' gratitude would take the form of spears in his gizzard. That was a reward he had no mind to wait to collect.

"Crom!" he snarled and spat on the ground. The Fish-Eater chief jumped back, as if he expected to see flames arise where the Cimmerian spat. Then he jumped again as Conan snatched up a spear.

That was not enough. Conan's throw sent the spear clean through the fancy headdress, impaling it like bait on a fisherman's hook. The spear flew on to sink deep into a tree trunk and stand there quivering, with the headdress dangling from the shaft.

Before the Fish-Eaters stopped gaping at the sight, the Cimmerian turned his back on them and strode off toward the stream. If the bear had left any fish at all from the ruined trap, he would carry off a few for food on his journey to the Bamulas.

Before he reached the stream, the thunder came again, a single clap, followed by a long rumble dying away into the ordinary sounds of the jungle night. Conan halted, weapons ready, looking back on his trail for signs of pursuit by Fish-Eaters, bears, demons, or anything else.

He saw nothing and heard no unnatural sounds, nor any further thunder. The bear might be dead, but whatever had brought it to the Black Kingdoms from the frozen lands of the north was still abroad in the jungle.

Four

So the Fish-Eaters did not follow you?" a Bamula whom Conan did not recognize asked.

Conan's brows drew together. He fought an urge to loosen a few of the fellow's teeth. Under their dark skin the folk of the Black Kingdoms had every virtue and every vice he had met elsewhere. One vice was asking questions asked ten times before, merely to hear the sound of their own voices.

"Is this a counting-house in Shem or a council hut of warriors of the Bamulas?" the Cimmerian growled. He looked at Kubwande. "Or has someone forgotten to tell others what I told him?"

Kubwande spread his hands in a placating gesture. "I have told as many as have asked."

"Well, the next time hold them down and shout it in

their ears, or I will do it for you," Conan said. He grinned, to take the menace from the words.

The Bamula warriors did not relax their guard. Stout fighters every one of them, they knew that none of them could have done half of what Amra had done. This made him the master of any warrior at the council, even if less than half of his tale was true.

"The Fish-Eaters did not follow," Conan went on, measuring the silence. "But if you think this means they bear me any goodwill or expect me to be their man among the Bamulas, think again. Or use your heads for brewpots, for they hold no wits!"

His look invited anyone who wanted to take the insult seriously to do so, as long as he had mourners enough for proper rites afterward. None of the Bamulas accepted the invitation, and after a moment more of silence, Idosso let out a gusty laugh. Beer-laden breath washed over the Cimmerian as the Bamula chief shook and quivered.

"Of course the Fish-Eaters would not follow this lion among men," he said at last. "They have the courage of she-goats, if that. And to think of a lion obeying the commands of such goats! Sooner think of *me* doing it!"

That signaled the other Bamulas to join the laughter. Conan looked around at the faces, noting how they watched Idosso. Clearly, these were the warriors and petty chiefs loyal to the big *qamu*. Just as clearly, both Idosso and his followers expected Conan to join their ranks in return for their offering safety among their tribe.

In that, too, the folk of the Black Kingdoms were like all other men Conan had met and fought.

This time the urge he fought down was to toss his beer in Idosso's face and follow the beer with a good measure of Aquilonian steel. Conan's dagger was much closer to his hand than any of these folk seemed to realize. His patience with their treating him as a witling was also much closer to its end.

No, there was one among them who seemed to see clearly. The one whose name he remembered as Kubwande was nodding. "I doubt that the bear left half the Fish-Eaters fit to walk, let alone fight. And who among us would trail this wounded lion with less than a score of comrades? Idosso maybe, but who else?"

Everyone seemed to decide that it would flatter Idosso if they agreed with Kubwande. Conan saw heads nodding and hands thrusting gourds and wooden cups of beer toward him. He accepted them all. A man could drink enough of this jungle brew to float *Tigress* without fuddling his wits, if he had any to begin with.

"More beer!" someone shouted. Others took up the cry, and one man began pounding a drum.

The grass curtain across the door parted and two women entered. Their clothing consisted of heavy ivory earrings and necklaces of scarlet wooden beads. Both were young and slender, just out of girlhood, but one of them moved like a crone of seventy winters.

Looking more closely, Conan recognized the two Fish-Eater women he had allowed Idosso to carry off. The slow-moving one in her turn recognized him. Her look carried a wish that the wrath of all the gods descend on the Cimmerian and the claws and teeth of fifty demons rend him. It was a change from the last time he had seen them, when they seemed to think *he* might sprout teeth and claws if they yielded to him rather than to Idosso.

"Ho!" Idosso shouted. "Fresh Fish, are you doing as I told you, when you look at a sworn guest that way?"

Conan could recall no guest-oath, but he did not care to call Idosso a liar to his face. The woman clearly re-

called much, and none of it agreeable. She knelt, and
Idosso surged to his feet, one vast fist clenched to descend in a blow that might have broken the woman's
skull or snapped her neck.

The blow never landed. Idosso had touched the Cimmerian's honor too closely already by giving those
bruises that Conan now saw on Fresh Fish's otherwise
smooth and well-oiled skin. Clearly, the big man's word
to treat them well had been worthless, and Conan
would not see them suffer further, even to buy peace
with the Bamulas. Either the suffering or the peace
would end.

Conan's arm shot out and five sinewy fingers clamped
on Idosso's wrist. The Cimmerian let the thrust of
Idosso's blow pull him to his feet. In rising, he jerked
Idosso off balance. The Bamula would have fallen on
his nose at the feet of the women had not the Cimmerian held him in front and Kubwande and others from
the rear.

"You dare—!" someone began.

Conan cut him off. "These women came to me. I allowed them to go to you because they seemed to fear
me and you promised to treat them honorably. Now it
seems that you have given them reason to fear you more
than me."

Idosso snarled, shaking himself free of his helpers.
"Any man would have done the same. Or is your blood
as milky as your skin, Little Lion, that you know nothing of women?"

Conan released his grip and stepped back. The
women gaped at him, horror warring with dawning
hope on their faces. "If you want to see the color of my
blood, Idosso, try to take it," he said. "Or take a Cimmerian at his word, and remember what you promised to
these women!"

Idosso looked ready to leap at the Cimmerian, until
he caught Kubwande's eye. Then he contented himself
with cursing eloquently. Finally he grabbed each woman
by an earring, jerked them to their feet, and all but
flung them at Conan. They fell back to their knees,
struggling with the pain of their bleeding ears, and each
grasped Conan's legs.

"Take them, then, and may you have much joy of a
better man's leavings!" Idosso snarled. "Take them, and
be out of Bamula lands before nightfall, or—"

Idosso's threat died unuttered as a sweat-drenched
warrior flung himself through the curtain and fell at the
chief's feet. The big man gaped at this portent, then
Kubwande signed the man to rise.

"What is it?" Idosso demanded.

"The demons struck again," the newcomer gasped.
"In Dead Elephant Valley, they have taken a village."

"Taken?" Conan exclaimed. "Carried off, you mean?"

Either the man did not understand him or did not
recognize him as one with the right to an answer. Only
when Kubwande (again!) signaled did the man begin to
speak.

Conan listened to a tale of a village assaulted by
beasts out of a nightmare. They had the forms of apes
but the scales and sharp teeth of gigantic lizards, as well
as the ravenous appetite of starving lions. A score of the
villagers were dead, as many more hurt, huts, grain
stores, and livestock ruined, and altogether as much
harm done as a band of hostile warriors could have contrived.

He also saw the eyes of warriors searching him for
some sign of foreknowledge. It seemed that the Fish-
Eaters were not the only ones who suspected him of being such an utter fool as to deal with demons!

Conan muttered curses under his breath, wishing

himself and the women a long way from the land of the
Bamulas. But wishes were not fishes, nor even Fish-
Eaters in strength enough to protect the women should
he return them to their kin and tribe.

The Cimmerian added curses on the whole race of
women, except one whose spirit now walked with the
spirits of other valiant warriors. Without the two
wenches, there'd be no cause for him to quarrel with
Idosso. It would be his choice, to stay among the
Bamulas or to set his feet to the nearest trail and blink
the smoke of their huts from his eyes for all time.

"Idosso, my friend," Conan said. "It is too great an
honor, these two fine women. I must do something
more to earn it before I can take them with a good
heart."

"So?" Idosso's growl was still that of a bear's, but one
disturbed from sleep rather than enraged or hungry.

"So I think we'd best all be on our way to Dead Elephant Valley and see this demon's work," Conan went
on. "If I help the Bamulas fight these demon-spawn,
then I will take the women for my household. But by
Crom, I will earn that household before I take any
women to it! Conan of Cimmeria accepts nothing like a
bone thrown to a dog, and the Bamulas had best remember that!"

It took much less than Conan's knowledge of men's
eyes to read those of the Bamulas. *Surely this quest will
prove Amra either a great warrior or a friend of demons,*
all the eyes said.

Only Kubwande's were unreadable. Conan measured
the lesser chief, wondering if his life among the
Bamulas might be easier if the man was not quick
enough to escape one of these demon-spawned lizard-
apes.

But to every man his fate. Conan would accept his

when Crom sent it, and not push another into death's path when that other had as yet done him no harm.

Then he looked down at the women. Their eyes were even easier to read than those of the warriors. The women's eyes held a wish that Conan be found worthy of some rank that would allow him to protect them. A short while at Idosso's mercy seemed to have left them indifferent to whether he was black or white, brown or purple, yellow like the folk of Khitai or spotted like the Dog Men of old tales, if only he could stand between them and the Bamula chief.

Conan drew the women to their feet and rested one brawny arm lightly across each set of slender shoulders. "Well," he growled to the assembled warriors. "What say the Bamulas? Or are they going to stand gawping, until I have to find my own spears and mealies and make the journey with only these wenches for help?"

After that, it seemed that the Bamulas could not swear to the bargain fast enough.

In the Pictish lands of the north, Lysenius had exhausted his curses. This was as well, as he had likewise exhausted his daughter Scyra's patience. She had even ventured to speak sharply to him about wasting his strength and frightening those Picts within hearing.

"Any Picts that close are weaklings!" was his reply. "Best I frighten them to death, before they breed weakling sons!"

"Some of them are sure to do so," Scyra said, smiling. "How many of them can marry me?"

Then her smile faded as her father cuffed her, not angrily but not lightly either. "No jesting, girl. There're ten clans that would follow us if their chiefs had hopes of getting sons from you."

She held the shadow of the smile on her face until her

father turned away. Even then she did not ease her stance or lower her head until she heard his footsteps passing out of the chamber, down the passage. . . .

Down the passage to the other chamber, where he would wrestle with his Stygian scrolls. Wrestle not altogether in vain, and always with great earnestness, as he sought true mastery of the spell of the world-walker. He wished not to merely use the spell about the world at random, but to master it so that he could pluck anything (or anyone) he wished from one chosen place and send it to another.

The girl shivered from more than the chill of the cave. She had heard in her father's nighttime mutterings hints that blood-sacrifices might help one master this and other spells. The blood of near-kin, by preference—and she was the only kin her father had yet living in all the world, let alone in this cold land to which she had followed him because she would have been doomed as he in the land where they were born.

The blood of near-kin—or the blood of *many* victims. Would she have to choose between being the sacrifice herself or being wed to some bandy-legged Pictish chief so as to buy the blood of a score of his warriors, wives, and slaves?

The shivering passed. Now what the girl felt was an inner queasiness. Also, deeper within, a firmer resolve than before to increase her knowledge of her father's wizardry.

He had said little enough, one way or the other, about her learning magick. What she had learned, she had learned carefully, because even before the quest for the demon's gate began, she knew that magick gone awry was an unforgivable crime.

That care took its price, though. She had to snatch her time with the scrolls and phials from her other work, work that was entirely hers from the time her mother died. Years before the yeomen of the land came with bows and ropes in search of her father's life, no servant would spend a night under the Cave Wizard's roof. She cooked and cleaned, washed and mended, and by candlelight after all was done, scraped up knowledge of a few lesser spells.

That knowledge would no longer be enough. Use those lesser spells to heat the soup or to lure birds into the snares? Why not? Every moment, every drop of sweat, saved from her work meant freedom to spend increasing her own knowledge.

Her father would not notice how she did the work. He would notice only if she failed, as had been his way even before her mother died.

Mother, you could have saved both me and Father, by not dying. He might not have heeded you, but alive, you would not need the vengeance that has consumed him.

But that was a foolish girl's wish, and her time for being either a girl or foolish was rapidly nearing its end. Every day brought her closer to the time when she would be either woman-wise or dead . . . or wishing that she were.

Somehow, Kubwande was not surprised when the man who answered to both "Conan" and "Amra" brought the two Fish-Eater wenches with him on the trek to Dead Elephant Valley. Anyone who would risk a quarrel with Idosso over such women was hardly a man to leave them in the very village where Idosso had a dozen sworn friends who would avenge the slight to his honor by killing the women.

Of course, such friends would not have won through. It would have been their blood trailed on the dirt of the village paths, and their hyena-gnawed bodies found on the edge of the forest in the morning.

Some of those Idosso thought were his friends were sworn to Kubwande by still more potent oaths (and many good cows had it cost Kubwande to purchase the binding of those oaths from the wizards and wise-women). Others were friends only to Kubwande and no other among the Bamulas. A man who feared the fate of those who stole from wizards or lay with their sisters would do far more than guard a pair of Fish-Eater women for the man who held their secret.

Shedding the blood of Idosso's friends to keep Conan among the Bamulas was gambling, of course. But since he first learned of the game of chance, Kubwande had never gambled save with bones he had carved or shells he had painted himself. Now his game-pieces were men, but he still took care that they were of his own making, unlikely to do anything to surprise him.

The only question, in the innermost recesses of his spirit, was whether the white warrior was not even more accustomed to gambling, and for higher stakes, than Kubwande or any other among the Bamulas.

Then, after two days' swift march, warriors and women alike came to Dead Elephant Valley, and there was no more time to play luck-games with men, or even to think about it.

Five

The village was a sight to daunt even the Cimmerian, who had looked on such more times than he had years, and sometimes when friends or allies lay stark and bloody in the ruins. This village at least was one of strangers.

Even from two long spear-casts away, one could tell that more than elephants now lay dead in the valley. Closer to hand, the stench rose like a wall, and the air seemed so thick with the reek of death that one could cut slices from it with a dagger.

Not all the huts were ashes, ruins, or the tombs of their inhabitants. Some yet stood, and in their shadowed interiors Conan glimpsed still more shadowy figures, furtive and fleeting.

Emboldened by the coming of the Bamula war party, a few of the hardiest villagers crept out into the gray dawn light and began to move about. They still avoided, as if it were the mouth of the underworld, the center of the village, for there the dead lay thickest.

As the sun climbed higher and burned off the mist, turning the sky from gray to blue, insects began to gather. One sight seared itself into Conan's memory: a babe who could not have seen out his first year, slashed open from throat to belly, and one leg ripped from its socket.

Flies hummed around the eyes of the tiny corpse, and other, less familiar insects crawled over the rest of the blackening body. Nor was the small corpse intact even apart from its wounds; other carrion-eaters had been there before the insects.

In the middle of the human corpses lay the body of one of the lizard-apes. Braving the stench, Conan strode forward to within a spear's length of the dead "demon" and studied it. Rather as he would have noted the armor and weapons of a dead foe from a host he had never met before, he noted the beast's apparent strengths and weaknesses.

It had an ape's long arms but longer legs than most apes Conan had met, as well as a stumpy tail. Short spines ran up its back from the base of the tail to the neck, then resumed on the head as a crest. With the butt of a spear, Conan prodded the scaly hide, more resistant to weapons than any ape's but clearly not impenetrable. Half a dozen spears, as many arrows, and a portion of skull crushed in deeply by a club swung with desperate strength, bore witness to that.

Conan shifted the spear-butt to the beast's mouth, prying open the jaws. Most of the teeth were caked black with dried blood and shreds of human flesh, but Conan saw that they were more like a leopard's than a gorilla's. In their native land, these beasts ate flesh.

"But not in this land," the Cimmerian said to himself. "By Crom, not in this land! Not again."

"Eh?" Idosso asked, then covered his confusion with a bellowed war cry. Carrion birds, feeding on corpses at the fringes of the village, flew up squawking and screaming. The villagers flinched as if Idosso himself had turned into one of the lizard-apes.

"Well, Amra, does all this sniffing and poking tell you anything?" he growled. "It is said you have more than a man's senses."

"Much is said, by those who know nothing," Conan replied. At Idosso's scowl, he added, "Wise men such as you and I do not listen to them."

The diplomacy acheived the effect the Cimmerian had hoped for. Idosso's scowl turned into nothing worse than the frown of a man trying to think what to do next. Conan already knew, and likewise was sure that Idosso would hardly welcome advice.

"The back, guard the women and bearers," the chief shouted. "Chest and belly, ring the village. Arms, to me." It was the Bamulas's custom to divide any large war party into four divisions, each named after a part of the human body. The arms were the vanguard, scouting ahead. The chest and belly were the main body, supposed to be the strongest and fiercest warriors. The back brought up the rear; its warriors were commonly either youths newly given their spears or older men not far from putting their spears into the roofbeams of their huts, the Bamula ritual for declaring oneself an elder.

It had not surprised the Cimmerian to learn that when both chiefs carried spears in another's band, Kubwande had marched with the arms and Idosso in the belly.

Conan held his tongue as the Bamulas moved to obey

Idosso. He also stepped back from the center of the village, so that he would not have to hold his nose.

The Bamulas moved in obedience to Idosso. Some were clearly swift, skilled, and alert enough to please any captain. Others were merely trying to pretend the best they could. It was the same mixture that Conan had seen in other hosts, save those who were either handpicked from proven warriors or rabbles snatched from the streets and farms by some lord's sergeants.

The Bamulas would hardly prevail against an equal force of seasoned troops from some civilized land, but then they wouldn't have to. Their warriors did well enough against rival tribes, and they held their own against the occasional slave-raider, darting in from the sea or across the Stygian frontier to pluck a village's worth of live merchandise. It remained to be seen whether they would be equal to the task they now faced, that of fighting demons, or at least creatures hurled into this land by sorcery as vile as any demon.

Conan strode over to Idosso. He made the greetings of one chief to another slightly higher in rank, as well as other gestures of respect he had learned from the Suba warriors aboard *Tigress*. He hoped that none of these were insults among the Bamula.

"Speak, Amra," Idosso said. He had command of his voice, but when the chief spoke, Conan could hear a hint of weariness—the result of the battle he had fought to become chief.

For once, the huge Bamula had the Cimmerian's sympathy. Conan's own early battles as a captain were not forgotten, nor the indescribable pleasure of facing the unknown and pretending that it was neither frightening nor confusing.

As a pleasure, it ranked just ahead of drinking bad wine or embracing aged serving wenches. It was also quite as common a part of the warrior's life, and Idosso was just going to have to take it as one more of the gods' favorite jests.

"I doubt that I've anything to say that you haven't long since thought of yourself," Conan said. "Have any of the folk of the village come forward to tell the tale of their slaying the beast?"

"No, but what can they teach our warriors?"

Conan almost forgave Idosso's arrogance for his saying "our." Being soft-spoken to pale-skinned strangers was clearly no pleasure to Idosso, but it was an art he was prepared to master if called upon.

If Kubwande thought the big man was too witless to be other than the smaller man's puppet, he might have a rude awakening in store for him. Probably in the last moments of his life.

"The gods only know, but I cannot help wondering," the Cimmerian said. "These lizard-apes look like natural creatures, the same as the boar and the bear. Warriors' weapons can take their life. But how many warriors will die in so doing?"

"Do you think Bamula warriors fear death?" Idosso did not raise a weapon. His voice made such a gesture needless.

"Less *even* than I," Conan said. "But *even* a Bamula warrior might think twice about dying before all the demons were slain. If we trade our lives for the lives of this band of lizard-apes, what happens when the next band comes through the demon's gate?"

Idosso looked as close to uneasy as his face allowed. Conan pressed his advantage.

"Any man might fear seeing his village used as this one has been—his women carried off, his sons gutted like that babe there."

Idosso looked, and his face worked. "Then let us find the demon's gate and close it."

"Aye, and with our own living flesh if need be. But we shall hunt it with more knowledge if we speak to the villagers first."

Idosso stood like a vast ebony image. Then his head jerked, hard enough to make the crimson feathers of his headdress dance like branches in a gale.

"Let the arms search the village," he shouted. "Bring all fit, to speak to me! At once!"

The warriors of the arms thumped their fists on the earth at Idosso's feet. He spat where they had thumped. They struck their foreheads with their open palms, formed into pairs, and ran off, spears in hand and shields on their arms.

"Am I permitted—?" Kubwande asked. He seemed to have sprung from the earth, but Conan was hardly surprised. The gift of silent movement was one a man like Kubwande would surely need.

"Not alone," Idosso growled. "You have no lizard-scales with which to keep a spear out of your unguarded back."

Conan neither smiled nor shouted for joy. He only said, "Would I be good enough to guard it?"

"Am I worthy of being guarded by Amra—?" Kubwande began, to be interrupted by the Cimmerian.

"Flatter one who will listen to it," Conan said.

The Bamula looked as though he had been slapped. The Cimmerian wondered if he had spoken too plainly, or perhaps said something he had not meant. His command of the Black Kingdoms' tongues grew almost daily, but it was far from perfect.

"I have been a warrior in many lands, and on the seas," Conan said. "I have not been a warrior in this land nearly as long as you have. You must know things I do not, if you are not a babe in arms."

"If he is, then a stranger babe was never born of women," Idosso said. "Go and seek what you may find, unless you both think *I* need nursing?"

Neither Conan nor Kubwande stayed to answer that question.

Conan and Kubwande found less to do than they had expected, until they reached the farther edge of the village. The folk from the nearer huts had taken the brunt of the lizard-apes' assault, and those who had not died had mostly taken to their heels. Those left were mainly the aged, the young, or those caring for them.

These the other Bamula warrior-pairs were vigorously seizing, dragging out of their huts, and all but beating with clubs to learn what had happened. Kubwande admonished a few warriors who seemed sure to attract more fear than knowledge, just before Conan would have done the same.

That was as well, the Cimmerian knew. The villagers were Lesser Bamulas, whose dialect was somewhat apart from that of the Greater Bamulas whom he had met first. The villagers could have offered to guide him to the demon's gate, and he might have been slow to understand. Also, it was too soon to put to the test the willingness of Bamula warriors to obey his commands.

The two men stalked onward. Each kept his eyes roving over the huts, livestock enclosures, and fields. Out here, the huts were mostly intact, if empty, but too many of the enclosures and fields showed the passage of the lizard-apes. Where the cattle and goats did not lie gutted and fly-blown in patches of dried mud mixed from blood and soil, the fences lay smashed flat and the freshly sprouted grain and yams trampled into the earth.

A few villagers peered out of huts, more boldly than Conan had seen before. Some of them were young women. He thought of sending back to the baggage train for his two maidservants. Perhaps they could get some sense, or even knowledge, out of these village wenches.

No warriors appeared, not even the graybearded or newly fledged. The bodies strewn on blood-hued earth doubtless accounted for a good many of them, and others had surely stayed with the fugitives. But Conan wondered if that was all the warriors that Dead Elephant Valley had boasted on the morning the lizard-apes came.

He said nothing and indeed put the matter almost out of his innermost thoughts. But his eyes now searched the huts with more care than ever. Also, when he thought the head Bamula was not looking his way, he cast an eye on Kubwande.

In the Pictish lands, Lycenius's wrath had long since taken him past cursing, into a morose silence. Before the silence came, however, Scyra had learned that he had a new problem with the world-walker.

Once the problem had been to keep it open. Now it was open at both ends and would not close. The gate ran from a remote part of the jungles south of Khitai to somewhere in the Black Kingdoms. Though this was more knowledge than he had usually possessed before, it was useless as a midwife's pain-charm for closing the gate.

It was not that Scyra cared much for the fate of the jungles and their remnant of a race from before the dawn of man. She cared hardly more for the Black

Kingdoms, full (or so she had heard) of fierce warriors to whom a score of monsters could hardly be more than a brisk day's martial exercise.

She did care very greatly that frustration and failure could drive her father ever closer to the edge of madness, or even over it. Nor was there a great deal she could do to prevent it. She might try to heal him if he slipped beyond that edge, or at least care for him, but to do either, she would have to be alive.

It was the knowledge that she might soon be at the mercy of her own resources, which were small, or of the Picts, among whom "mercy" was near-kin to a curse, that kept her at work. The hides were easily filched from the store in the cave; the spells she had largely fixed in her memory.

It was the herbs and unguents that gave her the trouble now. Neither could be easily filched from her father's stores in sufficient quantity without his being warned. Later in the year, if the peace with the Owl Picts held, she might gather the herbs herself, but now the Owls did not guard Lysenius's lands, which were just awakening to the new spring.

With the gods' favor (she had invoked all save Set), she would be apt for a short time of shape-changing. If that short time was not enough, she would face the choice of remaining in animal form forever or turning back to face her father's wrath.

She might even be driven to praying and sacrificing to Set, if she thought the Lord of Serpents could spare her that choice.

In time, Conan began to wonder if the "village" of Dead Elephant Valley stretched all the way to the Suba lands, or perhaps to the sea. Certainly he and Kubwande had already covered ground enough to hold some of Turan's smaller cities, or a merchant prince's estate in Argos.

At least they were leaving the slaughterhouse stench behind, which must be growing riper as the sun climbed higher. Now the orb blazed from above all but the highest treetops, stripping the last shreds of mist from the jungle and awakening those birds and beasts of daylight, who had slumbered until dawn. They added their sounds to the rising din of the jungle, until Conan could no longer hear his own footsteps and had to raise his voice for Kubwande to hear him.

He had noticed that no other Bamula searchers were in sight, and even their footprints were few and sparse. One could tell the Bamula warriors' prints from the villagers'—the villagers wore footgear that spread the great toe wide apart from the other four toes. Kubwande and the Cimmerian were some distance from friends, whom they might need should they meet enemies.

They met neither friend nor foe for about as long as it took a skilled dancer in a good tavern to divest herself of her garments. During that time, they reached a part of the village—or perhaps it was another village—where the huts thrust themselves deep into dense second-growth jungle. Or perhaps it was the jungle growing back among the houses.

However it came about, the few huts were low and rude, almost lost in walls of stunted trees and lank vines. The fields seemed to cower before the onset of the jungle. Only the cattle-pens and the fowl-runs rose stout and well-made, everywhere set about with thorns.

Conan had seen such care taken in other lands, where beasts of prey roamed close to human habitation. A babe or child, even a servant or lesser wife, taken by the leopards was of small moment. Loss of a cow, or even a calf, spelled disaster.

That at least was not the Cimmerian way. For a moment, Conan looked back across the years, as he might have looked down a well, to consider his involuntary leave-taking from his homeland. On the times he had returned, he had found nothing to make him less a wanderer. When he had found Belit, he had thought it might be a good sign that the gods blessed those wanderings.

Now she was gone, and again he wandered alone. He hardly cared where those wanderings ended, or when. But he had more than enough pride, to be sure that neither an oaf like Idosso or a schemer like Kubwande would make an end of him without a fight that storytellers would still remember when the world was old.

Conan shortened his stride until he was level with Kubwande, then a trifle ahead. He had no need to be at Kubwande's back, and indeed that might give offense without cause and bring a quarrel without purpose. Neither would he give Kubwande a clear look at *his* back. Enough that the women were a long way behind him, tending the baggage and no doubt well-guarded—as long as Idosso wished them so.

The ground began to slope down, and through leather-tough soles Conan sensed dampness underfoot. They passed a fish-trap that had once been very like the Cimmerian's, and was now rent savagely apart, as his had been, by the ice bear. Then the ground dropped away, and they stared down a path that broke the wall of vines, giving passage onto a shingle beach, and beyond the beach, a view of a muddy stream.

The stream was hardly more than thirty paces wide, but judged by the current in the middle, it was too deep to wade. Also, as with most streams in the Black Forest, it was doubtless home to crocodiles and river-horses.

Conan slung his shield and spear to free both hands, then leapt down the last few paces of path to the beach. Gravel hurled by his landing raised spray from the river and sent a swirling rainbow of fish darting for safety.

"What are you doing?" Kubwande sounded truly concerned for the Cimmerian's safety.

"Looking for boats. If anyone has gone on from here, they're in a boat. It may have left traces."

Kubwande's face hinted that searching for anything short of a pile of gold this close to the river was less than wise. Conan kept on with his search, kneeling at times to examine the gravel, being careful to turn his back neither on the water nor on Kubwande.

At last he rose and stared downstream. "Two boats were here, I think. Both are long gone. All the footprints look to be the villagers'. No signs of crocodiles or river-horses."

"What about the lizard-apes?"

"I'd not wager on recognizing their prints. But do you see signs of any kind of fight?"

Kubwande studied the beach and the path, then the masses of vegetation. He was plainly determined to prove as skilled a tracker as the Cimmerian, but also unwilling to pretend to see what was not there. An honest streak, or only enemies whom he feared might make common cause with the Cimmerian?

Conan laughed. Honesty in such as Kubwande was as rare as chastity in tavern wenches, whether they were white, black, yellow, purple, or green. The *iqako* had also mistaken his man if he thought Conan would stoop to making common cause with one set of intriguers against another. If matters came to that pass, he'd shake the mud of the Bamula lands from his feet and fight his battles elsewhere.

"What is the jest, Amra?"

It tempted the Cimmerian to give Kubwande a truthful answer. He might even have yielded had he thought for a moment the man would believe him.

"A thought came to me. Have the villagers fled the lizard-apes only to fall prey to river-horses?"

"Only the river-spirits know, and they seem slow to speak today." Kubwande shrugged and turned his back on both the Cimmerian and the river as he climbed the bank.

He had just reached the level ground when the vegetation rustled, tore, and disgorged a half-score village warriors. Some of the men of the village had survived demon-sent lizard-apes, fear, and any perils of the river, to seek vengeance with spear and shield.

There could be no doubt, either, about the object of their vengeance. "Slay the demon-master!" one screamed, and flung his spear straight at Conan. The Cimmerian's shield leapt up, catching the spear in midflight and knocking it into a wild arc. It soared high over all heads and vanished in the mud-hued river.

The next spear Conan met more boldly. He snatched it from the air, whirled like an Iranistani dervish, and flung the spear butt-first the way it had come. Also butt-first, it struck a warrior, just above his loinguard. He doubled over, dropping shield and remaining weapons, then sat down abruptly, gasping, groaning, and spewing all at the same time.

Three more spears followed, but Conan's feat had dazzled eyes and slowed arms. All three spears sank deep into the thick leather and tough wood of his shield; none of them came anywhere near his flesh.

"I am no demon-lover!" Conan shouted. "Kubwande, you speak their tongue. Tell them that. Tell them that I can give their spears back butt-first, so they can use them against the demons. Or I can return them point-foremost, if they try to kill me."

Kubwande shouted. It slowed a few of the villagers but stopped none. Four of them half-slid, half-fell, down the bank and came at Conan with spears held low or clubs brandished high. If they could not slay the demon's master from a distance, they were ready to fight, kill, or die at close quarters.

Fighting men who were determined to kill, without shedding their own blood, was the most demanding sort of fighting. It was also an art in which the Cimmerian was not as skilled as he now wished. For most of his years, his battles had been against those who sought his life, and there was no reason not to take theirs.

Matters were otherwise now. The villagers had lost scores of people to the lizard-apes' teeth and claws, and they would lose more to the perils of jungle and river before all the fugitives returned. Conan had no wish to weaken them further, or to make them enemies, when their strength and friendship might help solve the mystery of the demon's gate.

So he wielded shield and spear as he might have done in a tavern brawl, where honor rather than life was at stake. As he had the advantage of reach on all of the warriors, this went well at first.

Conan rammed the shield up under the jaw of one man, while thrusting with the spear-butt into the thigh of another. Both men went down. Then he swung the spear clubwise to the temple of a third man. The man's headdress, shield, and war club toppled, and a moment later he measured his length on the beach among them.

That reduced the number of opponents on their feet, and the ardor of those left standing. Conan saw Kubwande driving two others back up the path, shield and spear dancing almost too fast for the eye to follow.

He hoped the Bamula would have the wits to end the
fight without ending his opponents' lives.

Then three more villagers leapt down onto the beach.
That restored the enemy's strength, and they began
spreading out to either side, seemingly to trap the Cimmerian with his back to the stream. One of the newcomers was young, hardly more than a boy, and with the
rash courage of youth, he ran into the water, hoping to
outflank the Cimmerian.

Conan was trying to look in all directions at once,
when the splashing of the boy ended in a louder splash.
The horror in the villagers' eyes told him what made the
second splash, even before he heard the bellow of a
river-horse.

The Cimmerian whirled and leapt in a single motion,
landing clear of the circle of warriors. One obstinate villager thrust at him. Conan's spear danced and came
down across the man's wrist. He yelped like a kicked
dog and stumbled out of range, cradling his wounded
hand in his sound one.

The river-horse had the lad gripped in its massive
jaws now. But Conan saw that by some god's whim, the
boy was held in a gap between the beast's teeth. None of
the tushes, long as a short-sword and razor-edged, had
pierced his flesh.

Water fountained as the Cimmerian leapt into the
river. His club blurred in an overhand stroke that could
have taken a bird on the wing. Instead, it took the river-
horse squarely across the nose. The beast reared back,
jaws gaping.

Even Conan's thews protested as he lunged with one
arm to grip the boy by the loinguard and snatch him
from the jaws. With the other arm, he drove his spear
deep into the roof of the beast's mouth.

The river-horse bellowed like a dragon and churned

the river like a school of sharks in a feeding frenzy. It tried to snap at the boy, then at Conan, but the firmly embedded spear kept it from closing its mouth.

The Cimmerian held the boy at arm's length, examining him for wounds as he waded to the bank. "Here," he said, setting the boy on his feet. "Find a wise-woman for him and he'll do well enough. Better than you will the next time I find you naming me demon-master!"

The villager gaped. Then one of them ran forward and embraced the boy, which was all that kept the lad on his feet. Conan saw that the man's hair and beard showed gray, and judged he was the lad's father.

Meanwhile, the river-horse was thrashing about in the shallows, trying to be rid of the spear. Conan had thrust it in too deep for easy dislodging, but not deep enough to reach the beast's brain.

Maddened with pain like this, the creature might roam the river for days slaying many, before death came. Conan knelt to replenish his stock of spears, then turned and waded back into the river.

As the water reached his knees, he heard a mighty shout and a fierce splashing. Before he could turn, a rush of village warriors nearly knocked him off his feet. He had barely regained his balance before the villagers surrounded the river-horse, thrusting with spears, slashing and stabbing with daggers, even pounding on the tough hide with clubs as they might have pounded on signal drums.

The death-cries of the river-horse might have been heard as far as any drum, too. At last they ended, and the beast floated dead in bloody water. It took the united strength of all together, Conan included, to drag the river-horse out of reach of the current.

"Not out of reach of the crocodiles, though," Conan said. "Best we go back to the village and bring up a few more spearmen, and *all* the women to cut the carcase apart. I didn't wrestle that beast to give the crocodiles a banquet, by Crom!"

He had to speak three times before Kubwande seemed to understand. Even then, the warrior was slow to retrace his steps. The Cimmerian had time to receive the barely coherent thanks of the man whose son he had saved. The man was named Bessu, a lesser chief; his son was Govindue. Conan hoped both would speak for him in Dead Elephant Valley. There was precious little he could do in their land if he had to fear demons before and spears behind.

Conan also had time to prowl the bushes where the villagers had hidden. He found little that he had not expected, and only one thing that gave him any unease.

It was footprints leading to and then from the bushes. No villager's footprints, either, from the way the toes stood together. On a bush not far in from the bank was a blue feather. The villagers wore few feathers, and none blue that Conan had seen.

It was a rare Bamula warrior, on the other hand, who did not sport more blue feathers than any other color in the headdresses all were wearing today.

Conan's face was sober as he retraced his steps to the village, but all took it for the look of any man who has just escaped a death-grapple with a river-horse. None asked questions he could not readily answer, and soon the meat from the river-horse was roasting over cookfires and boiling in pots, sending more wholesome odors to war with the carrion stench.

Six

Conan climbed a hand'sbreadth higher on the branch, the height of a temple tower above the jungle floor. The branch swayed and creaked softly.

He climbed another hand'sbreadth. The branch sagged, and now the creaking held a sinister note, like the creaking of the ungreased hinges of a tomb door in the least-frequented part of a graveyard.

Conan considered that from where he was, he could see little. He considered that after a fall to the jungle floor, he would see even less, if he saw anything at all with living eyes.

Belit would not welcome him with open arms if he perished through a boy's folly. And speaking of boys—

"Govindue!"

"Here, Conan!"

"Where is here?"

"On the largest branch on—I think on the far side of the tree, from you."

It sounded to Conan rather as if the boy was in the next tribe's land, but the tree they had climbed was large. Also, the Cimmerian's ears had been accustomed to wide spaces, by land or sea. The jungle had a wizard's power to twist a foot snapping a twig, or even the fall of a drop of water, into something that sounded unnatural, whose distance one could not judge easily or sometimes at all. This made Conan no fonder of the jungle than before, but it was not beyond his power to learn the art of judging the distances in this land.

"Do you see clearly?"

"Yes."

"What do you see?"

"The tops of all the trees in the world, a sky that promises rain, and many birds."

"Any strange ones?"

Conan could almost hear the boy shrug as he replied. "There are many I do not know. But some are so far off that no one could make out their breed. Also, I do not know all the birds of the jungle."

"You see a trifle more clearly than some warriors twice your age, Govindue. You know what you do not know."

"Is this important?"

"Only if you want to live to twice your age, lad."

It sounded almost as if Govindue was laughing. Then Conan heard: "Are you coming higher to join me, Conan?"

"If I do, the next you'll be hearing of me is when I hit the ground and spatter like a ripe melon."

"Tell me when you fall, Conan. I want to watch."

"Your father said I might regret saving you. I begin to see that your father is a wise man."

From safely on his side of the tree, Govindue made a rude noise. Then he laughed, and the Cimmerian judged that the lad was resuming his watch over the roof of the jungle.

Conan and Govindue were not the only hunters for the demon's gate who were perched in tall trees, gazing out over sunlit treetops. Many other warriors, Greater and Lesser Bamulas alike, were aloft, not altogether certain of what they looked for but praying that nothing unusual would escape their eyes between dawn and dusk.

When all who sought the demon's gate had taken counsel together and all had spoken and been heard, it became clear that the demon's gate was not open at all times. When it was open, however, it had come to open very nearly the same place each time.

The first task, therefore, was to find this place. And the first suggestion Conan made was to begin the search from the high ground.

"There is no high ground in the jungle," a Bamula of Idosso's faction reminded them all.

"A watcher can do as well from atop a tree as from a cliff or the crest of a hill," Conan replied. "All he needs are sharp eyes and keen wits, which makes me doubt you could do much if we hung you by the heels from a cloud."

All laughed, even the man himself. Conan judged that a good sign. It was not within him to curry favor by meekness.

In Nemedia or Aquilonia (or so Conan had heard), a band of warriors such as the demon-hunters would note each coming of the demon-spawn on a map. The Bamulas knew nothing of maps, however. Conan had used maps in Turan and afterward as a mercenary, and charts while aboard *Tigress*, but he was not equal to teaching the art of the map to the Bamulas.

What the Bamulas did know was the jungle they had roamed since they were boys, and how to give Conan at least some of that knowledge. It was not hard to make in their minds a picture of a great circle, formed by the appearances of the demon-spawn.

A child could then understand that the gate must open and close somewhere within that circle. All that remained was to watch the circle.

Some of the Bamulas, currying favor with Idosso, and some of the villagers, bent on vengeance, wished to watch from the ground. To hide in trees like a monkey, they said, was for women, and for men with milk instead of blood in their veins. Some were bold enough to look at the pale-skinned Cimmerian as they said that.

Kubwande heaped scorn on those men like coals on a roasting fowl. "The jungle hides so much that all the tribes of the land together could not watch such a circle. Also, the demon-spawn are best not watched far from the ground."

"The ghosts of our kin will haunt us if we flee battle!" a villager snarled.

"If you watch from the ground, you will join your kin without a chance to avenge them!" Conan said. "None of these demon-spawn are fit prey for a single warrior. Face them alone, and you will prove yourself a brave fool. Face them with your comrades, and you will go to your kin with the foes' blood on your spears!"

He looked at the village chief. "Is not that the truth of it, Bessu? Did you not slay the lizard-ape while working together, after those who sought to be heroes were all dead?"

Govindue's father nodded. "Amra has seen the truth. By the spirit of my daughter, I swear it. These spawn must be fought by many against one. The many can come together only if they are warned. Only from the high places can the warning come swiftly."

So the watchers climbed aloft, the drummers settled down where they could hear the watchers and speak with their drums, and the warriors waited to hear the summons of both watchers and drums. All that remained was for the gate to again open itself, so that the watchers might see.

The demon-hunters had been watching and waiting now for ten days.

Conan had no intention of climbing down the tree and leaving Govindue to watch alone. Instead, he sought a more secure perch that would still let him see something besides a curtain of leaves.

He had just reached a point some five spears' length below Govindue when the boy cried aloud, surprise mingled with fear in his voice. Conan unslung his spear and gripped a stout branch with one iron-thewed arm. With the other hand, he used the spear to push the leaves aside.

It might have been a small bird close at hand. A hunter's instinct had told the boy, and now told the Cimmerian, that it was a giant far off. How far, Conan could not judge.

Plain to anyone's eyes, beyond the bird was an unearthly *shimmering* in the air above the jungle roof. It seemed a waterfall, all but solid with golden-scaled fish—which was impossible.

If this was not the demon's gate, then there were two creations of wizardry abroad in the jungle. Conan stared at the shimmering, squinting against the sun. He gave it his whole attention, trying to fix its position in relation to other visible objects.

It did not help that all those visible objects were the tops of trees. Conan's jungle lore grew daily, but he was not yet master of the art of telling trees apart at a glance.

He had just noted that one tree had a jutting three-sided crest, when Govindue shouted again. The branches quivered as the boy slid down to dangle beside him.

Conan now saw it also. The bird was sweeping toward them, as if it scented either prey or enemies. Conan had no intention of being the first, nor was he well-equipped to be the second, with only a spear and a dagger.

The bird turned in the air, seeming to stand on one wing. Each wing was the size of a ship's foresail. Turning, the bird revealed a repulsive belly the hue of dried blood, half-bare and surrounded by molting feathers of sickly gray and the green of swamp scum.

Its beak was the hooked weapon of a predator, and if that had not made its diet plain, a carrion reek wafted over Conan and his companion as the bird flew by.

Govindue lowered himself onto Conan's branch, which creaked but did not sway. With one hand, he gripped a light branch, with the other, he raised his spear.

Conan put a hand on the boy's shoulder and shook his head. "We will never have a better chance," Govindue said. "Warriors do not skulk."

"We are warriors with other tasks than fighting," Conan said. It went against every instinct hammered into him in his years of war to say this, but truth was as plain as the stink of the bird. As long as the bird lived, it might fly back to where it had come from: the shimmer, which might be the demon's gate, or whatever other place unnaturally linked this jungle with the bird's home.

Which "others," the Cimmerian wondered. He had

never heard of the jungles of Vendhya harboring birds the size of a war chariot, but even Vendhyans did not know all the denizens of their forests. Vendhya held wide expanses of rank forest where no man ventured lightly, and few of those who ventured at all ever returned.

As the bird flew past for a second time, Conan saw that the neck was even barer than the belly, and scaled as much like a serpent's as like a bird's. The eyes glared a venomous yellow and seemed to drip a pallid ichor.

Then the bird was coming for a third time, and it did not turn. Instead, it spread its wings wide with a thunder of air and a viler reek than before, and halted itself in midair. Long, claw-tipped toes, four on each foot, reached out for Govindue.

They never touched their goal. Warriors' instincts commanded both Conan and the boy. Each launched his spear simultaneously. A heavier weapon driven by a stouter arm, Conan's spear thrust deep into the bird's reeking breast. Govindue's flew straight to a more vulnerable target, one glaring eye.

Carrion breath nearly stifled the warriors, and the bird's shrieks of rage and pain almost deafened them. They clung like apes to the branches as the great wings thrashed wildly. Leaves, twigs, birds' nests, and the odd monkey showered down around them.

The bird plummeted away and out of sight, then reappeared farther off, climbing slowly. Blood oozed from one eye and added further hues to its breast. All but holding his breath, as patient as a great cat eyeing its prey, the Cimmerian waited. Waited for the bird to either flee toward that distant shimmering or return to the attack.

It did neither. Instead, it folded its wings and plummeted down into the jungle. Branches crackled and

splintered. Then came a mighty blow, making Conan's
tree shiver like a fence post struck with an axe.

Smoke poured up through the branches, greasy dark
fumes that reeked of burning flesh. Conan drew a scrap
of bark cloth from his loinguard and clapped it over his
nose. At last the unnatural stench faded. Govindue was
trying to look in all directions at once, as if he expected
another bird to fling itself at the tree. He gave little care
to a secure perch or grip, and Conan made ready to
catch him if he slipped.

Then the tree shivered again, worse than before. The
shivering passed briefly, only to return. This time it continued.

Suddenly Conan saw the horizon tilting, and heard
sharp cracks as wood fibers thicker than a man's arm
tore like threads. Somehow severed by the bird's funeral
pyre, the tree was toppling.

Conan reached up and grabbed Govindue. "Hold
tight, lad. There's no riding this one down. We'll have to
leap for it."

Govindue was silent. Limber and agile as he was, he
knew his master. He threw his arms around the Cimmerian's massive torso as Conan flexed his legs,
stretched out his arms, and leapt.

As their first tree fell away from them, they plunged
across open air and landed in a second tree. A branch
caught the Cimmerian across the chest, knocking the
wind from him and bruising Govindue's hands. The boy
used his feet to keep himself from plummeting to the
forest floor, then hooked one arm painfully over a
branch. The tree under the two swayed and creaked as
its falling neighbor tore vines, splintered branches, and
crushed everything beneath it into the forest floor.

Smoke and dust streamed up through the gap in the
forest roof, as if the bird's funeral pyre had reignited.

Conan and Govindue stared down at the corpse of the tree, seeking some traces of the corpse of the bird.

They saw nothing, save on either side of the severed trunk, a patch of ashes that might have come from wood, flesh, or leaf. Even the smell had vanished with what seemed miraculous speed.

No, with sorcerous speed. The demon's gate was letting greater and viler magick into the jungles each time it opened. This latest trespasser had immolated itself without harming more than trees. The next one might be as deadly as the snowbear, and as tenacious of life as a great serpent.

As Conan clambered down the tree, it struck him that learning where the demon's gate was might not be so great a victory by itself. Not if the gate was defended by creatures such as had come through it thus far, or even by more formidable ones.

There would indeed be grief among the kin of the hunters for the demon's gate before the hunt was done and the gate closed.

That night Lycenius cursed softly and fell asleep in his northern cave long before his daughter Scyra.

When she at last also slept, she knew still more about the world-walker, and much of the new knowledge gave her sinister dreams. The gate was transforming creatures that passed through it, a little more each time. Never in nature would that bird have burst into flames as it had.

Her father had never been fully master of the world-walker's powers. Now those powers were growing in ways that it was not meant for mortals to understand. It seemed that her father had tried to link the world-walker with the Pictish Wilderness instead of with Vendhya, and then close it. The link was uncertain, but there could be no doubt that the world-walker remained open. Was it to remain thus until it had sown chaos in whatever lands it might link?

Scyra slept then, and dreamed of the gate twisting so that it linked the Black Kingdoms and the Pictish Wilderness. She dreamed of warriors leaping—unchanged, by some sorcerous logic—through the gate and striding up the hill, led by one gigantic in stature, if blurred in features. A broadsword swung at his hip, she knew, and long black hair flowed from a nobly held head.

If he was coming for her, at least he was no Pict. Indeed, he looked fit to fight the warriors of any three tribes of that ill-natured race.

Seven

Conan and Govindue were not the only gate-hunters to see the shimmer above the treetops. Indeed, other watchers had studied it longer, not having to contend with giant birds. (One man was bitten by a tree adder and died of it, but this was an uncommon fate for those who searched the jungle, nor did it smell of sorcery.)

Each of the climbing watchers described what they had seen, some with more care than others. Kubwande listened to all alike with great attention, and beside him sat Idosso, seeming to listen as intently.

Conan also listened, and was pleased to recognize a fair number of places where he had wandered before the demon's gate opened. It was good to know that he had not lost his power to swiftly learn the lay of a battlefield.

Of course, he had intended the jungles to be a refuge from the sea and all the bitter memories it held. It was distant and malignant sorcery that had turned the land into a battlefield, and the demon's gate that held the key to defeating that sorcery.

Now it seemed that the warriors held the key to finding the demon's gate. Or so Kubwande said.

"We should watch the slope dawnwards of River-Horse Crossing on the Afui," he said. "Some should watch aloft, some from the ground. All will need their finest weapons, and hearts girded with courage."

"Then we are ready for the hunt," Idosso said. "All are armed and brave, and let no one doubt it."

Conan could have laughed at Kubwande's face, which was a study in hiding his anger at being chided by his friend. It would have been unwise, however. Plainly, the two chiefs were rapidly becoming as much rivals as allies in the quest for the demon's gate. The honor of closing it would be a warrior's dream, and past friendships would be of little account.

Such rivalries were nothing new to the Cimmerian. In many lands over many years, he had snatched everything from pearls to chieftainships. One day he might snatch a throne, although that was not something he valued as much as some did. A king was not nearly as much his own master as folk thought, and he was a fixed target for his enemies.

What prize Conan might find in the Black Kingdoms he hardly knew and did not much care, as long as it made him no more enemies than those with whom he could contend. That would be more than he had so far, of a certainty.

The Black Kingdoms bred stout warriors. Cimmeria bred still stouter ones.

They marched to the banks of the Afui in a dawn that hinted of rain not far distant. Mist rose from the trails and spiraled upward, to veil saffron-hued flowers and clusters of drumfruit, a deep, glossy purple worthy of a royal robe. Insects chirred and whined high and low.

Conan marched in the vanguard with the arms. He had not seen the two women since the night before last, but they had showed no hurt then. They might have grown a trifle thin-flanked, carrying waterskins and mealie sacks, but their bruises had healed and their eyes rested approvingly on the big Cimmerian.

The party split to move along three trails as it approached the Afui. Conan judged that this might take the men on each trail out of reach of help from the others. It would also bring more warriors up to the river at one time. Time and the gods would tell which was the greater risk.

Idosso seemed in rare good spirits this morning. He even tried to sing, until Kubwande gently urged him to silence. Conan knew the lesser chief's prompting was due to the nearness of wild animals, but doubted that was the only reason. The Cimmerian had no great ear for music, but even to his ear, Idosso bellowed as loudly and harshly as a rutting bull.

The ground sloped for the last few hundred paces, the paths winding down toward the riverbank. At last Conan led his warriors out into the open ground, where once there had been a sizable village, but long before the demon's gate opened, a tribal war took it. Now the jungle was taking back even the ruins.

There were plenty of hiding places, but few of the men chose to use them. Most stood on the bank, staring across. Ripples in the water hinted of river-horses, crocodiles, and carnivorous fish lurking in the sluggish depths.

Beyond the water lay a circle of clear ground. Something like the foot of a beast still more gigantic than an

elephant had stamped it out, crushing small trees,
bushes, flowers, ferns, and vines into an ill-smelling
paste.

Conan studied the clearing from the near bank. It was
not pressed into the earth at all. Only the vegetation had
suffered—and, Conan saw, nearby trees. More than a
few of them showed signs of branches lopped and bark
peeled with unnatural precision. A great fungus, an unwholesome white—blotched still more unwholesomely
with umber and black patches—stood half-whole, half-
crushed, with crawling insects further blackening the
crushed portion.

When Conan saw the other parties appear in the
open, he began studying the bank, looking for a way
across. He had no intention of swimming that river, nor
of examining the mysterious circle without a line for
swift retreat. If that circle was not the demon's gate, it
was still something with no rightful place in the jungle.

The Cimmerian cupped his hands. "Ho!" he shouted.
"Bearers with axes forward." The heads of Bamula axes
were of an iron too easily dulled for Conan's taste, but
there were many of them, and the Bamulas were skilled
in all manner of woodscrafting. It would not take long
to fell a few small trees and bind them with vines into
a light bridge.

Not long, after the axes came up . . . so where were
they? Conan cupped his hands to shout again; then his
hands fell to his waist, clenching into fists as they did.

The axes were coming, bound across the backs of the
two women. One of the wenches limped, the other had
one eye swollen almost closed.

"Crom!"

Conan's gaze swept the riverbank as he turned in a
full circle. His hands remained clenched, but he kept
them away from his broadsword. Too many spearmen

stood about him, ready to throw before he could reach them.

Idosso met the chill rage in the northerner's eyes with a set jaw and level stare of his own. He also kept his hands from his weapons, but challenge was in every muscle and in every feather of his ornate headdress.

Conan knew that Idosso (urged on by Kubwande?) had set him a direct challenge. Moreover, it was one that he would find it hard to meet either way. Fight Idosso and even if he won, the band would be divided and forced to accept a stranger for leader on the eve of battle. (If challenging the demon's gate was not a battle, Conan wished some kindly god would tell him what it was!)

Refuse, and Idosso would preen himself as one whom even mighty Amra dared not challenge. Also, the lot of the women would be even more wretched, and this latest beating far from the last or the worst.

Conan understood that Idosso was the kind of man who needed a firm hand the moment he challenged you. There had been some like him aboard *Tigress*, until Conan and the mates reduced them to order. Others too, many others, stretching back to Cimmerian villages. . . .

He should have met Idosso's challenge the first time it was offered and laid him out next to the dead Vendhyan! But—better late than never.

Conan unbuckled his sword-belt and let it fall. A gesture brought the women over, one to pick up the fallen weapon, the other to hand the Cimmerian one of the axes.

Idosso looked bewildered. Good. Kubwande was not whispering in his ear. Or perhaps this challenge really was no idea of the *iqako*'s?

"I am Amra. I'll not take the advantage of a sword against a spear."

"Ha!" Idosso sneered. "You'll take the edge of my
spear, and when you do, no woman will look at you
again."

Conan shrugged. "Better than you. No women ever
looked at you, save as one who sees a snake in her bed."

Idosso's mouth opened, but no sound came out.

The silence told Conan that work on the bridge had
also ceased. He rounded on the wide-eyed men by the
stream. "Keep at work instead of gaping, you mud-
grubbers! Or I'll be after you when I'm done with this
overgrown lout!"

Silence replied. Fearing treachery in the silence,
Conan turned. His eyes widened. He also found his
tongue frozen, and a bitterly cold sense of the presence
of ancient evil crept along his backbone.

A golden shimmering was growing in the air over the
cleared ground. Already it was higher than most of
the trees, and climbing higher still, in utter silence. The
golden light dappled leaves and struck sparks on even
the murky water of the Afui.

Conan detected a spiral motion beginning in the
golden shimmer, but heard no thunder, and indeed, not
the slightest sound. He saw Bamula warriors per-
forming rites of aversion and young Govindue staring,
his jaw sagging halfway to his chest. But the lad had his
spear raised in one hand and his shield advanced on his
other arm. Whatever ancient horrors might be rising
along this river, he would meet them like a warrior.

For a moment, Govindue made Conan feel ancient.
The Cimmerian himself had been no older than the boy
when he first knew war. He wished for Govindue at least
as many years and as much luck as he had enjoyed, and
shifted his stance. He would not willingly take his eyes
off either the apparition across the river or Idosso on
the near bank.

The huge Bamula stood with his spear trailing on the ground and his shield halfway down his arm. Either he did not fear treachery from Conan or he was too bemused to think of his weapons.

A moment later, however, everyone had cause to think of their weapons. Not all had time to use them before death struck.

Death burst from the trees in the form of the most gigantic of all lizard-apes. Its glaring red eyes could have stared into those of an elephant, and its claws and teeth torn out a bull's throat.

It limped, from a festering wound on its left leg that oozed yellow. A spear had left a barely healed gouge across its ribs. One eye was half-closed by the scab over a scalp wound. Clearly, the beast's sojourn in the alien jungle had brought it across the paths of humans more than once. From the brown smears across its muzzle and on its forearms, none could doubt the fate of those humans, dying even as they left their mark.

Its ordeal might have slowed the beast, but it had also taught it cunning. It approached silently, so that it was almost upon the rearmost men before they knew their peril. Then it charged into their midst, kicking and clawing wildly.

Hammer-blows of clawed hands flung bleeding warriors to the ground. Kicks sent others flying. Some landed rolling and leapt up to rejoin the battle. One, slashed open from throat to belly, landed almost at Conan's feet and did not move. The Cimmerian snatched up his fallen sword, leapt over the body, and closed with the lizard-ape, sword in one hand, axe swinging in the other.

Spears flew wildly, flung by desperate men who had forgotten that friends stood between themselves and the enemy. One spear skewered a village warrior in the buttocks. He leapt and howled, then cried out in a different voice as the lizard-ape ripped open his shoulder.

With the courage of desperation, the warrior reached behind, snatched the spear from his body, and thrust wildly. The spear-point sank through scales into flesh, but a furious buffet from one long arm flung the valiant villager aside. He fell and lay still, his skull crushed out of all human semblance.

A woman's scream checked the Cimmerian's rush into battle. He slowed, searching for the wench without taking his eyes off the lizard-ape. New wounds had slowed the beast further, but those of its ilk seemed to be as tenacious of life as any creature he had ever fought. He thought it had clutched one of the women, but it lumbered forward with bloody paws empty.

Not the lizard-ape, but Idosso had brought forth the scream. The big man held Chira, one of the two women, with his fingers wound in her hair. She struggled and spat at him, but he mastered her as easily as he would a child.

Then he gripped her by loinguard as well as hair, lifted her high, and *flung* her straight at the lizard-ape. She screamed again. The beast caught her before she struck the ground, and its teeth fastened themselves in her throat. The screaming crescendoed in a welter of blood.

In the next moment, the ghastly meal ended as Conan lunged forward. He plunged the axe's blade in the massive skull, then slashed the beast across the muzzle to force it to turn. Beast's blood and woman's blood both showered Conan as he struck again, this time a thrust through the ribs with all his gigantic strength behind it.

The fine Aquilonian steel was bent and nicked when the Cimmerian withdrew the blade, but the lizard-ape was as dead as the Empire of Acheron.

Conan jerked the axe free next, then glared at Idosso over the two corpses, beast and woman. He lifted the axe, ready to throw, judging its balance. He really wanted to choke the life out of the brute with his bare hands, but anything that left Idosso dead was better than nothing.

The axe never flew. Idosso roared with surprise and pain and whirled. The other woman—Vuona, Conan remembered—leapt with a gazelle's grace from the reach of Idosso's arms. In her hand she held a small but well-made dagger. Its blade dripped Idosso's blood.

The huge Bamula lunged at Vuona. He only hooked her loinguard, tearing it away. Nudity did not slow her flight.

Idosso flung the spear he had held ready for the lizard-ape, but it only grazed her ankle. Then she was running with the speed of mortal fear down to the river.

Whatever might be in the river terrified her less than Idosso did. She leapt into the water without breaking stride, then splashed furiously across. Bare and dripping, proud and slender, she rose from the water.

Idosso snatched another spear from the nearest warrior. He raised it to throw, but Conan closed and chopped down, wielding his sword left-handed and holding another axe in his right hand. The blade might need a smith's attention, but it could hack through a Bamula spearshaft as through straw.

Conan stepped back and tossed his weapons, snatching the sword out of the air with his right hand, the axe with the left. He spat on the ground, then put his foot on the spittle and rubbed it into the earth.

"Come on, Idosso, brave against women. Come, and end underfoot like that."

Idosso roared a wordless challenge filled with mindless fury. Then a great cry arose, freezing the warrior to the spot and making Conan turn.

Vuona still stood on the opposite bank, but now her hair rippled as if in a strong wind. She stared at the demon's gate with the gaze of a bird ensorceled by a snake. Conan thought he saw sparks of light dancing over her skin.

"Vuona!" he shouted. "Back!"

She seemed to hear—at least he thought he saw her shake her head. Then she took two steps forward, lengthened her stride with a third, and broke into a run.

Ten paces brought her to the edge of the golden spiral. Its light now gilded all her dark skin to the hue of fine bronze. Conan shouted again, and this time she showed no sign of hearing him or anything else.

Without breaking stride, she vanished into the spiral. Conan thought he saw it waver, and he cursed women turned witless by fear as he waited for the gate to vanish behind Vuona.

It did not. Instead, Idosso loomed up at Conan's shoulder. By pure instinct, the Cimmerian whirled, fists clenched. No steel touched the Bamula, but one weathered fist sank deep into the pit of the chief's stomach. As he doubled over, the other fist smashed into his jaw. He fell sideways into the bloody mud around the dead lizard-ape.

Conan now cursed his own temper. He could have slain Idosso with steel and lived with a clear conscience, and not a Bamula would have complained until after their mission was done, if then. Now he had made the man helpless, and it was not in Conan to kill a senseless man in cold blood. Nor, most likely, was it in the Bamulas to peacefully see him do it. Least of all was it in Idosso to learn wisdom from a mere crack on the jaw.

Conan wished Idosso in Crom's nethermost and coldest afterworld, where fools and traitors stood encased in blocks of ice. He wished any Bamula who followed Idosso all the lice of all the ill-kept taverns in Zingara.

Then he sheathed his sword, ran down to the bank, and took a running dive into the water. Shouts rose behind him as his head broke the surface, and he felt something rough scrape his leg. But the crocodile—if it was one—fell short in its first lunge at the Cimmerian. Before it could turn for another attack, Conan's powerful strokes had carried him across the river.

He scrambled onto the land and gazed at the demon's gate with the care of a hunter seeking the weak points of a beast he has never seen before. A golden spark settled in his hair; he brushed it away as he would a persistent fly. His hand seemed to tingle where the spark struck it, but the tingling faded quickly.

Shouts rose behind him again, louder than before. He recognized Govindue's voice, and thought he heard that of Bessu as well. If they were trying to tell him to stay away from the demon's gate, they were wasting their wind.

The gate had not compelled his will, as it seemed to have done with Vuona. It had done nothing except swallow the woman—who would not have been desperate enough to pass within it had she not been fleeing Idosso.

Nothing compelled Conan except his own honor. An honor he had allowed to be stained by not dealing with Idosso the way the chief deserved, and in the moment he saw what the man was. In honor, he owed Vuona rescue, as well as Idosso's death . . . if he ever returned to the Black Kingdoms.

And if he did not? Well, Crom promised nothing to

even the best warriors, but left their fate in their own hands. If no more, he could at least see that Vuona did not die alone.

Conan drew his sword, wiped it on the grass to remove a trifle of water from the blade, and strode forward into the golden spiral of the demon's gate.

Eight

The boy Govindue was the first to follow Vuona and the Cimmerian. He flung his spear across the Afui to free both arms for swimming, then leapt into the water. The head of a crocodile broke the surface just behind him, but the boy reached land before the tooth-studded jaws could close on him.

Spears rained upon the crocodile. Few penetrated the ridged, scaly hide, but one struck an eye and another the sensitive flesh of the nose. The creature hissed like porridge boiling over into the cookfire and sank out of sight.

The boy made a ritual gesture of dedicating himself to conquer or die, hands over heart and head bowed. Then in silence he turned and walked into the golden swirling that had swallowed Vuona and the Cimmerian.

Bessu let out a terrible cry, like a half-score hyenas all

at once. The birds not already driven from the banks of the Afui by the demon's gate flew up screeching and chattering. Then he was tugging the one lopped tree trunk forward, toward the narrowest stretch of the river.

Bessu had help from the others toward the end, but he did most of the work himself. His lank frame seemed to have been endowed with a strength greater than that of the vanished Cimmerian. Sweat poured from him and his breath came in gasps, but he was the first across the bridge, running lightly as a monkey to the far side.

"Warriors, I follow my son!" he called. "Join us and battle the demon's gate and its master. Stay, and let all know that you are less brave than a woman, a white-skinned outlander, a boy, and an old man."

Then he ran forward, to become the fourth person swallowed in the golden swirling.

One foolish warrior raised a spear to bring down Bessu, but a wiser head struck that spear out of the wielder's hand. With a shrewd blow of his war club, Kubwande slapped the second man on the shoulder, then ran across the bridge.

He did not rush straight off on the trail of the others, though. He carried over his shoulder lengths of branch hastily hewn into stout pegs. These he drove in on either side of the log bridge with the blunt side of an axe. On the near end of the bridge, others did the same.

The thudding of axes on pegs woke Idosso. He lurched to his feet with all the grace of a beer-swollen river-horse and stared about him as if those he saw had fallen from the sky. Then he shouted at Kubwande.

"Where is that dog of a Conan?"

"No dog," Kubwande said, "but one who has led where we must follow."

"Whaaaaa—?" Idosso's roar would have stunned in

the air any birds not already startled into panic flight by the uproar before the demon's gate.

"Yes," Kubwande said. Being no fool, he had seen the look in the other warriors' eyes after Bessu vanished into the demon's gate on the trail of his son. The village chief's appeal to everyone's honor was not one to resist.

Also, Idosso's offenses against Conan's honor, as well as against many taboos, were great. Kubwande recrossed the bridge, stepped close to the large man, and whispered this message into one large scarred ear.

Idosso's nostrils flared, like those of a leopard scenting prey. He raised one fist, then put the other hand to his aching head.

"Of course, if the outlander struck you so fiercely that your wounds demand I summon the village women—" Kubwande began.

"Shall I tell you what to do with the village women?" Idosso muttered. Kubwande pretended not to have heard.

The last pegs were driven in, and the first warriors crossed the bridge. They moved slowly, and not only because the log was slippery and the crocodile might be waiting below, wounded and wrathful.

On every man's face was a common look. No one rejoiced that Conan's honor had taken them through the demon's gate on Vuona's trail. No one seemed ready to let his own courage be doubted, by refusing to follow the northerner into whatever lay beyond the demon's gate.

Kubwande was of a mind to blame that eager lad, Govindue, more than he blamed the Cimmerian, and perhaps the lad's father likewise. Conan was a stranger, and one could always say he was not worthy to be followed—until a boy said otherwise, then led the way.

There would be a reckoning with son and father,

Kubwande vowed. He hoped there would also be no reckoning with Idosso for shaming him into action, but knew Idosso's temper was as certain as a crocodile's hunger.

But Idosso was grasping a spear and strapping his zebra-hide shield to his other arm. He tightened his war belt of crocodile hide set with river-horse teeth. Then he raised his spear and flung it with all the terrible strength of his right arm. It flew across the river, skimming over the heads of the men on the bridge, and bit into the ground just short of the demon's gate.

"Where Conan leads, any warrior must follow!" Idosso shouted.

Kubwande was on the bridge ahead of Idosso. Then the big chief was on the log. It groaned and swayed, in spite of the pegs. Kubwande half-hoped that the gods would spare him a host of burdens by snapping the log like a twig and dropping Idosso into the crocodile's jaws. Undoubtedly Idosso was not the only war chief of the Bamula who might allow himself to be ruled by Kubwande's advice.

All the men were now across the river, save a few too hurt to fight but able to remain behind and tend the dead and dying. Briefly, Kubwande envied them. Their scars would tell all that they had reason not to go battle demons.

He was almost ready to prod Idosso forward with the point of a spear when the big man leapt ahead, snatching up his spear and flinging it again, straight at the heart of the demon's gate.

It flew into the golden swirling and vanished. A moment later, Idosso was striding forward, and a moment after that, he had likewise vanished.

"We have a chief to lead us into the demon's land," Kubwande called. "Forward, warriors!"

No one ran at that call, but none dared hold back, and in the time needed to heat a pot of stew, the far bank of the Afui was empty. As the crocodile rose again, its remaining eye and slit nostril alone showing above the water, the swirling of the demon's gate became swifter. The golden light darkened, and a roar as of a mighty cataract battered at the hearing of the wounded.

They clapped their hands over their ears and opened their mouths. As they did, the spiral grew tighter and a wind from beyond nature churned spray from the Afui, drove the crocodile into the depths, and scattered leaves and lengths of vine.

Branches and whole trees snapped, unheard in the roar. Nuts pelted the cowering wounded, and a branch flew down and ended the suffering of a dying man by crushing his skull.

The wounded murmured words they had been taught, but they knew that a score of the greatest wizards of the land would have been powerless. The demon's gate had gained new strength by devouring those who sought a warrior's reputation by entering it. Soon it would leap across the Afui and devour them, then go on to ravage the land.

Between one breath and the next, the roar and the sinister glare died. The wind eased, the last few leaves drifted down from the sky, and the log bridge slipped into the Afui with a gentle splash.

Those whose eyes had not been dazzled or ears deafened thus far saw a thin spiral of smoke rising from the circle in the ground, and heard the faint cackle of flames in dried leaves. Little else except the wide eyes and trembling hands of the watchers remained to tell the tale of how the unknown had entered the jungle, then departed with more than a score of warriors.

* * *

Conan walked at a steady pace through the demon's gate. He would learn what lay on the other side soon enough, if there was another side. Meanwhile, a wise warrior took care when he could not see the ground under his feet and barely feel it (if indeed it was ground; it felt more like a half-frozen marsh).

The golden light was all around him, and in his ears sounded a low-pitched drone, like an immense swarm of bees the size of pigeons, returning to a hive the size of Aghrapur. Then the light and the drone began to fade, and Conan stood ready to draw his sword to face whatever might await him on the other side of the gate.

Whether he faced demon, wizard, or peasant with a flail and outrage against the stranger trampling his crops, Conan was prepared (although he would rather not kill the farmer, who could not be counted a real foe, and perhaps would be willing to tell him much useful about the local wizard).

Chill wind blew on Conan, the golden light gave way to daylight, without the emerald tint of the jungle, and he seemed to fall the length of his sword. His hillman's swiftness of hand and foot, eye and sinew, would have guarded him, had his sensibilities not been blunted more than he realized by the demon's gate.

As it was, he felt a steep slope under his sandals, and gravel sliding away, taking his balance with it. He threw himself backward, thrusting out his spear like a Gunderman mountaineer's climbing staff. The spear-point met rock and rebounded, not sinking in even the length of the first joint of a child's finger. Conan had the sense of being about to slide over the edge of the precipice, and in his ears roared the unmistakable din of rapids below.

Then something snagged his hair. It gripped so fiercely that for a moment he feared his hair would tear loose from his scalp or his scalp from his skull. Then his slide ended, the pain faded as the golden light had done, and he was able to look about him with a clearer vision.

His hair was tangled in a low, thorn-studded branch of a bush growing seemingly out of the bare rock. Below him, a slope strewn with boulders and patches of gravel dropped sharply to a stream thirty paces beyond. White foam boiled over more boulders as green water seethed past them, and stunted trees thrust gnarled brown branches toward the sky.

Conan carefully sliced away hair with his dagger until he was free, then stood up. The sky was largely hidden by the sides of the valley, although the slopes were not as steep above as they were below. Seamed and weathered rock sparking with bits of quartz bulged outward to either side of a ravine that gave Conan his best view of the sky.

It had a northern look to it, a hard blue that found a reflection in the Cimmerian's eyes. Under such a sky had he been born, although the clouds marching by on the wind were softer than those of his native sky. It still had to be a long journey to the north from the Black Coast, or from whence came the breeze that crept even down into the valley and blew cool on his bare skin.

The demon's gate might never have existed, for all that Conan could see of it. Nor was there any trace of Vuona. She could not be far ahead of him, but what did the demon's gate do to distance?

Also, what might it have done to her senses? Bare as she was, she could not have passed quickly over this rocky ground even had she been sound of mind and wits. Fuddled by the demon's gate, she might well have fallen down the slope and now be a corpse, battered out of human semblance against the rocks in the rapids.

Conan did not know what gods ruled in this land, nor which of them would help him if petitioned. So he merely asked that cold Crom, if he took care for a warrior's honor, would allow him to return to the Black Kingdoms. That the god would further allow him to find Idosso alive, and to then end the man's life. It was the least he could do for Vuona, he vowed, although he suspected he might have an exceedingly long journey from this land to the lands of the Bamulas.

Having made the vow and seen no signs of disapproval that he recognized, Conan considered how well he was prepared to face this land. He was no worse-clad than he had often been when facing harsher weather. Sandals protected feet, while a belt held weapons and a pouch of pressed meat and beans (hard as wood, as enduring, and tasting hardly better, to Conan's mind).

His weapons were sword and dagger, with the spear now hardly more than a staff or club. Its soft iron head had not met hard mountain rock in friendship or survived intact. He would have given much for a bow, had he thought there was anyone in this land able to accept the offer. Seeing no bowyers' or fletchers' shops hidden behind the rocks, he resolved to seek out sinew and flint, feathers and branches, to make his own. Also a sling, a weapon he had small use for on the battlefield but one that he had found handy for filling the pot in any wilderness (and for poaching in more civilized lands).

Conan shifted his spear to his left hand and drew his dagger with his right. Then, putting his hillman's knowledge to the test, he began to climb toward the ravine and the sky beyond.

Scyra had waited long, but only silence came from her father's chambers. Indeed, the whole cave was more silent than she had ever known it, even when her father had simply fallen asleep in the course of nature.

When he did that, his body at last commanding his sorcery-clouded mind, he always snored. She remembered vividly the snores that raised echoes not only in his chambers, but outside them, when she went in to draw blankets over him.

Scyra's eyes grew moist at the memory, and at other memories from years farther back, before exile, the wilderness, and all that came with it. Her father had tucked her into bed during the year of her mother's illness. Then she had begun tucking him in, when his grief after Mother's death threatened to unman him.

Had it in fact done so in the end, turning him into what he had become, all but a slave of his own powers? At least she prayed to lawful gods, when she could remember their names, that it was only to his own powers. Had he been grief-stricken beyond common sense, and thought of nothing but avenging his wife (or of at least sending her the message that he loved her, words he had so often left unsaid in life)?

Scyra did not know. She knew only that unless her father called out by voice or spell and said that he was dying, she had to flee this cave for a while. In time, she would return, to be the dutiful daughter while also working along her own paths, to perfect her own magick as well as to master her father's. Not so dutiful as to submit to wedding a Pictish chieftain, but there was much else that she could do before she had to openly refuse that last bargain.

The air in the cave seemed hotter and heavier than usual, and she smelled a pungent hint of sulphur. Eager as she was to flee to the fresh air, she did not do so in foolish haste. She had been spellclad for studying the scrolls, in case she needed to actually cast one to test them. Now she drew on breeches and undertunic, overtunic, belt and dagger, wrapped her auburn hair in a rawhide hood, and pulled over everything a rawhide cloak in the Gunderman style.

Staff in hand, she made her way out of the silence and stink to the outer cave. She paused to salute the votive lamps at the mouth, and to kiss the upheld hilt of her dagger. Then she flattened herself against the wall and sidled toward the daylight.

The Picts were her masters in woodscraft, as they were the masters of most folk, and if they dared to lurk near the cave, they would see her before she saw them. But if the Owls were daring to draw close to the cave, much else had gone awry, and the best she could hope for was to live long enough to bring word of their presence to her father.

If he had not indeed allowed them to close in, echoed in Scyra's mind. The wind from the cave mouth seemed suddenly to bring more cold than cleansing.

The echo grew louder, and she realized that it was not of the making of her mind. Borne on the wind with it was the sound of Pictish drums. They were not close, but had the volume of a clan-sized war party at least.

She would still go out, but stay close to the cave. Even a Pict commonly wary of sorcery would lose fear of wizardry and all else in his war-frenzy, and slay what stood before him without caring much what it was.

The boy Govindue was glad that everyone believed he was as brave as he wished to appear. Even his father seemed to be deceived. But then, his father had suffered much. He would be slow to believe ill of his only remaining son.

In truth, Govindue (and no doubt the gods) knew that he was both as excited as when he had taken his first woman and as frightened as the first time he had hunted a leopard. He had been fortunate both times, pleasing the woman and killing the leopard. Remembering such good fortune was about all that kept his limbs moving as he trod the road through the demon's gate. It felt like a muddy trail, and adding to Govindue's unease was the feeling that at any moment the mud would turn liquid and he would plunge downward, out of even the golden demon-light and into a darkness without end.

Then the mud seemed to dry and the golden hue faded from the light. A moment later, Govindue sensed something harder and colder under his feet than he had ever before felt. He had heard of walking on bare rock, with wind colder than the winter rains about you, from certain elders who had reached the Mountains of the Moon and returned. He himself had never left the Bamula lands; he could only believe the tales of the elders as a boy must, to show respect.

Govindue went to his knees, then sprang up and ran. He did not know what lay before or behind, except that any foes who lay before should have a moving target. Also, he could seek out any foes laying ambushes for those who might come behind him.

Govindue ran fifty paces before he realized that the ground was turning into a steep slope. Also, he was bumping into the trunks of stout trees, and their lower branches were lashing him across the face. He halted and studied the limbs.

Instead of leaves, they had clusters of fine needles, and instead of nuts, they had clusters of little brown scales. Once he had seen an old warshirt taken from the body of a Stygian slave-raider, a shirt made of iron scales shaped much like this. Also, he had heard of such trees, again from those elders who had walked in the Mountains of the Moon.

Well, even if the demon's gate had taken them no farther than the Mountains of the Moon they would have a long journey home and not all of them would complete it. They would have to fight hostile tribes, to say nothing of the demon's servants who were surely close at hand, ready for their master to call them into use—

Drums sounded from up the hill. The drummers were lost in the trees, but Govindue was accustomed to judging the place of a drummer half a day's march away in the jungle. These were five or six of them, beating small drums and no more than ten spear-throws uphill and to the left.

Thunder rolled, although Govindue saw nothing amiss, neither golden light nor indeed any disturbance of the air. He did see a man stagger into the open and go to his knees. More men followed, until there were nearly as many as he could count on his hands and toes.

Might the demon's gate be invisible from its far side? With such powerful wizardry, anything might be possible. If that was the truth, then whoever mastered the demon's gate also had a mighty way to send warriors wherever he wished, into the very hut of an enemy chief—

Govindue swallowed a cry. He had recognized the first man through the gate. It was his father, Bessu. Others of Dead Elephant Valley were with him, likewise some Greater Bamulas. He recognzed Kubwande, and less happily, Idosso.

The boy began to work his way down the slope. He was relieved to see that the warriors seemed to have their wits about them. They had fallen swiftly into silence and had readied their shields and weapons in response to the drums.

His relief faded quickly as he saw his father and Idosso quarreling. They kept their voices low; he heard no words. But he knew his father's face well enough to read it even from this distance. Also, Kubwande was not taking sides, which weakened Idosso but also Bessu, and indeed, weakened the whole band by allowing the quarrel to go on.

Govindue began moving faster. His place was at his father's side, all the more because his father had followed him through the demon's gate. He moved so swiftly that on the rocky ground his foot turned and he would have fallen had he not been able to brace himself against a tree.

From a bush ahead, a man rose into view. Govindue saw him clearly, although no one unused to hunting in dense forest would have recognized the form of a man. Govindue not only recognized the form of a man, but saw that he was naked except for a loincloth and a necklace of human teeth. Save where he was tattood or painted, he was brown-skinned, about the hue of some Stygians, and carried a bronze-headed war-axe and a short bow with a quiver of flint-headed arrows.

The man's dark eyes quested about, searching other bushes and trees for the source of the drumming noise. Govindue had the eerie sense that the tree he had sought the moment he slipped was no protection from the man's gaze, let alone his arrows. Did the man have potent magick. What if all his people had the same?

But if the man had magick, it was not enough to reveal Govindue to him. He needed no magick, however, to see the Bamulas gathered in the open, or to signal to what were likely his comrades. The axe rose and fell three times. Only those behind him could have seen it, they and Govindue. The boy also saw more bushes quivering slightly; the man had at least a hand of comrades. If they all had bows—

If they all had bows, Govindue knew what he must do. He would be alone among at least six of the enemy, and he would die there. But if he died giving a warning, his father and others would live. If in time they knew he had given the warning, the ancestors would be told and would honor him.

Also, Idosso would know what kind of son Bessu had, and perhaps accept his leadership. If Idosso did not, Kubwande might.

The man was rising again, with his bow ready and an arrow in his hand. Standing, he turned his side to Govindue. He was smaller than the boy, but his exposed side seemed as generous a target as the flank of a buffalo.

Govindue's spear flew. As it struck, Govindue cupped his hands and shouted: "*Wayo, wayo, wayo!* The enemy comes! *Wayo, wayo, wayo,* the son of Bessu calls!"

Conan had been creeping downhill ever since he reached the ridge and heard the drums. He could have used more time on the high ground spying out the land, but even a brief look had been enough.

This was indeed far from the Black Kingdoms, a higher, colder land way to the north. The trees were pines and firs, giving the terrain a darker hue than that of the jungles of the south. The sky was harsher and the sun milder than in the land of the Bamulas. Far away a line of slate-tinted sapphire slashed across the horizon, a sea very unlike the warm blue of the waters Belit had sailed.

For a moment, Belit seemed to die all over again. Conan shook his head, letting the wind whip his hair about his shoulders—a wind such as he had often felt in his native land, but never on the Black Coast.

The sorrow passed, and grim resolve took its place. The demon's gate had brought him not to some other part of the Black Kingdoms, nor to any party of Vendhya. This was an unknown northern land; his first task after finding Vuona was to make it known. Somewhere under one of those crags or in a stand of straight-boled firs might lie the master of the demon's gate.

Conan was looking for any sign of Vuona's passage when he heard the drums. He at once resolved to seek out the drummers and watch them from hiding. If they appeared friendly, he could learn their land and ways around a fire, and over meat and ale seek their help in finding Vuona. He doubted that any tribe inhabiting such a land as this would refuse help in the hunt, and abundant meat had a way of loosening tongues.

If they were hostile, on the other hand, he would make one a prisoner, then learn as much in a less friendly manner. He might then know Vuona was doomed, but also from whom to take vengeance.

The last of the befuddlement had left the Cimmerian's head. He stalked down the hill with the silent grace of a hillman on the prowl, never bringing his foot down where anything might snap or roll. He passed in silence through gaps between trees one would have sworn would not pass a squirrel, and all this while moving swiftly as well. It was not long before he was in sight of the first of the folk of the drum, and knew his enemy.

They were Picts, which meant "enemy" to any Cimmerian. Conan had learned much from men who had fought in the Pictish Wilderness, both Cimmerians and those of other races. Many of them bore scars, likewise the memories of friends hideously slain; none bore any goodwill toward the Picts.

"Which is something no god would ask anyway," Conan remembered one mercenary in Argos saying. "Because the Picts bear nobody any goodwill, including mostly one another, I think. If they'd better weapons, they might do us all a favor and kill one another off. As it is, they'll be a plague long after my grandson's a gray-beard."

Masters of woodscraft, the Picts were, lightly armed, and certainly no match for Conan in single combat. But they would be a hundred to his one in this land, and they had bows.

The drums continued, the rattle and thud shifting as if the drummers or the wind or both were on the move. Conan judged that he was upwind of the main body of the Picts and that the breeze would hide any slight noises he made.

He wanted to close with them unseen and unheard, before they launched their attack. If their intended victims were civilized, he would know who might be grateful for his aid. If this was only a brawl between Pictish clans, neither side would be a friend to strangers, but one side might yield a talkative prisoner. Also, the Pictish prisoner would save Conan the work of making a bow for himself.

He judged where the flank of the Picts would be by where he would have placed hillmen himself when launching such an ambush. Nor was he wrong. A solid mass of Picts was not slow to appear, well-hidden from below but naked to the keen blue eyes studying them from above.

Conan was about to drop to his knees to crawl closer, when he saw a slim, dark figure rise from cover farther down the slope. Fugitive sunlight sparked on a spear-head as the slim figure threw. A Pict thrashed out his life, and Conan heard a Bamula war cry.

The cry was still echoing on the wind when the Picts close to Conan leapt up and charged downhill. In the next moment, the Cimmerian recognized the village boy, Govindue, as the spear-thrower. Now the lad was facing his last moments of life, with only one who might deserve the name of friend to share them with him.

Conan gave the wildest of all Cimmerian war cries, and his legs were churning even as his sword flew from its scabbard. Then he was on his way downhill, crashing through bushes like a rolling stone, leaping boulders, altogether like an avalanche about to strike the Picts.

Nine

Govindue did not see Conan for some while after the Cimmerian began hammering his way into the rear of the Picts. There were too many trees and not a few Picts between him and Conan. Also, the Picts were busy trying to kill him and he was equally busy trying to stay alive.

The boy's first man-kill had certainly drawn the attention of all the Picts about him. They sprang into the open, snatched up bows, nocked arrows, and shot. Those without bows threw spears. Only his fleetness of foot and a few intervening trees saved Govindue from being brought down at once.

Instead, he opened a gap of thirty paces or more between himself and the Picts. As he ran, he sought a hiding place. It was not in the gods to give him one where these smelly, snarl-haired hillfolk might not see him.

But perhaps he could find someplace that would let him fight them on more equal terms, even killing a few more of them before they brought him down. He had only one more spear besides his war club, but he might be able to capture a weapon from some dead foe.

He had already done better than he would have expected, killing one enemy, drawing others on to him, and still being alive. If he lived only a little longer, the songs they made of his deeds would not console his father for being sonless, but would make his death-rites more pleasing.

A spear rattled against a branch and plunged into a bush an arm's length from Govindue. He risked a look backward, and nearly paid for that look with his life. His foot came down on a branch so rotted that it snapped under even his youthful weight. A broken stub gouged his ankle.

Seeing his prey slowed, the leading Pict slowed in his turn. That mistake cost him dearly, giving the boy just time to snatch up the mis-aimed spear, judge its balance, and throw.

The Pict was snatching his bow from his back when the spearhead drove into his ribs. He threw up his hands and fell across the path of his comrades, blood spurting from his mouth as he choked and coughed out his life. At last his thrashing limbs were still. Four live, full-armed Picts faced a Bamula lad with only spear and war club left to make the songs about him worth hearing.

That they would be sung, Govindue had no doubt. Behind him, the trees gave way to open slopes, with broad spaces where a rat would have trouble hiding. Boulders crowned the hill, but the hillmen would bring him down one way or another long before he reached the rocky shelter.

In boyish bravado, Govindue made an obscene gesture at the hillmen. "Govindue, son of Bessu, gives you this greeting to take back to your women. Maybe they will regret the better man you slew, and take your parts to put on my grave."

The Picts did not understand a word of the Bamula speech, but they understood that they were being insulted, and they howled with fury. One nocked an arrow.

Then the odds changed in a moment, as a stone flung seemingly from nowhere crushed the archer's throat. A demon's howl made the surviving Picts flinch, even as the dying archer toppled. They were looking about them to see what had risen from the earth when Conan stormed through the trees and into their midst.

Against Conan, three Picts had no more chance than three goats against a lion. None of them ran, so they died all the more swiftly. Conan threw a spear that impaled one Pict through the back of the neck, until the spearhead burst from his mouth in a shower of blood and teeth. He threw another stone that caught a second Pict just above his loincloth. The Pict stumbled and ran into a tree hard enough to knock himself senseless.

This left the last Pict alone, with nothing to do but fight. He did this with a warrior's courage, but he faced both Govindue's spear and the descending sweep of Conan's sword. The Bamula spear pierced the Pict's thigh in the same moment as the Aquilonian steel sheared through shoulder and ribs into the man's belly.

Conan put his foot on the last Pict's ribs and jerked his sword free. His grin was a leopard's.

"Never throw that close to a swordsman."

"Forgive me, Conan."

"I will, since you didn't hit me. Now let's see what your father and his friends have left of the rest of these ill-smelling rockscrabblers."

"Who are they, Conan?"

"A folk called the Picts. What more I know, I'll tell you all later."

As if to remind them of further work at hand, the drums sounded again from farther down the hill. Only briefly, however—the clash of weapons and the war cries of both peoples swiftly drowned them out. Amidst these sounds, Govindue was sure he heard men's death-cries as well.

He needed no second command to follow Conan.

Conan knew enough about the Picts to have some notions about fighting them. He also had his strength, speed, and instincts, all honed like a fine sword by many years' fighting in more than a dozen lands against a score of different enemies. Some of those foes were hillmen like the Picts, although the Pictish Wilderness was more heavily wooded than the Ilbars Mountains or the wastes of northern Iranistan.

Conan led Govindue across the slope just inside the tree line. They could have gone faster in the open, at least until the first Pictish archer made good practice against them. The trees hid them and the Picts from each other, and Conan trusted that he was a match for any Pict they might stumble across at close range. More than a match, with a second pair of eyes and another fighting arm at his back, each ruled by sharp, if youthful, wits.

Dead Elephant Village would be well-led, if no more demons came to further ruin it before Govindue was of age to succeed his father as chief.

Conan judged correctly in thinking that the Picts had a second party opposite the one Govindue found. Thus placed, the Picts could have caught the Bamulas in a deadly hail of arrows from both sides as the warriors

came uphill. More than once, Conan had laid such an
ambush himself. Just as often, he had fought his way
out of one, commonly carrying dead or wounded comrades and, at times, a few holes in his own hide. Ambushes were no mystery to him.

Govindue, however, had drawn the first band of Picts
out of their intended position. Then Bamula and Cimmerian together had slain them so swiftly and silently
that their comrades below had no idea of what had befallen them. Fierce but ill-disciplined warriors, they
were shooting from behind their trees at the Bamulas
behind theirs, when Conan and Govindue came down
upon them.

Again the attack had the force of a rockfall crashing
onto a hut. This time, however, the Picts had greater
strength and less courage. Some turned at bay, desperate as wolves, bold in their refusal to retreat from only
a handful. Others turned to flee. The two crossed one
another's path, hurled curses and stones, and sometimes
came to blows.

Conan and Govindue waded into the confusion, slashing, thrusting, and flailing about with total impartiality
between the two factions. Neither courage nor fleetness
of foot helped those Picts who found themselves within
striking distance of the pair.

The Cimmerian wielded a spear in his left hand and
his sword in the right. He thrust an axe-man through
the shoulder and split his skull as the man dropped his
axe. Reversing the sequence, he hamstrung an archer
who had turned his back, then rammed the spear between the man's shoulder blades. The spear stuck in the
Pict's ribs. Conan put one foot on the small of the Pict's
back, snapping the man's spine in the process, and
jerked his spear free.

Then, in a single motion, the Cimmerian whirled,

smashing the spear butt-first into a Pict's jaw. As the man reeled back, two of his comrades valiantly tried to close with Conan and give their friend time to flee.

They failed. The Pict stumbled and fell before he completed three steps. At the same time, Conan's sword whistled left, right, left, in three cuts. The neck of one man gaped so that his head lolled like a drunkard's. The other screamed and clutched at his thigh, dropping guard and weapon. Conan split his head with a fourth stroke.

Govindue had nothing except a bent-headed spear, but he killed one Pict and drove a second back. A third came on to the attack, shrieking like the spawn of demons and wielding a rude stone-headed axe. Govindue leapt in under the swing of the axe and slammed his spear up against the Pict's arms.

The Pict howled and dropped the axe. Govindue shifted his grip and thrust hard before the Pict could draw clear. Blood oozed from around the spearshaft, and sprayed from the Pict's mouth as the breath tore from his punctured chest. He jerked until he twisted the spear from Govindue's grasp.

Conan kicked at the Pict but the man fell back, taking the spear with him. The Cimmerian stood guard against two more Picts while the boy picked up the axe and tested its balance.

"Near enough to a war club," Govindue said. He swung furiously, with more energy than skill. One of the Picts chose that moment to lunge forward. The axe caught him across the bridge of his nose and he fell, without even a scowl crossing his ruined face.

By now, Conan and his companion had cleared a respectable space about them, empty of living, or at least of fighting, Picts. Howls and cries from among the trees suggested the nearness of other Picts, and also foretold that the Bamulas downhill were fighting their way toward the Cimmerian.

It was as well, Conan realized, that the demon's gate did not fuddle the wits of those who passed through it, or change *them* into demons. If the Bamulas had walked through the gate too bemused to fight until after the Picts had sprung the ambush, he might have been facing a long and solitary search of the wilderness for Vuona.

Now he had twenty or more comrades to help him search for the girl, fight the Picts, and seek out the master of the demon's gate. There was loss with the gain: the twenty would be harder to hide than one, few of them were used to northern lands or cold weather, and some might not be wholly trustworthy.

Conan signaled to Govindue to open the gap between themselves, and they worked their way down the hill. The arrows came thicker now that the Picts below had no fear of hitting friends who were either slain or fled. But the Picts were less than polished archers. A score of men in any Turanian band of mounted bowmen would have been their masters. They trusted to showering foes with arrows and had ill success when they needed to rely on sharpshooting.

A tree at a time, Conan and Govindue worked their way into the ranks of the remaining Picts. They slew three, and in time the remainder abandoned their archery, once more afraid of hitting comrades. Conan picked up a bow and used it to good effect. He told Govindue to watch for other bows, and also for fallen arrows still fit for use.

"We will be in this land long enough to need some meat, and the bow outreaches the spear for hunting," Conan said.

"You have fought before in this land?" Govindue asked.

"In ones enough like it that what I remember from them is worth doing here," Conan replied. "Also, men come from many lands to serve the Aquilonians along the Pictish frontier, and talk freely when their service is done."

"The gods grant that is enough," Govindue said. For a moment, he looked close to his age, the courageous boy far from home rather than the seasoned warrior.

Conan slapped him on the shoulder. "Hurry with that arrow hunt," he said. "I'll watch for any Picts fool enough to linger."

Before the thud of the Pictish drums faded from Scyra's ears, the unmistakable din of a battle replaced it. The sorcerer's daughter at once went to ground. Picts this far inside her father's lands were rare; a battle was unheard of. Learning who was fighting whom and bringing the knowledge back to her father would go far to earn her a pardon for leaving the caves.

She would balance curiosity with caution, however, lest she die with her knowledge sealed behind her lips. The Picts were her masters in woodcraft, but she was not helpless. One born in the Bossonian Marches knew one tree from another, and ground that hid from ground that revealed.

Scyra formed a picture in her mind of the location of the battle, then judged the best route to follow to see it. She considered casting a spell of invisibility, or at least of confusion, but such a spell would not last long, and might reveal her at the worst possible moment, close to the enemy and defenseless. (The spell of invisibility she had learned needed to be cast spellclad, without so much as a sharp pin from her hair for defense.)

No, the simple prowl of a cat stalking a bird would teach her the most with least danger. She crouched and began to crawl forward on hands and knees, to cross the patch of ground where only bushes offered cover. Thirty paces farther on, the trees began, reaching all the way up the slope to her goal.

Scyra had covered only fifteen of those paces when she saw something move under a bush. She ceased her crawl and held her breath, waiting for a further movement. It came, and now it seemed unmistakably to have a human source.

She listened for sound from beneath the bush, and also for any sign of lurking Picts. It could be that two tribes of the hillmen were fighting—a band of Snakes or Wolves breaking the taboo against being on the white shaman's land, and a band of Owls defending the holding. Scyra had no illusion that she would be truly safe with either tribe, but the Snakes would surely kill her, and not mercifully. The Owls might be slow to kill the shaman's daughter, if they recognized her in time.

Quickly she realized that the battle was making too much noise for her to hear any lurking Picts. But this had to be true for Picts listening for her, too. She drew her dagger and crawled toward the bush from which the sounds and movement came.

Branches crackled and gravel sprayed as a dark-skinned figure scrambled frantically into the open. It was just leaping to its feet when Scyra clutched it firmly by both ankles. She was not a trained or accomplished fighter, but she was calm, not terrified, and also sturdily made from birth and strong from years in the wilderness. The figure toppled, almost on top of her. From less than the length of her dagger's blade, Scyra stared into the wide, rolling eyes of a dark-skinned young woman.

The sorcerer's daughter would have given ten years of

her life now for a spell to both silence the other and persuade her that she faced no enemy. The best Scyra was able to do was to clamp a hand over the woman's mouth and make soothing noises into one ear. The ear, she noticed, showed clotted blood where an earring had been ripped away, and the dark skin bore bruises and grazes. Some of them might be the work of the rocks; others surely were not.

Beyond those minor hurts, the woman seemed unharmed as far as Scyra could judge. She hoped that was far enough, for the woman was of no race she had ever seen, darker than either Pict or Shemite, with rounded features. She was also well-formed—with the look of a girl just come into womanhood—under dust, dead leaves, and bruises.

Was she from the Black Kingdoms far to the south? Most likely, from what Scyra had heard of their folk. But then what was she doing in the Pictish Wilderness, farther from home than Scyra cared to imagine, far even from any shore where a ship might have landed her?

The answer was plain. The world-walker had linked the Black Kingdoms with the Pictish Wilderness, whether by Lysenius's intent or by pure chance. This woman had wandered into it—or been drawn like so many others by the mind-compelling power of the spell. Had she come alone?

The woman wore neither clothing nor weapons. Hardly garb for flinging oneself into the unknown. A madwoman? Scyra looked at her companion's eyes again.

They were still wide and fearful, but no madness as Scyra recognized it showed in them. She pointed at herself. "Scyra," she said.

The other's eyes widened farther. She pointed at her breast. "Vuona," she said.

"Vuona," Scyra repeated, pointing at the woman. The dark one nodded vigorously.

All this while, the battle had faded into the back of Scyra's mind. Now it returned to the forefront as a man's death-scream cut through the trees and seemed to soar into the sky like an arrow.

"*Wayo, wayo, wayo!*" Scyra heard. It came from the direction of the battle, an exuberant chant from a dozen robust male throats. She had heard the victory chants of Picts before, but this was nothing like theirs. Deeper, fuller, and somehow more wholesome, it was like nothing she had ever heard or imagined.

Vuona jumped as if bitten by a serpent.

"Bamula!" she cried. Scyra tried to restrain her. Picts three clans away must have heard that cry, if they had not already heard the battle. Rushing off to where you thought friends were was often a short way to death in a Pictish ambush.

The woman fought with surprising strength, and now Scyra wished for a Pictish war hammer. A good buffet on the head—

"You Bamula?" Scyra asked. Could that be the name of Vuona's tribe? Had a war party come through the demon's gate and fallen among the Picts?

The chant went on, now almost as loud as the battle. Not a Pict could be heard, only the Bamulas. Perhaps it was a case of the Picts falling among the Bamulas?

Silence swallowed the hillside. It lasted long enough for a deep breath, then a new chant was taken up.

"*Ohbe* Bessu, *ohbe* Bessu, *ohbe* Bessu!" The new chant was no softer than the first, but slow and dirgelike. Vuona listened attentively, then scratched a shallow trench in the ground, pushed in a small pine cone, and covered it up.

"Bessu," she said, pointing at the mound.

The victory had not been without cost, it seemed. A warrior named Bessu was honorably dead. Again the chanting sounded more worthy of a warrior than did the Pictish howling.

Vuona pointed up the hill. Scyra sighed. It appeared that the woman wanted to go up there, badly enough to face the arrows of any lurking Picts alone if there was no other way.

Scyra studied her intended path again. At least Vuona would not have to go alone. Then perhaps she might in turn be grateful enough to return to the caves with Scyra, for a hunting smock to cover her skin and lotions for her bruises, if nothing else!

Then, who could know what might follow? Scyra lacked spells for learning Vuona's tongue or teaching her Bossonian, let alone reaching into her thoughts and reading them without words. Those were in scrolls she had never touched, let alone read, if indeed her father had not so firmly embedded them in his memory that he needed no scrolls to cast them.

But if they were embedded in his memory—? Vuona might speak, might see Scyra and Lysenius as friends, might lead the other Bamulas to them—the other Bamulas, who had survived a passage through the demon's gate in a condition to fight Picts!

Scyra had long since vowed to either defeat or win over her father. Old love let her prefer the second. The Bamulas might give her the key.

Ten

Govindue allowed Conan to lead the way down the hill toward the place of the Bamula warriors. The village lad walked proudly, for this day he had won a name that would last even if this was his final fight. He wondered if Conan's tribe—the Kimmerala, was it?—had the custom of praise-songs, and if Govindue of Dead Elephant Village of the Lesser Bamulas would ever be mentioned in the praise-songs about the fires of the Kimmerala.

It was as well for Govindue that he allowed Conan to lead. The Cimmerian was first to see the leaves trembling, revealing a lurking live Pict where others might have seen only the dead. There was no shortage of dead Picts, and from one of them Conan snatched up a short-handled axe. Not well balanced for a swift throw, it still plunged through the concealing bush.

A pantherlike scream froze all except Conan. He was

126

still moving when the mortally wounded Pict leapt into the open. One arm dangled useless, but the other held a spear and retained its strength and cunning. The spear flew toward the oncoming Bamulas.

Most of the men had the wits or the time to fling themselves to the ground or to raise their shields. Bessu had the wit and the swiftness of eye and hand to fling his own spear, but he had no shield, having given it to a warrior who had lost his. Before he could think to defend himself, the Pict's spear was in his throat.

Bessu fell backward, half-flung by the spear, half-falling as strength deserted his legs. His own spear sank clean through the Pict's broad chest, so that the weapon burst out his back. It was slaying a dead man, but the Bamulas shouted as if Bessu had killed the enemy's war chief.

Govindue knelt beside his father while all the rest joined in the chant of *"Wayo, wayo, wayo,"* then moved on to *"Ohbe* Bessu. . . ."

"Honor to Bessu." Yes, much honor to a man who had followed his son through the demon's gate and into a strange land, to die there in battle. Honor Bessu would not hear except with his spirit ears. His face was set and his eyes wide and staring; he must have died as he struck the ground.

Govindue set his own face into a mask as hard as polished wood over his grief and gripped the spear. It was custom that if a dead warrior had blood-kin in the band, that kin should draw out the death-weapon and do whatever else might be needful for the dead man. If blood-kin was not present, then the eldest living warrior bound to the dead man by a blood-oath had this duty. Either man still received a spirit-burden that needed lifting after the battle, but a lesser one than would some total stranger.

The lifting would be far in the future, Govindue realized. He saw trouble from that, not far in the future, when the other warriors also realized it. They too might be uneasy about the fate of the body of Bessu and of any other dead in this distant, cold land of savage men who seemed near-kin to demons.

"We must also honor Conan," Govindue said. "Without his arm and sword, we would have suffered more. Without his knowledge of this land, we might still be in danger."

Govindue looked at the black-maned warrior, hoping he had kept the desperation out of his voice and eyes alike. Conan shrugged.

"I can't do much about the Picts, for I've heard they swarm like wild bees and are about as hard to kill. But yes, this land is more like my homeland than yours. I know something of what a man needs to live and fight here.

"Also, we're better placed in one way than I expected. This is not some demon's realm from which the only way back is through the demon's gate. The gate's sorcerous master may not be our friend, but we may not need his friendship. Somewhere at the end of this wilderness is the sea. On the sea are ships, to be hired or, if needs be, taken. Remember that I have sailed as Belit's right hand, and I know ships."

Idosso stepped forward. He was shaking his head. Govindue hoped it was because he was still befuddled by Conan's blows, not because he was working himself up to a fighting rage.

Idosso's first words dashed that last slender hope. "Are you saying that you lead here now, *Amradulik*?" One did not call a man one wished peace with "Lion Dung," not even as a jest—and it did not seem to Govindue that Idosso was jesting.

"I am saying that I know the ways of this land and you do not," Conan said. "Does anyone care to dispute that? I can find a path out of the wilderness and a ship to warmer lands more easily for myself and Vuona than for all of us together. If it is your wish that I do that, only say so now and plainly, and there is no quarrel among us."

The thought of being abandoned to freeze, starve, or die under Pictish onslaughts clearly appealed to no one. Even Idosso looked a trifle daunted.

He also seemed to find something in certain faces, something Govindue was too young to put a name to, not too young to dislike. "Are we supposed to beat this wilderness for Vuona, until we find her with a Pictish arrow through her ___?" the chief challenged.

The obscenity drew faint laughter. Conan shrugged again. "If you think that is the best way to find her, go and seek her yourself. Only, I doubt that you are the man to find her, unless she is dead or too hurt to move. You coming after her will make her run faster, and one day she will run faster than you."

"No woman can fear me," Idosso growled. Govindue saw his fingers begin to twist. He also saw Kubwande begin to look openly uneasy. Unfortunately, Idosso's back was to the lesser chief. He seemed to read nothing in any of the faces he saw before him that would deter him.

"Truth," he went on, "is that Vuona should welcome a return to me. In Amra, she has had only the kind of man who makes his bed with such as Govindue."

A killing light flared in the ice-blue eyes. Conan took a step forward, fists clenched. Idosso stood with legs apart, waiting for him to strike with hand or steel.

The blow never landed. Conan merely said quietly, "Well, then, if I am supposed to favor Govindue, I will prove it. Lad, you are now second to me. Idosso, you will obey his orders as you would mine."

Conan turned his back on the big warrior. For a moment, Govindue thought the uneasy peace would hold.

Then someone laughed. Kubwande glared around the circle, plainly seeking who had been so foolish as to laugh at Idosso when the big man was in such a temper.

Govindue also sought the laughter. If he was to be leading these men, it would be well to know who was foolish and who wise among them, without learning everything from Conan.

Neither chief nor youth finished their search before Idosso bellowed like a rutting buffalo and flung himself at the Cimmerian.

Idosso's bellow of rage was probably intended to slow the wits and limbs of his opponent. Against many other men, it might have done so.

Against Conan it merely gave a warning, and cost Idosso the advantage of surprise. Insofar as he needed every advantage he could gain, this was not the act of a wise warrior. But then, Idosso had never been famous for his wisdom.

Conan knew at once that he faced a formidable opponent. If Idosso managed to get in one shrewd blow with fist or foot, or a firm hold on a limb, let alone on Conan's neck, the fight would bode ill for the Cimmerian. He had seldom faced barehanded an opponent so nearly his equal in size, strength, and speed, with that speed, if anything, increased by the man's rage.

The Cimmerian kept the distance open for a few moments, long enough for him to get rid of his sword. He hoped Govindue would guard it, but had no time to look where the blade fell. He could not wear it in this chief's bout of honor, and not only because it would go against Bamula custom for this sort of fight.

If Idosso once had his massive hands on the blade, the temptation of easy victory might outweigh the fear of public dishonor. It would not be an easy victory, of course, and it might be no victory at all. But Conan doubted he would gain much if he defeated Idosso at the price of being too badly hurt to lead the warriors out of this Pict-ridden land! These wanderers needed one leader, and he a born northerner who was also fighting-fit.

The sword clattered to earth somewhere. The onlookers hissed and pounded their fists together, the Bamula form of applause at such bouts. Conan hoped they would not be so enthralled by the fight that they forgot to post sentries. He doubted that all the live Picts were gone even from this patch of forest, and knew they must swarm in the forests beyond it.

Idosso came on, and Conan let him close. As the Bamula chief neared within striking distance, it was Conan's turn to leap. A fist buffeted the side of Idosso's head. It was a blow that had it struck full and fair would have stunned an ox.

The Cimmerian's opponent was not without cunning, however, at least in this kind of fight. As the blow was launched, he was moving sideways, swiftly enough that it only bruised his cheek rather than crushing his skull. His reply was a kick that might have shattered Conan's knee, but the Cimmerian also saw the menace and moved so that Idosso's great foot only grazed instead of landing full-on.

Around and around the two men went, neither able to gain any advantage that the onlookers could see. Nor did Conan himself think he had much of an advantage. A single stumble, not impossible on this rough ground, and he might take a blow that would slow him. The first man to be slowed would be the first to die.

Few arts of personal combat were strange to Conan, a warrior since his fifteenth year. If he did not stumble, he had little fear of the outcome. What he wanted was a swift victory that would settle all doubts among those he must lead out of this land. If the fight lasted long enough, they might wonder.

Also, the Cimmerian might take grave hurt in a long battle and be unfit to lead. Nor could the Picts be ignored. The longer the fight drew the attention of the warriors, the more time for the Picts to gather 'round.

Conan could not abandon the fight and flee to the forest. Neither honor nor good sense allowed that. So a swift victory or death were his choices, and he resolved to gamble his life on the swift victory. Not only his life, but the lives he might save by thus winning.

It was a matter of waiting until Idosso gave him an opening. The wait only seemed to last until sunset. In truth, it could not have been more than the time needed for a hungry man to gnaw the meat from a chicken leg, before Idosso offered Conan that opening.

Conan pretended to stumble. Idosso, turned half away from his opponent, whirled. He did not guard himself as the Cimmerian rolled back on his shoulders and kicked out with both legs.

One leather-soled foot caught Idosso where Conan had aimed it. Against such a kick, a loinguard of zebra-hide was no more protection than a lady's silken shift. The steel plate of an Aquilonian knight's guard might have been enough, but even it would have been dented and the wearer uncomfortable for days.

Idosso doubled over, but he still had the determination to clutch at Conan's ankles. Conan broke his hold with a swift half-roll and kicked again. This time a Cimmerian foot caught Idosso's knee, and Conan felt bone give.

He also heard a cry, and not from Idosso.

"Beware, Conan!"

Conan recognized the voice as Kubwande's and the note of warning in it. He rolled again, and his own sword in Idosso's hand slashed down through the space where he had been. The blade bit deep into the rocky ground, and Conan spared a moment's thought for the new nicks it would be taking. Much more of this and he would need either a blacksmith's forge or a good stout club to take the place of a useless blade.

Conan sprang to his feet, and with one foot, kicked the sword from Idosso's hand. It flew, Conan neither knew nor for the moment cared where. Then he brought both hands clenched together down on the back of Idosso's neck. Skull and spine alike gave under the blow. Idosso fell facedown, rolled onto one side, then over onto his back as the light went out of his eyes.

The noise of another fight, or at least of a scuffle, now reached the Cimmerian's battle-sharpened ears. He moved until he had no one at his back and a clear view of Govindue and a village warrior rolling over and over together. Conan bent to pick up his sword, and Kubwande raised a warning hand.

"Ha, Conan! Hold your sword. This is a chief's bout like yours. Iron has no place in it."

Conan considered placing iron, or even steel, in Kubwande's skull or belly, but held his hand. It was not impossible that Kubwande might have the wits to follow the victorious Amra, at least until Amra had led the way out of the Pictish Wilderness. Honor was probably not in the man, but any treachery he contrived back in his homeland, Conan could meet with either sword or a swift pair of heels, as he saw fit.

Meanwhile, Kubwande was a warrior of some prowess, and there were not so many like him in this band
that one could be spared merely because of what he
might do. That was one of the rules of wise leadership
that held true for all men, white, black, yellow, brown,
or green with purple stripes if there were any such!

Conan could not put a name to Govindue's opponent,
but he determined to ask the man a few sharp questions
if he won. If he slew the lad, Conan resolved to make
those questions still sharper, with the aid of his sword.
It would give any blacksmith an apoplexy to measure
the damage to the blade, but it would serve well enough,
even for one so thick-skulled as to further divide these
lost warriors by a chief's bout.

Strength was equally matched in the contest, but the
opponent clearly had more experience. Govindue, however, had youthful swiftness and suppleness. He also
seemed more in earnest. He could not have been fighting harder if his victory would have brought his father
back to life.

The thought made Conan look toward Bessu, whose
body still lay where it had fallen. There had to be other
bodies as well. Now that Idosso was no longer among
them, it was time to find all the corpses and hold proper
rites, lest the Picts carry them off for rites of quite other
kinds.

Conan knew little about Pictish ways with their foes'
dead, but he doubted they practiced anything he had
not already met among his foes. Any man who had
come upon a patrol staked out, gelded, and even more
indescribably mutilated in other ways by the fierce warriors of the Afghuli, did not expect to be surprised by
anything the Picts did.

Conan was also certain that nothing but proper rites
for their dead would ease the minds and hearts of the

Bamulas. They were a long way from home, so far distant that even spirits might have a daunting journey to the Black Forest. Anything that eased their minds would ease Conan's task.

As if Conan's thoughts had summoned up new strength in the youth, Govindue wriggled like an eel, breaking his opponent's grip. Sweat streamed from him as he leapt up and kicked at the other's throat. The kick landed, not hard enough to crush the windpipe, but hard enough to make the man clutch at his neck with both hands.

Govindue jerked one hand away from the bruised throat and twisted it. "Give over, Bowenu," he snarled. For a moment, his voice sounded like that of a man ten years older and chief for all of them.

"It is not my place to decide for you, Bowenu," Kubwande said, "but if it was—"

Bowenu's reply was neither coherent nor polite. Govindue drew the man's other hand away from his throat and pinned him to the ground.

"Now do you give over and swear to follow me as chief over our village?"

"Ah . . . eh . . . over those of the village . . . here, led by Amra. Is . . . enough?"

Conan hoped Kubwande would have the sense to be silent and Govindue to accept. The boy certainly was of an age to succeed his father, and his work on this day would give him a claim going far beyond blood. Asking for everything in one bowl, however, might not be wise.

"Then you accept that Conan leads here?" Govindue demanded.

"I will . . . swear blood-oath . . . offer anything I do not need in this land of monsters!"

"Good sense, Bowenu," Conan said, laughing. "We will all need everything we have with us or can steal

from the Picts, to live until we find a way home. Govindue, what say you?"

The boy—no, Conan would not call him that again,
the *young chief*—rose to his feet and looked down at his
former opponent. "I accept, Bowenu. Although I hope
you at least do not challenge me again, even when we
reach home. I would not gladly fight such a brave warrior and thus weaken our village."

"I will bring birds' eggs for broth for your first-born
son," Bowenu said, speaking clearly for the first time in
a while.

Conan looked on the young chief with approval. He
was showing a brew of skill, mercy, and resolution that
should serve him well. The Cimmerian hoped for but
few troubles from the six or seven warriors of Dead Elephant Village among the band.

As to the rest. . . .

"*Iqako* Kubwande. I ask no oath. I only say that I
have no quarrel with you, and I trust you have none
with me. Idosso was your friend, but not mine."

"He was friend to none of us for challenging you as
he did," Kubwande said. "I will not unsay praise I have
given him, before both men and gods. I will say that he
lived with more honor than he died. May the spirits reward him for his life and forgive him the way of his
death."

That seemed to satisfy the Greater Bamulas. It did not
wholly satisfy Conan, but he knew when he would gain
nothing more from the man. He resolved to keep a dis-
creet guard against Kubwande and not allow the man
any closer to his back than necessary.

"We know who leads," Conan said. "You know the
kind of man I am. And I know that our first work is to
gather our dead, tend our wounded, and find a safe
place for the night."

"Is there one?" someone asked.

"There may be, or there may not," Conan replied. He raised a fist. "But there will be no place safe from me for any man who disobeys."

Kubwande raised his fist, and Govindue did likewise. The ritual gesture served its purpose. No one spoke, but instead, all scattered to relieve the sentries, seek moss and leaves for the wounded, and find any dead not lying in plain sight.

Scyra now needed no common language with Vuona to understand what was in the woman's mind. Vuona had only one thought there: to rejoin her people, or such of them as were abroad in the Pictish Wilderness.

It seemed to Scyra that this urge was stronger than it had been, before the two tallest warriors fought and the northerner conquered. Had the black champion been an enemy to Vuona? It did not seem impossible; Scyra could not read thoughts precisely, but she had some art of recognizing evil by what it did to a man's face. The big black warrior had been, if not evil, at least in too much of a rage to either lead or follow.

If this had been as it seemed, a fight over the leader's place, the Bamulas had chosen the better man. The big northerner had a kingly air to him even in his garb as a Bamula warrior, with nothing of it lost to the blood, dirt, and bruises. He would have looked equally well as a greenclad Bossonian archer or an armored Aquilonian knight. Not in any sorcerer's garb, however, for he looked a creature of the open land; or even of the wilderness itself. He also had about him a forthright quality that Scyra once thought only her father possessed among sorcerers, and now knew that even he lacked.

Scyra was so intent upon the tall northerner that she had less attention to spare for Vuona. Vuona, no fool,

soon recognized this. The first warning Scyra had was
Vuona's leaping up and running toward the Bamulas.

The men were just lifting their dead and wounded on
improvised litters of poles and branches when one of
them saw Vuona. He shouted and waved. Vuona let out
a shriek of happiness, which turned to a shriek of fear
as an arrow struck a tree a hand'sbreadth from her ear.

The tall northerner shouted a single command, and
his warriors spread out with the speed and sureness of
seasoned fighters. They could not see the Pictish archer,
however. He was behind rocks, so close to Scyra that
she could have touched him with a long stick.

Instead, she touched him with her knife. She was not
a skilled knife-fighter, but she had surprise, fury, and
enough strength for the purpose all working for her. The
Pict died, and she made sure that he died in silence by
clamping a hand over his mouth until his last breath
had passed.

Scyra lay motionless beside the Pict until she was certain her kill had drawn no Bamula's attention. She
searched the body until she discovered the tattoos of the
Red Adder Clan of the Snakes. She was hardly surprised
to see her previous suspicions justified. The Snakes had
never been entirely happy with her father's peace with
their Owl rivals. Now it seemed that their unhappiness
was driving them to treachery, if not to open warfare.

She began to crawl backward, intending to be well
away from this place before the warriors came searching. Then she considered that it might not hurt to let
herself be found. If she could speak to the northerner,
she might learn more of him and his band of warriors.
Such a band might prove useful if they needed to earn
their way home and had the prowess to earn it in defense of Lysenius and Scyra.

Scyra's arts of concealment were like her knife-

fighting, sufficient for many purposes. They were sufficient to hide her until the Bamulas, called back from
the hunt by their leader, gave up the search for the Pictish archer. She was ready to weep in frustration when
she saw the slope empty.

She had not meant to be out of the cave this long, and
besides, she had given her cloak to Vuona, now marching off with her people. Scyra saw no alternative to following their trail. Let them go, and they might as well
be on the moon for all her chances of finding them
again without either the Picts or her father knowing.
She had to be first here to know what the Bamulas were
about, or she would be going to the marketplace with
an empty purse.

She took bow and arrows from the body of the Pict,
and searched the other dead tribesmen until she found
one who also wore a cloak. It was of Bossonian work,
stiff with dirt and grease, reeking from long wearing by
Picts who never bathed unless they were caught in the
rain, and probably the prize of some bloody-handed
border raid.

Still, she wrapped it around herself. It was just barely
large enough; her Bossonian blood made her as tall as
the common run of Pictish men. But the wool was
warm, and from a distance, it might deceive the hasty
eye.

There was no food to be found, save the bodies of the
dead Picts—and even in jest, the idea made Scyra gag.
But some of the edible ferns were green, there were fish
in the streams, and the Bamulas could hardly travel too
far their first night in this land, no matter how the
northerner led (or drove) them.

With those hopes lightening her step, Scyra set off on
the trail of the Bamulas.

* * *

It was agreed on the march that one of the three chiefs would always be on watch. Conan, Govindue, and Kubwande drew twigs for who would begin the night, and Govindue drew the shortest twig.

Not that there was much to see in this nighted forest, either of friend or foe. A cloak from a dead Pict kept out some of the wind, but even the gentlest breeze in this land seemed to pierce like an arrow. Govindue had never been so cold, not even during his manhood ordeal, which had sent him into the jungle during a particularly severe autumn season of rains.

It was as well that Idosso was dead. He would never have been an honest follower to Conan, the young chief decided. Kubwande might be, if only out of fear of starvation, Picts, and Amra's fist.

More surely still, Idosso would never have had Amra's knowledge of how to live in this land. Live, fight, even win free of it. He had not been so stupid that he would not have learned, but before he learned (or Kubwande taught him), many might have died. Perhaps too many.

Conan had the soul of a great chief, and with such a soul, his skin did not matter to the gods, still less to Govindue, son of Bessu.

The footfall was loud enough to have reached ears much less keen than Govindue's. More seasoned as hunter and tracker than as warrior, he heard the sound as clearly as he might have heard a boulder falling from a cliff. When two more footfalls gave him a sense of the intruder's direction, he had plenty of time to hide where he could see the path.

It seemed as if the intruder either wished to die or thought the Bamulas were friends approaching. In the darkness, it was hard to tell what the oncoming shapeless cloak concealed, and Govindue would have given a year's yam harvest for a trifle of moonlight. Had he been sure it was a Pict, his spear would have pierced the intruder's belly after the third step.

Then the intruder stopped and threw back the cloak. Govindue's breath hissed out, and he began a ritual of aversion. Pale-skinned, pale-haired—a ghost had come upon them!

His hiss found an echo. Then he knew it was not an echo. No echo of his ever spoke in words he had not uttered.

"Bamula? Vuona? Bamula? Vuona?" The questioning note was clear. So was the kind of voice. Not a ghost, after all, but a northern woman. Coming for Vuona? Why not? If the world was mad enough to hold such things as the demon's gate, why not a northern woman coming for Vuona?

Govindue rose, but did not step into the open. The woman might be honorable, but the Picts were not and could be following the woman.

"*Ohbe* Bamula," he said. "*Ohbe* Bamula. *Ohbe* Vuona. *Ohbe* Vuona." Then he called, "Woman," using the word for an elder's wife. If she was one of power, it would please the gods, and if she was mad, they would not care.

"Bamula," the woman said, sounding somewhat like Amra when he spoke his own tongue. Then she stepped forward. Govindue saw that she wore a knife at her belt and a bow and quiver on her back, but held her empty hands out in front of her.

Govindue stepped out to face the woman, holding his hands as she held hers. Then he pointed back over his shoulder toward the camp.

"Bamula! Vuona! Bamula! Vuona!"

She understood his message. Still holding her hands before her, she walked up the hill toward the band's night camp. Govindue had barely time to call one of the

other guards to take his place ere he hurried after her,
lest she vanish in the darkness.

Conan and Vuona sat a trifle apart from the others,
without being outside the circle of the guards. The Cimmerian had left no one in any doubt of what he would
do to them if they wandered off and the Picts did not
save him the work.

Vuona squatted on her haunches and leaned back
against a fir bole. The moonlight silvered her bare
shoulders. She wore rawhide leggings taken from a
dead Pict, but was bare otherwise. She had returned
wearing a rawhide Gunderman cloak, but had given
that to one of the wounded.

They would have to hunt for both food and garb,
Conan knew, and soon, even if all the Picts in the wilderness came at them. For him, this night was as mild as
a summer eve in Cimmeria, but the Bamulas only just
kept their teeth from clattering loud enough to wake
Picts a day's march away!

"I ask your forgiveness, Amra."

"If you wish it, ask it of Conan. 'Amra' is a name that
sounded well aboard *Tigress*, or from Belit's lips."

"Is it your true name?"

"Were you thinking to bespell me with it?"

Even in the darkness, Vuona's expression of horror
seemed real enough. "No!"

"That's as well. I've a habit of putting my sword in
people's gizzards faster than their spells can slow my
arm. I would hate to have to do it to you."

"It would be . . . justice. I . . . if I had not—"

"Oh, plague take your quaverings of conscience, girl!
Leave them to the priests. You're not the first woman to
make a mistake about a man. Since the wrong man's
dead and I'm alive, what ails you?"

"Being here, when we could be somewhere safer. It is my fault."

"Very likely it is, but past mending now."

She slipped out of the crouch and knelt before Conan. "Not even by a woman's gift?"

Conan looked her up and down. She needed no darkness to hide faults; her lithe form had none. He realized that he was looking at her as at a woman, and that this was the first time he had done such a thing since Belit's death.

Also, Vuona needed a place in this band, and a chief's woman was the most honorable she could hold. Conan had begun this whole mad affair to save her. . . .

She climbed into his lap and twined her fingers in his hair, raggedly barbered after his encounter with the thorn bush, but still giving any woman a good grip. Almost too good a grip, for she had strong hands.

Conan ran his own hands from her shoulders down to the small of her back, and beyond. Fingers that had wielded a deadly sword earlier in the day now undid the leggings. Vuona leaned forward; Conan felt youthfully firm breasts—

"Amra!"

"My name is Conan!" he snarled. Vuona slid off his lap. The Cimmerian took a deep breath, then realized that it was not Vuona who had spoken.

"Govindue, you are away from your post." Those were the first words that came into his mind. Had he thought at length, he would doubtless have spoken more sharply.

"Forgive me. Amra—"

"He wishes to be called Conan."

"You're not a chief's woman yet, girl, so let Govindue speak."

"A woman has come."

"I've heard of Pictish women. Doubtless the guard who saw her fell dead at the sight of her. Take her captive, put another man in the dead one's place, and leave me in peace."

Conan thought the young chief was trying not to look at him or Vuona. "Am—Conan. The woman is not a Pict. She looks like you. Her name is Scyra, and she knows we are Bamula and that Vuona is among us."

Vuona jumped to her feet as if she had sat on a viper. "It is she, the magick woman!"

Govindue made gestures of aversion. Conan rose, took Vuona under both arms, and gently lifted her off her feet until his nose and hers were a hair'sbreadth apart. She flinched at the look in the blue eyes.

"Vuona, I can forgive you for choosing the wrong man. I will not forgive you for hiding something like this from me—" he waited until she looked ready to faint, then added "—a second time." When he set her on her feet, her legs quivered and threatened to tumble her into the fir needles.

She found her voice, however, and could hardly talk fast enough. When Vuona was done, Conan donned his sword-belt but drew the blade. It seemed to compel Vuona's gaze.

"Remember what I said about sorcerers with swords through their gizzards? This woman had best prove herself our friend, and quickly. Govindue, take me to our guest."

"As you wish, Conan."

Interlude

The Pictish Wilderness, in the reign of King Conan the Second:

Sarabos was the first of us to fully regain his wits. To speak more precisely, he had lost the fewest of them at the sight of the cave, and even of the statue. Therefore he had the least ground to cover before he could command his voice.

He still spoke more than a trifle distantly, as though he were recounting something he had experienced in a dream and whose reality he could not altogether trust.

"Let us all believe that what we see here is really here. Believing so, has anyone heard even a faint smell of rumor that might explain it?"

He might have been talking to the statue, and the living men gathered around it made as little answer as if they also had been stone. I was glad to see that this was not wholly because they were standing with eyes wide and staring, jaws hanging and gaping, and their powers of speech quite gone.

Some of them were cleaning and dressing their comrades' wounds. I heard a stifled scream as one man cut down for an arrow in another's thigh. It was deeply embedded, and I prayed to Mitra that it would not drain the man of blood when it came out.

Others were unpacking supplies and cleaning weapons. As unwholesome as this cave appeared, it was still dryer and freer of Picts than the world outside. Also, these were veterans of the border wars, some of them old enough to have served under Conan at Velitrium, had they been in the Aquilonian service at the time. Unless the ancient Stygian magick—or whatever other spells had produced the image—awoke, I had no fear of my men or for them.

I saw by the torchlight men looking at each other. I held my tongue. I suspected that I was about to learn things that it would have been as well to know beforehand. But there are always things that the soldiers, particularly Marches born, will not willingly tell their officers, especially those born and reared far from the Marches.

"What we hear tonight stays with us," Sarabos said. "No matter what you confess, we will leave it to the gods."

The men continued to look at each other in silence. One or two flinched as the man with the arrow in his thigh let out a scream that was anything but muffled. The echoes were slow to die, and I saw men looking toward the rear of the cave.

Their faces said that they hoped nothing lurked back there to waken at a human presence after so many years, and come forth hungry and horrible. I did not find that hope quite without reason, but I chose to put a better face on the situation.

"This is no very pleasant place, but let us remember that it seems to be taboo to the Picts. They will not come in, but our comrades will have no such fear. Remember too that the last time Conan the Great found himself in such a place, he came away with the treasure of the pirate Tranicos and put himself on the throne of Aquilonia with its aid."

Somebody muttered about putting himself in bed with a comfortable wench and a jug of good wine being quite enough. I did not find that without reason either.

One of the men finally spoke up. "There is something that I heard from my mother." He was a Gunderman by his speech, but he looked dark enough for a Shemite . . . or a Pict?

As if he had read my thoughts, the man went on. "Yes, I have Pictish blood. My mother is half-Pict, though my father was all-Gunderman. She had some of their speech and knew some old tales.

"One of these, she said, was taboo among the Picts. There was a curse on anyone who told the tale, almost as great as on anyone who entered the cave. She told me, because she thought I had best know it, and also believing that my Hyborian blood should weaken the curse."

Nobody dared ask one question, and again the man seemed to have the power to read thoughts. "My mother bore five healthy children, the last when she was hard upon forty, and was living yet last fall in her sixtieth year. I have fought in five campaigns, without loot or honors, but also without grave wounds. If there is a curse, I think my mother spoke the truth about it."

"Well, then, speak the truth about what she told you, and we will listen," I said.

"It may not tell you much—" the man began.

"Anything you tell us will be more than we know now," I said firmly. "And a storyteller should have a name. Forgive me that I did not learn yours."

"I am Vasilios, son of Ayrik," he said.

"Then speak, Vasilios. We are all listening."

Vasilios cleared his throat; the air was much dryer in the cave than outside, as well as a trifle dusty. He sipped water from his bag. Then he folded his legs, rested his hands upon his knees, and began.

"It was in the time of my mother's father, the Pict, when a sorcerer lived among the Picts and a statue came to life and walked. . . ."

Eleven

The Pictish Wilderness, many years before:

Conan listened to Scyra with great attention even after she admitted to being the daughter of the sorcerer Lysenius.

"I have never heard of him, not that I make it my affair to count the world's wizards," Conan said. "Nor do you look much like a sorceress. You're dressed too shrewdly, for one thing."

"We have lived here for five years," Scyra said, voice taut with indignation. "I was barely a woman when we arrived. Assume that I am not a fool and hear me so."

"I ask your pardon, Scyra," Conan said. He translated her remarks for Govindue and Kubwande. They nodded, then frowned when he added that Scyra and her father clearly had either great powers or friends among the Picts.

If Lysenius and his daughter had magick enough to stand off the whole Pictish nation, dealing with them would be a chancy matter. They would be too cursed powerful! And if so powerful, why did they need help?

If they had Pictish allies, helping them would mean fighting alongside Picts. Conan had no blood-debts owed to the Picts, unlike many Cimmerians had, but the ancient feud between Cimmerian and Pict was nothing he could easily forget. Nor did it necessarily matter what he wanted; the Picts might choose to slaughter the Cimmerian in one moment and the Bamulas in the next.

These things were true. It was also true that Conan's band had small chance of fighting their way to anything more than a warrior's death. They would be twenty-odd men fit to fight against all the Picts in the forests, Picts who knew these forests as they knew their own hands, shot arrows from cover one would swear could not hide a mouse, and did not shiver on a mild summer night!

Conan had walked into the demon's gate because of his duty to Vuona. It should not come hard to do worse than fight beside Picts, to save Vuona and all the rest who had honored him by following in his footsteps.

"Can your father conjure us up some warm clothes and hot food if we enter his service?" Conan asked. "We will expect more, but those we must have before we can do enough to earn it."

"Can your men not hunt, cook, and clean hides?"

"All of these things take time, Scyra. Time the Picts may not allow us. Do you think whatever friendship you have for them will save us?"

"Do not call the Picts my friends. At best, they are allies."

She sounded as if she expected to be believed, and for Conan not to ask "Against whom?" Conan decided that it did not matter. Anything that took his band closer to safety would help, and to obtain that, he would swear any oath. If Lysenius needed their aid at all, he was not powerful enough to punish them for breaking such an oath, and the band could take its chances with the Picts. Fed and garbed for this wilderness, those chances would be better than they had now.

"As well. I will never call a Pict my friend, but I may take a day off from killing them if they do the same for me."

"That I believe my father and I can promise. We have furs and hides, salt meat and dry nuts, and a part of the cave where you will be safe from the Picts as if you were at home in the Black Kingdoms."

"Also, I'll be bound, where you will be as safe from us." Scyra looked indignant, but Conan held up a hand. "No insult taken and I hope none given. In your place, I'd do the same. We've no need for a Zingaran love-temple feast, as long as we understand each other."

Conan watched Scyra sidelong as he translated for Govindue and Kubwande. She seemed to understand what he was offering and what his doubts were. He hoped he would not have to put into words his intention to end both her and her father at any sign of treachery. That would be a sad waste of a fine woman, apart from everything else.

The two Bamula chiefs each had to go apart and talk to their followers, while Conan and Scyra sat cross-legged facing one another. She assumed that posture as easily as any Pict or Khitan, and seemed as calm as if she had been waiting in a nobleman's hall for the horses to be brought up.

Out of the corner of his eye, Conan saw Vuona flatten

herself against a tree, as she thought out of his sight. He wanted to go over and shake some sense into her. If she wandered about by night in this land to spy on him out of jealousy, the Picts would be making magick with her skull before three dawns, if they found anything in it.

The other chiefs returned.

"Will the wise-woman swear blood-oath to treat us with honor, even if she must go against her father?" Kubwande asked.

"That demands too much!" Govindue exclaimed. "The gods would frown on—"

"The gods would spit on us from a high cloud if we did not at least ask," Kubwande said. "Lad—young chief—not all fathers are as yours was. I learned that before my manhood ordeal."

There was some dark secret about his childhood lurking in Kubwande's voice, one Conan would have given a barrel of good Nemedian wine to know. Doubtless also it was something that torture could not wring from the warrior.

Conan turned to Scyra and translated the question. He saw her flinch, and even in the darkness he could see her face lose some of its color.

"Please. If my father knew—"

"Does your father not know about your coming here?" Conan wanted to roar loud enough to crack branches and shake birds' nests out of the trees. He had wits enough to realize that would only frighten Scyra out of hers, besides warning Picts half a day's march away.

"He doubtless knows by now that I am not in the cave," Scyra said. Conan heard the effort it took for her to control her voice.

"Then you do not come here by his command?"

"I do not come here against it, either."

CONAN AT THE DEMON'S GATE   153

"You might have said that."

"You, my friend, might have asked." She had the impudence to grin. Conan resisted the urge to shake her, then suddenly could not resist the urge to grin back.

"Scyra, I think you'd have the courage to go against your father if needs be. If these chiefs will take my word for it, you need swear no oath."

He translated. Govindue was almost eager to forget the oath, Kubwande reluctant. The older man at last yielded—however, muttering as he did, that he seemed to spend all his time running about on matters begun by women. . . .

About this time, Lysenius's ghost-ear came within hearing of the meeting place by the cliff. Tonight it was carried within an owl, because the Picts most likely to be about were of the Owls and the bird was taboo to their hunters. Lysenius had not forgotten the time he sent a ghost-ear hawk into the land of the Snake Clan and next saw it as feathers on a chief's headdress.

The sorcerer had enough command of the owl's keen night-sight to recognize Scyra. He also saw what proved his judgment about the men of the band with whose leaders Scyra was meeting. Their ghost-voice was that of folk of the Black Kingdoms. The world-walker had finally won him what he wished most of all: warriors with no kin in the Pictish lands or anywhere close enough for them to reach him before he had done his work.

He would brew his vengeance with their blood, and then his daughter would see him as he truly was.

Was she, in her delusions about him, warning them? And if she was, were they believing her? The ghost-ear should warn him of that much, even in the modest brain of an owl. Better by far was a man, even a Pict, but Lysenius had decided against that before he went into his ghost-ear trance. The Owl Clan would not be pleased if these black warriors slaughtered one of their men while he was too bespelled to defend himself.

The owl swooped low, as it might have swooped chasing a squirrel on a low branch. It passed within easy ghost-ear hearing of Scyra and those sitting with her.

The bird should have sent all their secrets across the nighted forest to Lysenius, waiting on his pallet of scented needles. Instead, it heard nothing closer than the warriors by the cliff.

It was as if Scyra and those sitting opposite her had no ghost-voices, which was impossible. Everyone had a ghost-voice, from the gods down to the lowest insects, even to the worms crawling beneath the earth. Sometimes it was all but impossible for Lysenius to separate the voices of those he wished to hear from the din of all the rest.

Now, however, Scyra and three men might have been outside the common world for all that the ghost-ear could hear them. On his pallet, Lysenius twitched, writhed, bit his lip for self-command, and contrived to avoid losing his mastery of the spell.

He sent the owl past them again, and this time he watched through the bird's bodily eyes. He saw Scyra, he saw two black warriors facing her, he saw a black girl hiding behind a tree.

He also saw in the middle a man taller than all the others by at least a head, of a northern fairness, with cold blue eyes and ragged black hair. The man's muscles were in proportion to his stature, and when he moved, it was with the control and mastery of a warrior. The scars on his tanned skin would have said as much had he remained perfectly still.

Was this the man with no ghost-voice? Did he not

only lack one himself, but bind those close to him into the same silence? Mystery piled upon mystery, and none of them to Lysenius's liking.

No, that was not altogether true. The man might have no ghost-voice, but everything else about him suggested a warrior's spirit. A strong warrior's spirit, able to feed the sacrifice more than any other two men put together.

The northern warrior with Scyra might remain a mystery, but he would have his place in Lysenius's plans, as little to his liking as that place might be.

Conan was not entirely persuaded that Scyra had merely wished to surprise her father with the gift of the service of the Bamula warriors. His two chiefs were still less so. None of them cared to call her a liar to her face. She still held out a better hope of a passage home than any they could make for themselves. The later the hour, the more the two Bamulas shivered—three, counting Vuona, who had not moved from her place by the tree.

A soft hoot and the thump of a falling body made all turn. An outsized owl lay on the ground, a spear through its breast. Its outspread wings were broader than Conan's shoulders. Its beak clicked twice, its eyes stared about with what seemed to Conan more than a bird's intelligence, then it shuddered and lay still.

"Good throw, eh?" came a cheerful voice from behind a tree. Bowenu stepped into sight, knelt, and retrieved his spear. Only then did he seem to notice that Scyra was regarding him with a face of distaste, even of fear, that needed no translation.

"Why did you kill it?" Conan asked.

"It was swooping so low I could hardly miss, and it is big enough to make a meal after a good plucking and roasting."

Scyra looked as if she wished to spew. Bowenu's gestures had also needed no translation.

"What's dead is dead, Bowenu," Conan said. "But this is a new land. We don't know what's safe to eat and what is not. This wise-woman would rather you had not killed the owl. I will trust her. And if you do not trust her, then trust me to leave bruises everywhere Govindue did not. And hold your spear!"

Bowenu went through the most elaborate of the four Bamula rituals for craving pardon, and Conan finally granted it. He had some difficulty keeping a straight face, and Vuona behind her tree was struggling to hold in giggles. Conan vowed to spank her soundly if her laughter broke the peace with Bowenu. They needed even warriors whose arms were swifter than their wits.

"We are in the lands of the Owl Picts," Scyra said. "The only worse thing you can do in their eyes than kill an owl is to kill a warrior in hunting paint and hang his head up."

"Just as well we were too busy to take heads this afternoon," Conan said dryly. "Although I seem to remember they were in war paint, if I know anything about Picts."

"They were, and they were of the Snakes, who have a long feud with the Owls. But I did not think they would trespass on our land."

That told Conan more than he had known before about the sorcerers' friends and foes among the Picts, if not as much as he would have chosen to know. It seemed to him that Scyra was no great hand at hiding secrets, at least not from one who had survived the intrigues of gilded Aghrapur in Turan.

"Well, Scyra. I think we've talked as much as makes any sense when there's neither wine nor beer to wet our throats. I trust you've no plans for returning to your father tonight?"

"The Owls would not—"

"The Owls may not be able to see in the dark as keenly as their totem. They might mourn after they feathered you with arrows, but you'd not get up from the bier for all that. I also much doubt that we've seen the last of the Snakes, and they'll be no friendlier to you after today than they were before."

Scyra nodded. "There is truth in that." She sounded both reluctant and gracious.

"Good. Then come share our fire, if you won't share the owl. All the warmth that's about here tonight is with us, and most of your hope of waking up with your throat unslit."

Scyra followed Conan to the camp, but she lay down well away from both the fire and the pile of sleeping Bamulas, huddled together to share the warmth of their bodies. Conan thought she was watching him as he also lay down, with Vuona curled against his chest, but sleep took him before he could be sure.

Twelve

By good fortune, the Bamulas were either dead or fit to march, even to fight. They performed as best they could the rites for their dead, gathered their weapons, and departed camp with Scyra as guide.

Conan's band came to Lysenius's caves on a fine spring evening, after two days of stiff marching for the barefooted Bamulas. The Cimmerian noted the need for footgear in this rock-strewn land; some said a host marched on its stomach, but they were bards, not captains in war.

The frowning rocks made the Bamulas look at one another, and Conan knew that some were looking within themselves to find the courage to continue. A hillman born, he had scaled such cliffs and explored such caves before he had seen his tenth summer. The Bamulas were hardy enough in their own land, but their own

land was not as harsh as the north, and they were as
their homeland had made them.

"Come along, brothers," he called. "Most of us have
crawled into lions' dens and come out alive, and no sorcerer is worse than a lion."

He did not entirely believe that himself, but the cheerful ring of confidence in his voice inspired the Bamulas.
They began climbing the ladder to the mouth of the
cave Scyra had said would be their quarters.

Conan and Scyra were the last to go up. They stood
briefly side by side, gazing at the forest that lapped like
an emerald sea against the foot of the sorcerer's hill.
Conan knew that Pictish eyes watched them—had been
watching them, indeed, all during the two days of the
journey.

There had to be some truth in Scyra's tale of peace
with the Owl Picts. In two days, a hostile tribe could
have conjured out of the ground a hundred warriors for
every Bamula and buried Conan's band alive under arrows and stones. But though black eyes had watched
from behind trees and under bushes all along the trail,
no arrow or spear had flown, no war cry had risen, and
no drum had throbbed except far off toward the sunset,
as a signal.

As if Conan's thoughts had called to them, the drums
began to thud again, barely heard above the wind even
by the Cimmerian's lynx-keen ears. Scyra shuddered,
and without thought save to warm her, he put an arm
around her. She shuddered again but did not shake
off the arm, and after a moment, relaxed into his comfort.

"It is still no easy thing," she said, "to hear those
drums and not be afraid. When I grew up, to hear them
meant running for the horses if you had them, snatch-

ing boots and bread if you didn't. The Picts were never far, or at least not far enough."

"What did your father learn that gives him a hold over the Picts?" Conan asked. "Or is that a secret?"

"It is. He has not shared all of it with me, and would not be happy if I shared even what I know with you without his permission."

Conan thought the happiness of a sorcerer would never be high among his cares, but then, he was not a sorcerer's son, Crom be praised! Also, this sudden reticence aroused a fighting man's suspicion. Scyra had been frank enough before Conan's band had entered her father's domain. What did she need to hide, to keep them there?

But it was as true as it had ever been that through this domain lay the best road home. A score of stout and wary Bamulas might daunt even a sorcerer's urge to treachery, and if worse came to worst, they were as well off dying here as among a howling horde of Picts.

"The more I learn, the happier I will be," Conan said plainly. "And the happier I am, the happier the Bamulas. They expect to leave here bound for home, and will be angry otherwise. Your father may have arts, but are they equal to twenty angry Bamulas?"

"I pray to Mitra that none of us ever need learn that," Scyra said. She climbed onto the ladder and scurried quickly out of sight.

Conan watched her go, then watched briefly as an eagle circled against a western sky rapidly turning blood-hued as the sun sank. He did not tarry long; this land was uncanny enough by day. By night, one did not need a barbarian's fine-honed instincts to sense awful evil creeping about on unwholesome business.

Even a sorcerer's cave had something over the Pictish forests by night.

* * *

The western hills swallowed the sun. Only stars, and a moon too new to give much light, served the world beyond the illuminated circle around fires.

This was as well for the thing that hunted in the darkness. The *chakan* had been sent by the shaman of the Owls, to trail the band of demon-men going to the rock house of the white shaman. It had a man's form but an ape's hair and a great-ape's strength, enough to snap most men in two as a boy snaps a twig.

It had no command to kill, however. Or at least not tonight. It was to trail, climb, and if it found a suitable place, to hide. What it heard, saw, and above all, smelled, the shaman Itha Yarag would draw from its mind with his magick.

When he had done that, the Owls would know more of the mage who had served them so well. They might even know if he would continue to serve them as well in the future, or if the coming of the demon-men meant he had found new friends.

If so, it would be time to take all of the loot in the cave, sacrifice the white mage in the old way, and pass his daughter round among the chiefs of the Owls, and even of friendly Picts such as the Lynxes and Eagles.

Spring turned into summer, and summer ripened the life of the forest. Fruits and berries began to show other hues than green. Streams lost their spring fullness, and the hunting around the remaining ponds was bountiful. The Picts gorged on the summer's plenty and lay about, sated and as at peace with the world as it was in the nature of Picts to be.

Conan and his Bamulas were quite content to let sleeping Picts lie, save for those they joined in raids toward the east and south. This they did with some effect,

as they were well-furnished from the storerooms of
Lysenius's caves.

They saw little enough of the sorcerer himself, which
was not altogether good, to Conan's mind. The more
they saw of him, the more they would learn. Lysenius
had other senses than the common human ones with
which to learn about the Bamulas; he could know without seeing.

When first they came to the cave, they heard that
Lysenius was ill. Scyra told Conan that someone had
slain the bearer of his ghost-ear and that he had been in
a healing trance since.

Conan passed that tidbit on to his band, and Bowenu
began to crow about his spearwork. Govindue promptly
told him that he would be wrestled into submission
again if he did not keep his tongue between his teeth—

"—if he has any left when I'm done with him," the
Cimmerian added. "A good warrior's tongue is bold,
Bowenu. It does not charge about like an elephant
drunk on overripe pears!"

Bowenu held his peace for some days thereafter.

He might well have done so because, like the others,
he was too busy accustoming himself to the new clothing, weapons, and food the Bamulas had received so
lavishly. Clearly, Lysenius was not stinting his new allies,
and had not stinted his former ones.

Just as clearly, he had been gathering more than the
loot of Pictish raids in these caves. Magicks, trade, or
friends beyond the border? About the first, Conan
would not even hazard a guess; he left in peace sorcerers who did him the same favor.

Trade was possible; there was one chamber so heavily
sealed that it practically shouted its name as the
treasure-house. With the eyes of a seasoned thief and a
prudent captain alike, Conan noted at least three ways

of breaking in. But he made no attempt on the chamber now. He wished peace with Lysenius and Scyra, and opted for no encounter with the magickal protections the sorcerer had surely put on his treasure.

Friends beyond the border seemed almost as likely a source of Lysenius's hoard. It was no secret to Conan that there were Hyborians who dealt with the Picts at the expense of their own kind, although there had never been many such in Cimmeria, and fewer still long-lived. That harsh land had its own harsh punishments for those who went against their blood.

In other lands, such men flourished, or at least were not spied out as readily. They were a kind that made Conan wonder more than once if the southern men had bred true. He would leave them to their intrigues, however, and keep his Bamulas free of them, the gods allowing. The intrigues of the Black Kingdoms would be enough for him for some years to come, if he and his band ever returned thence.

Clothing of rawhide and fur, tanned-leather sandals and woolen leggings, Pictish spears and war-axes, Bossonian bows and Gunderman armor—all came forth in abundance. So did more jerked meat, dried nuts and berries, and a pungent ale. The Bamulas pronounced the ale as good as their native beer, and were not backward about draining a whole barrelful before Conan put a halt to that.

"The Picts are still out there, those who pretend friendship and those who do not even pretend. We are more fit to meet them than we were, but they are still a hundred to our one and they know this land."

The Bamulas learned quickly, being seasoned warriors eager to begin carving a road home through Lysenius's enemies. Thrice Conan led them out on raids, and brought them all back.

They did not march with Picts on these raids, save one or two who acted as guides. This was as well. Conan knew the Pictish way of war, and would not have his Bamulas learn it. His people would return to their land with no screaming girl-children violated before their burning homes, and no graybeards left with skulls broken and unseeing eyes staring at the sky.

Then the day came when they raided across the borders into the Marches, and the Picts marched with them..

From a high branch, Govindue's birdcall came. It was the call of a Black Coast bird, not a native of this wilderness. Conan doubted that the caravan guards were woods-wise enough to notice the difference. Or if they were, that they would have the time to put their knowledge to any good use.

Forty Picts lay in wait along one side of the road. Conan's Bamulas lay in wait along the other side. This let both bands attack at once, but kept them apart until the moment of the attack.

That was just as well. The Picts looked askance at the "demon-men" as much as the Bamulas looked askance at the Pictish warriors. Bad blood had been avoided; although Conan and the Pictish chief had not a word in common, each was a seasoned captain who could plan a battle with gestures and scratches in the dirt.

The caravan was well into the trap now. Definitely its guards were not woods-wise, or perhaps the raiders had truly outrun their warning. The Bamulas had attacked nowhere and the Picts set upon only one isolated farmstead on the way across the border, and the forest could hide sixty men from even the most keen border patrol.

Now, if only the Picts would not shoot arrows with their eyes closed (as it sometimes seemed they did), and the Bamulas would remember that even a friendly arrow could kill—

A Pictish war yell gave the signal for the attack. Conan leapt from cover, brandishing his sword. He had smeared his face and other exposed skin with berry juice, darkening his complexion until he did not stand out among the Bamulas. Bad enough to be fighting on the side of the Picts; worse still if tales came that black warriors with a white leader fought in alliance with the Picts. That sort of tale could turn out a host to sweep the borders clean. Conan doubted that this would please Lysenius, and was certain that it would not speed the Bamulas' homeward journey.

He leapt into the road and snatched at the bridle of the caravan's lead guard's horse with one hand. With the other, he blocked three downcuts by the rider, who had more speed than skill and no strength sufficient to get through Conan's defense.

The horse reared. Conan ducked under its belly and came up on the guard's off-side. He struck with his sword, pulling the blow so that it only stunned through the helmet rather than splitting helmet and skull. With the other hand, he gripped the rider's belt and heaved. The man flew out of the saddle and crashed into the ditch. Conan noted with regret that he fell on the Pictish side; with luck, he would recover his senses before the Picts found him.

Conan reined the horse and thrust a foot into the stirrup. The mount reared again, nearly snatching him off his feet. A guard thrust at him under the horse's belly. The point of the blade only nicked Conan instead of sinking deep. He kicked the sword out of the man's hand, swung into the saddle, and slashed down with his sword. This time, skull gave as well as boiled-leather helmet; the man fell, and the horse's hooves finished the work begun by the Cimmerian's sword.

From horseback, Conan had a better view of the battle along the trail than anyone else. The guards to the rear had formed a shield wall, and those forward were retreating toward it. Not all of them reached their goal; Pictish arrows and Bamula spears were thinning their ranks. Conan even saw the one Bamula who had truly mastered the bow find a victim.

It seemed to Conan that the guards had decided to save their lives and let the wagons and packhorses go. Either that or they planned a trap.

Then he saw a flurry of fighting around one wagon that clearly had not been abandoned. He raked the horse's flanks with his heels and charged down on the men there. An arrow nicked his neck, the shaft of a spear thrown awry slapped the horse's flank, then he was up to the wagon. The arrows from the trail ceased; either the Bossonian archers feared hitting friends or the Picts had beaten them down.

Three men were struggling against four Picts and a Bamula. The guards had leather corselets and mail caps, and no little skill with their swords, which meant they were holding their own until Conan came up. He kicked one man in the back of the head without reining in, and smashed another across the helmet with the flat of his sword. Both went down.

The third man scrambled into the wagon, thrust his arms under the cover, and came out with an ironbound coffer. Small as it was, it was plainly heavy. The man staggered as he jumped to the ground, then staggered again as a Pict thrust a spear into his thigh. In spite of the wound, the man broke into a run, so swiftly that between one breath and the next, he outdistanced his assailants.

He did not outdistance Conan, on horseback. Before the archers behind the shield wall could draw and loose, the Cimmerian had overtaken the man. One massive Cimmerian arm swooped down like a kingfisher on a minnow and plucked the coffer from the man's hands.

The man squalled like a mating tomcat and stabbed at Conan with a vicious poinard. Steel tore flesh and, weighted with the hilt of his broadsword, Conan's fist stretched the man senseless on the ground.

He wheeled his horse and rode back toward the head of the caravan, to see Govindue on the trail, waving his arms. With only twenty Bamulas, there could be no division into four parts, not without keeping men out of battle in a way that the Picts would call dishonorable. But there could be a young chief with sharp eyes and a cool head perched in a tree unseen by Pictish friend and Bossonian foe alike.

"Horsemen coming!" Govindue shouted. The actual words he used were "six-legged warriors," since horses were unknown in Bamula lands.

Conan thought that he'd either scented a trap or that luck was with the caravan. Just as well, too. Without a fresh enemy to fight, the Picts' bloodlust might lead them to beat down the shield wall with their arrows and massacre everyone. As it was, anyone from the caravan left alive now might well see tomorrow's sunrise, and as many more as fate allowed.

He waved to the Bamulas. Picts also saw the gesture, but their chief had not signaled them. Drums and shouts held them where they were. Conan cursed. He had no wish to be impaled on the horns of this dilemma: either desert the Picts or stay until they also saw the Bossonian reinforcements, when that might be too late for the Bamulas, who were closer to the new enemy troops.

Conan shouted for the Bamulas to return to cover on either side of the road. That might give the newcomers a clear path to some of the Picts, but it would let the Bamulas survive long enough to fight back, and perhaps to rescue their northern *swozhu*. (That was an expressive Bamula word meaning "friends-for-one-raid," and it was not altogether praise. It was also the most common way the Bamulas had of referring to the Picts.)

The Bamulas had barely regained the shelter of the trees when the Bossonians charged out of the shield wall. Either the rearguard had been stronger than Conan realized or more survivors of the men forward had reached the wall. Regardless, they swiftly reached close quarters with the Picts.

The Picts were not ones to fight at close quarters against armored opponents, unless they had a great advantage in numbers. This they did not have, but they had an open road into the woods, where no horseman could go. They took that road, and in moments there was not a living Pict in sight.

Since the Bamulas had to take the same road, Conan dismounted, slapped his horse on the rump, and sent it cantering off toward the reinforcements. Then he sheathed his sword and gripped the coffer with both hands. Even for the Cimmerian, it was a trifle on the heavy side for one hand in rough country.

Conan made sure that there were no Picts within sight, and none hiding close enough to see, before he opened the coffer. He did this by seeking a hollow tree, the last remnants of what must have once been the size of a good temple and older than most such built by the hands of men.

While Kubwande held a tuft of burning moss tied to a stick, Conan attacked the coffer's hinges with his dagger. They gave only just before the dagger was too blunt for use. Whoever had contrived this coffer had wanted to keep what lay within exceedingly well-guarded indeed.

The lid opened with a faint and more than slightly eerie scream. Conan at first thought nothing was inside at all. Then he saw that within, the coffer was lined with black velvet and stuffed with black silk. He drew out the silk and noticed a faint reflection from Kubwande's light. He put in his hand, felt around, and gripped something smooth that had two textures, metal and stone.

He held the object up—a square-cut crystal so transparent that it had looked black against the black velvet, but it was betrayed by the age-darkened gold of its mounting. To Conan's eyes, it looked as if it might once have decorated a sword-hilt or a helmet, but there was something about it that made him uneasy.

"Hunh," Bowenu snorted. "Not enough gold in that to make it worth carrying."

"Not enough wits in your skull to make you a good judge of such matters," Kubwande replied. "If we do not wish to leave it, let us give it to Lysenius. He may find some value in it."

"That he will, from the way the guards were fighting to snatch it free," Conan said. "Whoever has lost it may pay a fair-sized ransom."

He felt an urge to have it out of his hands as quickly as possible, but he was not wholly sure that Lysenius was the right destination. The jewel had a smell of sorcery to it, and that meant the farther it was from both honest folk and Lysenius, the better.

What about an honest woman? Scyra seemed to have her doubts about some of her father's schemes. Conan would trust her more if she had concealed less about them, but his trust for her was still as a gold coin to a brass piece compared to his trust for her father. He trusted no sorcerer wittingly, but for the Bamulas' sake, he would give Scyra as much trust as he thought she had earned.

"We have crystals like this in my homeland," Conan said. "They have power, but it is women's magick. Vuona is a woman, but not adept with power. Scyra, however, is both a woman and a mistress of magick. She is fit to receive the crystal."

"What if Lysenius is angered?" Bowenu asked.

"Then," Govindue said in the tone of one instructing a child (although Bowenu had to be five years his elder at least), "we shall hold our tongues about it until Scyra has been given it."

Thirteen

Lysenius did not resemble the usual notion of the sorcerer, but then, Conan had acquaintance with many sorcerers (although liking few) and knew that they were as varied as were common men.

Scyra's father was nearly as tall as Conan, and had he led an equally vigorous life, he might have been nearly the Cimmerian's physical equal. As it was, a stout belly bulged under a silk shirt that could have begun life intended for a Barachan sailor. Other signs of good living thrust out blue hose cut in the latest Aquilonian style. A short green Bossonian forester's cloak hung from broad shoulders, and the curious array was completed by a massive rawhide belt, clearly Pictish, with an equally Pictish bronze dagger thrust through it.

The broad face above the garb was almost too youthful to belong to the father of a woman Scyra's age. Or it would have been save for the altogether bald pate and the splendid beard, mostly gray shot with streaks of black. The eyes were Scyra's, an intense blue that almost seemed the image of Conan's—but the Cimmerian had the same uneasiness about what lay behind those eyes as he did about what lay in a pouch slung to his own belt.

"I am well-served by you," Lysenius said. He spoke with what Conan had come in his wars to recognize as an Aquilonian accent. "Very well-served."

He used that last phrase three more times before Conan started translating for the Bamulas. The Cimmerian translated it only once. There was no cause yet to share his doubts about Lysenius. His instincts led him to wariness, and he trusted those instincts; had he done otherwise, he would have been long dead. Being neither god nor priest, however, he did not call them unfailing or perfect.

Conan's doubts grew as slowly as moss for some while as Lysenius rambled on. It seemed that he had come to the Pictish Wilderness in flight from first Aquilonia, then from his native Bossonia. In each place he had practiced the magick arts in a way that offended the powerful, and in Bossonia, their wrath had claimed his wife, Scyra's mother.

With nothing but his lawful knowledge of magick, he had come to the Pictish Wilderness. Conan vowed to believe that when he saw ships floating in the air. The Stygian priests had long reaches and much gold with which to buy friends. Lysenius had befriended the Picts by using his magick in ways that did not cast doubts on the powers of their shamans.

Now it was time to take his revenge on those who had exiled him and deprived him of his wife. He would find the Picts a champion. The statue of an ancient warrior lay in a distant cave. Vitalized by Lysenius's spells, the statue would come forth, an invincible protector of the Picts. They would swarm across the border, and those who had wronged Lysenius would rue the day they did so, as they listened to the screams of their kin before their own throats were cut. . . .

Lysenius went on at considerable length about the red ruin the Picts would leave in their wake. Conan, who had seen more such campaigns than most men twice his age, listened with grave attention. He was not learning much about Lysenius's plans, but he was gleaning a good deal about the sorcerer's mind.

Mostly, he decided, he was recognizing that Lysenius was mad. Whether the mage had been so before (and Conan had even less use for Stygian magick than for most other kinds), he certainly was so now. Mad from loneliness perhaps, and even perhaps with some cause, but there could be no cause for unleashing the Pictish nation on the Bossonian Marches.

Conan was about to ask what part he and his band might play in this scheme, when Lysenius seemed to pluck the Cimmerian's thoughts from his head. It was so uncanny that Conan dared not look at the pouch on his belt to see if Lysenius had also plucked the crystal from it by sheer force of will.

"I cannot give to any one tribe or clan of the Picts the honor of entering the cave of the statue. Not without making all the others jealous enough to fly at my throat, or at least at the throats of the tribe so honored. I am already unfriends with the Snakes more than I could wish, and there would be others in like case."

Again Lysenius rambled, evoking the vision of the Snakes returning to loyalty and trust once the statue walked and victory seemed assured. Conan began to wish that the Snakes would demonstrate their lack of friendship by raiding the cave in this moment. Fighting Picts would surely be less tedious than listening to a sorcerer with more ambition than sense (the most common kind, in Conan's experience).

"It will fall to you and your warriors of the Bamula to travel to the cave. You are of no nation among the Picts. You are proven in valor and skill. Above all, you have already passed through the world-walker, and what you have done before, you shall do again."

It took Conan a moment to realize that Lysenius was referring to the demon's gate. He used that name when he translated, and he heard hisses of indrawn breath all across the chamber behind him. Lysenius, fortunately, seemed to take these as signs of eagerness, and Conan thanked various minor gods that the sorcerer knew nothing of Bamula customs.

"Let honor be done to Lysenius," Conan said. The Bamulas hissed again and began to chant.

"*Ohbe* Lysenius. *Ohbe* Lysenius. *Ohbe* Lysenius."

Conan rather hoped they would be allowed to continue until they had gone on as long as the sorcerer. However, it seemed that only one man in these caves was allowed to be tedious. Lysenius made an unmistakable gesture of dismissal, and Conan arrayed his men, bowed in the Hyborian style, and led them out.

They passed down three corridors, and on the fourth and final one to their quarters, Conan signaled to Kubwande.

"Yes, Conan?"

Conan tapped his pouch. He had kept the crystal on his person even while in the chamber with Lysenius as he wished no other man endangered for possessing it. Sorcerers had tried to kill him more often than he could count on fingers and toes together; the Bamulas were not so seasoned.

"I am taking this where we have agreed that it belongs."

"Take care, Conan. The Bamulas need you more than they need Scyra. I do not mean only the Bamulas here, either."

"Time enough for the others when we see them again," Conan said. The man's transparent flattery had lost its power to anger him. Kubwande was no fool, and indeed a fine hand in battle, but intrigue was in his blood as much as vengeance was in Lysenius's.

Lysenius had not precisely discouraged roaming about the caves, but he had made it clear that it was not without its dangers. He did not describe these dangers, so Conan had no idea whether they were magickal, human, animal or simply holes in the floor ready to tumble the unwary into the abyss.

Being seasoned at skulking in the darkness from his days as a thief, Conan cared little for vague menaces. He was not slow to learn his way around the tunnels. Before the band had been ten days guests of the sorcerer, Conan had learned the tortuous way from the warriors' quarters to Scyra's private chambers as thoroughly as he had learned the way to the well when he was thirsty.

He did not enter those chambers. Scyra seemed to have told him all that she cared to, and he had no wish to strain her loyalty by asking for more.

He also did not wish to give Vuona cause for jealousy. Well-bedded as she now was, she would have little cause, but women did not always need cause for jealousy. Nor was Vuona powerless to make her jealousy dangerous, if she chose to betray the band to Lysenius. Doubtless some Bamula would spare Conan from having the girl's blood on his hands, but he would rather she returned alive and hale to the Black Kingdoms with her comrades.

Now Conan intended to cover the whole path to Scyra's chambers and meet her there—if needs be, waiting until she returned. In spite of what he had said to Kubwande, he had no plan to give her the crystal without demanding knowledge of what it was. If he had any doubts that she could be trusted with it, he would guard it, with his life if necessary.

He told Kubwande that if he had not returned before dawn, the Bamulas were to seek safety by themselves. He did not instruct the man on how. Kubwande certainly had fewer scruples than the Cimmerian, and might gladly think his best hope was serving Lysenius. Govindue would most likely not be able to prevail against him.

If it had not been for the mystery of the crystal, Conan might not have risked seeking Scyra. But two duties to his people now weighed in the balance, and the mystery of the crystal was the heavier.

Turning down a side tunnel, Conan quickly came to a crack in the rock. On the outside, it was large enough to admit him if he slipped through sideways, though not without some scraping of hide. Inside, it broadened into a chimney. The chimney offered only a few cracks as finger and toeholds, but for much of its way, Conan could go up it feet against one side, back against the other. He tied his lantern, a brass casing holding pressed moss soaked in oil, to his belt and began his climb.

He finished it with more care for silence than usual. It was his experience that sentries were always the most alert when you could least afford their attentions. He still made good time and was soon padding along the tunnel above.

This led to a corridor carved by an underground stream, which still flowed waist-deep through the premises. Conan stopped at the hole giving entrance to the corridor, and wrinkled his nose. Smell could tell of danger where eyes and ears failed, and he smelled something rank that had not been there before.

He heard nothing however, and the light of his lantern revealed even less—only the bare rock of the tunnel, eroded by the stream over the eons, and the chill, dark water flowing past at its usual swift pace. Conan put a finger into the water and tasted it. No trace of anything uncanny, or even foul.

There were several ways to Scyra's chambers beyond this tunnel, but here it was the only path, unless one could burrow through solid rock as easily as a mole through fresh-turned earth. Lacking that power, the Cimmerian slipped into the water and began his advance, breasting the stream that seethed around him. He held the lantern high and his sword in his free hand, and his eyes searched both ahead and behind, while his feet sought firm purchase on the tunnel-bottom with each new step.

It was well he used such caution. The foul odor grew stronger with each step, and now he began to hear what seemed to be breathing that was not his. He held his breath; silence did not return. He advanced; whatever lay in wait suddenly had the wits to halt its own breathing.

Now Conan felt a chill from more than the water. Obviously, what lay ahead had sensed his approach. It could choose the time and place of its attack, and he could only meet it with precious little warning, and possibly with less room. That was still better than having to pursue it through the caves, or worse yet, having it roaming the darkness ready to attack less robust prey.

The Cimmerian passed the narrowest portion of the corridor without incident. He thought he heard a scraping from ahead and well off to one side, and remembered that several dry branches led into the tunnel just beyond.

He stepped forward—and the tunnel rang with a hideous scream as a massive weight surged against him. Water sprayed, the lantern hissed out, and darkness swallowed the battle.

Conan recognized at once that he faced two assailants. One, bolder than its comrade, clutched at his left arm, then tried to twist, claw, and pull all at once, without securing its grip. Conan pivoted from the hips, breaking the enemy's hold and dashing the creature against the wall behind him.

That gave him a respite for a moment only, but all he needed. He rammed his free hand, clenched into a fist, into the darkness where he judged the other's throat to be. At the same time, he slashed, clumsily because of the angle, dangerously because of his strength and the newly keen edge of his sword. Aquilonian steel came hard across the back of the neck of the being in front. It howled again, and its fetid breath stifled Conan.

The first attacker now tried to seize him from behind. But once again it was slow to secure its grip, overly eager to do its victim injury. Conan brought both feet up and kicked hard at the attacker in front, at the same time driving himself backward against the foe behind.

He heard a crack as the rear attacker's skull met the tunnel, and felt its grip weaken. Now he had a hand free with which to draw his dagger, and he stabbed furiously into what lay before him. Another scream, and this time a spray of blood mingled with the reeking breath. Conan stabbed again and more blood sprayed, but no scream came. He stepped from between the assailants and brought his sword down, feeling bone give once to the right, once to the left.

Then only the echoes of the death-screams remained, and the gurgle of the water washing over two hairy bodies, carrying away two streams of blood.

Conan sheathed his weapons and climbed out of the water. He thought he had suffered no great hurt, although he felt as if he had been pounded with clubs and flogged with nettles. Whatever he had faced had been strong, quick, not highly intelligent, but far too dangerous to be allowed to roam the tunnels.

That made one more question he was going to put before Scyra, and demand that she answer before he handed over the crystal. He touched his belt to see that it was still in its pouch, and assured of that, began the next stage of his journey.

Conan had no way of rekindling his lantern, but no need to either. The last part of the way to Scyra's chambers was so easy to traverse that any apprentice thief could have done it without light. The Cimmerian's scrapes and bruises had barely started to throb before he was at Scyra's door.

He drew his dagger, sheathe and all, reversed it, and tapped on the door with the hilt. He heard movement— faintly, for the door was heavy wood bound with brass, some of the brass forming curious figures that might have been runes in a tongue Conan had never encountered. He heard a faint *ting*, beyond doubt the opening of a peephole, then a sharp hiss of indrawn breath and the sound of a bolt being drawn.

With a creaking of hinges that seemed as loud as the war cries of an army, the door opened. Scyra stood there, her dagger in one hand, a cloak of supple rawhide thrown hastily about her. It left her feet and lower legs bare—as well-formed as Conan had suspected. It also left him certain that she wore nothing under the cloak.

"Conan! What brings you here?"

"Curiosity."

"About me?" In another woman, that might have been flirtatious. Scyra's sober expression and level voice gave the lie to any such notion.

"About something I took from the Bossonian caravan."

"You fill *me* with curiosity. The more so, coming here looking as you do. You look as if you have fallen down a cliff. My father said there were dangers in roaming our tunnels." She beckoned him into the chamber and he followed.

"There are more dangers than your father believes, unless he has turned loose giant apes in the caves," he said. Scyra's eyes widened. Conan continued, describing his foes as best he could without having seen them clearly.

Scyra had turned pale before he finished, and was silent for a moment afterward. Then she said slowly, "You met *chakans*. Pictish wizards tame them and use them for tracking . . . and killing. They are not allowed in our caves."

"Tell that to whoever sent them," Conan said brusquely. "And meanwhile, keep your door locked and barred, and a dagger ready to hand. Or a spell, if you have one potent against those brutes. One of them could tear you limb from limb without breathing hard."

For a moment, Scyra seemed about to faint. The cloak nearly slipped from her shoulders, and she seemed not to notice when Conan rearranged it. She sat down as if her legs had failed her, and hung her head for a moment.

"Is your peace with the Picts breaking?" Conan asked,

seating himself beside her. He wanted to shout, but forced himself to speak as to a child. Scyra had wits and courage, but tonight was bringing her much bad news all at once.

"If they have unleashed *chakans* on us, it may well be," she replied. "What else did you come for?"

Conan drew out the crystal. Scyra's eyes grew even wider, but her voice was steady as she spoke.

"That was from the caravan?"

"Yes, stoutly coffered and well-defended. Three Bossonians looked ready to sell their lives to keep it."

"I understand why."

"Then if you do, tell me, and I will understand also. I hardly think we have time for riddles."

She shook herself. "No. We do not." She reached for the crystal. Conan hesitated for a moment. If this was something of sorcery and gave her new powers when she held it—

But his sword and dagger were ready and could deal with Scyra—or anything she could turn herself into—well enough. He drew the dagger and rested his other hand on the hilt of his sword.

For a moment, Scyra seemed to have eyes for nothing except the steel, and no power of speech. Then she held out her hand again, and Conan put the crystal in it.

Silence, long enough that Conan feared other *chakans* would find their dead comrades and come prowling in search of vengeance. Scyra seemed to be in a trance. He hoped she was finding some answers with these delvings into other worlds, and might in time condescend to give them to him.

Before his impatience forced the Cimmerian to speech, however, Scyra stood up. She seemed calmer, although the hand that gripped the crystal was clenched so tightly about it that the knuckles were white.

"This is, by its appearance a Crystal of Thraz," she said.

"That tells me nothing," Conan said.

"Forgive me. Such crystals are very old, said to be Atlantean, but of course everything that old is blamed on Atlantis, even when there is no mention of it in the chronicles of—"

"Scyra, I have no time to listen to you imitate your father at his worst. What does the cursed thing *do*?"

"It can increase the power of a sorcerer. It can also clean temples or other holy places of the taint of dark sorcery."

"Useful little device, isn't it?"

"Please. There are only six of them known to exist. I never dreamed that one would come into my hands."

"Then you intend to keep it?"

"Do you mean, to keep it from my father?"

Conan grunted. Scyra was too shrewd by half. He was almost tempted to snatch the crystal back and smash it on the floor. He doubted it was harder than the mountain stone, and a few shrewd cuts with his sword would finish the work.

"You're the best judge of your father's honesty. Would it help him use the demon's gate—the world-walker—to send us to the cave of that image he's planning to bring back to life? If it will do that, I won't ask you to keep it from him. It's my life and the Bamulas's at stake."

Scyra's eyes widened again. They were very fine eyes, and Conan would not mind seeing them widen on a pillow, but he wished the woman would find words more quickly.

"He is sending *your* band to the cave?"

"So he said, in words I understood. Which of us is astray in his wits?"

"No one. You heard . . . you heard the truth, but not all of it."

"And the whole truth is?"

Scyra took a deep breath, and now the words came swiftly and clearly. There was a woman of sense under that fidgety exterior, the gods be praised!

"The statue must be animated by a blood-sacrifice. Either the nearest kin of the sorcerer, or twenty-some other folk. My father considered sacrificing me. He then changed his mind and wished to sacrifice twenty Picts."

"How was he going to persuade them?"

"I was to marry a Pictish chief. My bride-price would be the lives of twenty of the chief's warriors."

"The chief wouldn't live to the next day's sunset after that. Your father may know magick, but he knows less about Picts than young chief Govindue knows."

"He was desperate. Also, the other Picts might have forgiven him after his magick brought them victory."

"The victory of turning the Marches into a howling wilderness. You wished that?"

"He is my father. He loved my mother, and saw the Marchers as her murderers. Vengeance comes easily when you look at the world thus."

"Madness comes even sooner, and I think it has come to your father." A suspicion buzzed in Conan's mind, like a marsh bug whining in his ear. It grew louder, then turned into an ugly certainty.

"My band goes to the cave in the world-walker, and then *we* become the blood-sacrifice? No Picts killed, none turned to enemies, and the statue on the march? Is that your father's scheme?"

Scyra nodded. "He has not said so plainly, but from what I have heard and what you have said—I can hardly doubt it."

"Nor can I," Conan said. "Scyra, if I give you this

crystal, can you keep it out of your father's hands? I think you have need of some defense against him, even if you do not choose to fight him. I would not ask that. But I swear I will destroy it if you do not swear to keep it, and if you betray us, you will join us in death."

It always made sense to arm a friend in the enemy's camp. It was ever a question, though, whether the friend would remain one and any weapons given him stay out of the enemy's hands. Conan's luck in such ventures had been mixed. He wanted to trust Scyra, and if she could be trusted, she might do much good.

If not, she might be the doom of them all, and not only himself and his band. Bossonian corpses would be piled high before the Picts were beaten back across the frontier.

"I will swear, Conan. While I am thinking of the oath, I would like to tend to your wounds. The *chakans* did not bite, did they?"

"Not so I've noticed, but they have claws and muscles in plenty."

"You were fortunate as well as strong. Their bite festers so that only spells can remedy the wound. Warm water and a herb poultice for the scratches, a potion for the pain of the bruises—"

"No potions."

"You do not trust me?"

"I need to trust my wits. I've never yet taken a potion that didn't slow them, and my arm as well. Those may not be the only *chakans* about."

"Very well. Turn your back."

Confident that she could not stab him without warning, Conan perched on a low stool. It creaked ominously under his weight. He heard bare feet padding across the floor, and then warm dampness touched his back. So did something else warm—the bare breasts of a woman.

He spun on the stool, raising his legs as he did. They swept Scyra off her feet. He caught her and dragged her onto his lap. She wore only a Pictish loinguard, and all the rest of her was as fair to look at as were the feet and legs.

She shook her head, making lights dance on her hair. "Is this enough of an oath?"

"For now . . . but I thought sorceresses needed to be maidens."

"A man who has no ghost–voice cannot weaken a woman's magick," she said.

"No what?" Conan asked.

She explained. The explanation was long, but this time Conan did not mind the length. She remained in his lap, kissed him, sponged down his wounds, and in due course, removed her loinguard. They were in the bed shortly after that, and entwined almost at once.

How long they remained thus, Conan never knew. He only knew that Scyra had cried out for the third time, when a fierce shock made the chamber quiver. *Earthquake*, he thought at first. The bed creaked and swayed, the stool toppled over, sponges and the water basin fell to the floor. As the quivering faded, Conan heard the rumble of stone, and then a cry that could have come from no human throat.

He rolled from the woman's embrace and bed and snatched for his clothes, steel, and the crystal. All were where he had left them. Neither Scyra nor any minion of hers had used this moment to steal the jewel. He might ask the woman more, *should* ask more if there was time.

"Scyra, I will trust you to be no enemy to us even though you be none to your father. The crystal is yours. It is best you and it remain here, though. I am taking my people away. We may be fighting *chakans*, Picts, and the gods alone know what else."

She looked up at him with eyes that were no longer wide but half closed, even sleepy, with satisfaction. "Conan, for a safer journey, look to the chest over there, by the hanging with the blue castle. It is not locked."

The chest contained a motley array of goods, but only three were of interest. The first was a new lantern. The second was a packet of oiled parchment, holding a map of the wilderness, embroidered on the thinnest of Khitan silk. Conan judged that with a little time, he could master it.

The last was a heavy purse. Conan opened it briefly, judged that the coins were gold all the way down, and added it to his load.

Scyra had neither moved from the bed nor donned her clothes. Conan threw her a final admiring look, and she writhed with pleasure as if the look had been a caress.

"Go swiftly, Conan. If you are beyond my father's reach soon enough, he may not punish me."

"You haven't seen swiftness, Scyra. Not until you've seen a Cimmerian and a host of Bamula warriors running for their lives!"

Fourteen

Govindue woke the men when he heard the distant sounds of a battle. In this jungle of stone, it was hard to tell where and how far away the battle was fought, but it seemed to lie on the path Conan had taken.

The men were sleepy, many of them, and not pleased to be awakened. Nor was Kubwande friendly to the young chief.

"Conan said that we had until dawn to await him," the *iqako* said. "Until then, we should rest and save our strength."

"Rather than save Conan, if he needs it?" Govindue asked.

The young chief was pleased to note that even some of the most heavy-eyed men nodded at those words. Some among the band had the same notions of honor as he did, which was as well. By now, they all owed their lives to Conan more than once, and Govindue was sure they would owe much more to the man who would not be called Amra before they saw the Bamula lands again.

"We do not know where he is—" Kubwande began again.

It was Bowenu who interrupted. "We know that where the battle is, Conan will be found. Never was there such a chief for finding the enemy, or they finding him."

This time everybody nodded, even Kubwande, although he seemed uneasy. Govindue made ritual gestures of gratitude at Bowenu and vowed that when he had it in his gift, the man would have more than gratitude.

"Then some of us should go," Kubwande said. "I will gladly lead them."

Govindue shook his head, and he was glad to see distaste for that idea on most of the other faces. "We will not divide our strength, not in an unknown place and facing an unknown enemy. We will all gather what we wish to take from this place, and when we leave this stone hut, we will leave together. Nor will we divide ourselves on the way to find Conan, or afterward, save by chance.

"We have been together this far, and it has meant life to all of us. If now it means death, then that is as the gods will it, and we will meet the death they send like warriors of the Bamulas. In this land, too, people will cry 'Ohbe, Bamula!' "

It was the longest speech Govindue had ever made in his life, even longer than the one at his manhood ordeal. It also seemed to strike home more than he dared expect, with warriors some of whom were almost old enough to be his father.

The gods touched those whom they wished to lead, it seemed. He would have to be worthy of their trust, as well as that of the men.

Then there was no more speech, only the scrape and rattle of men preparing to strike out for war.

Conan moved openly through the tunnels now. Speed was everything, to take him back to his people before anything could happen to them. Treachery by Lysenius, attack by *chakans*, another earthquake—anything was possible.

Anything except panic among the Bamulas. Not all of them had showed equal prowess in battle, but all of them had followed him through the world-walker and on after that. It was not in them to give way to fear.

At one point, the roof of a tunnel gaped open, a crack wide enough to swallow a boy running up into nighted depths. Conan could have sworn that the wall was also bulged out. Just as well he was moving openly through the wider tunnels. The narrow passages of the secret route he had taken to Scyra's bed might have become a trifle *too* narrow for a well-grown Cimmerian warrior.

Conan realized that the way he was following now led past the treasure-room. He also realized that there were smoke and dust in the air, and a foul odor he had no trouble recognizing. *Chakans* lay ahead.

This time he was ready. He set down the purse and map and advanced burdened only by lantern and weapons. Around the first bend, the smoke and dust swirled thicker, seeming ready to swallow every beam of light from the lantern. Around the second bend, his sandals grated on stones, and a block fallen from the roof lay half-barring the passage.

Conan crouched, listening for any sound from beyond

the block. If the *chakans* were lying in wait, that would be the best place for them.

Only silence came, broken once by the faint, distant clatter of rock falling. The reek of the *chakans* seemed to be weaker now, and another odor was joining it. That one was even more familiar to Conan. It was the smell of death.

Whose death? The only way to learn was to go on. Conan drew both weapons and sidled past the block, back to the wall, his eyes seeking friend, foe, or even knowledge of what had befallen the treasure-chamber.

The chamber opened off a larger one, and when Conan entered that larger chamber, he found himself on what seemed like a battlefield. Fallen rock was strewn about, likewise gobs of half-melted metal and pieces of charred wood, all still smoking and adding to the choking miasma.

Among the other debris were several corpses. They had almost human shape, but the proportions of the limbs were subtly wrong and no human ever sported such a peaked skull. Conan also saw on those corpses that were not charred black far too much hair for any human being.

Beyond the rubble-strewn floor, the arched entrance to the treasure-chamber gaped. Smoke curled out of it, and more from the remains of the doors still dangling from either side of the arch. Beyond the entrance, smoke and dust swirled so thickly that the light of Conan's lantern could hardly penetrate farther than into the stone itself.

He had seen enough, however. A band of *chakans* had come prowling this way, and with their half-bestial intelligence, had found the treasure-chamber. What they had thought it to be, the gods alone knew, but they had surely made some attempt on the doors—vigorous enough to draw the chamber's magickal defenses on them and cause a minor quake.

Or had that been entirely magickal? Lysenius had not seemed to be any master of the mechanic arts, Scyra still less. But these caves and tunnels were too extensive and well-shaped to be altogether natural; what powers had made them in the eons before Lysenius came to the Pictish Wilderness? What had those powers left behind?

Conan knew one thing that he was not going to leave behind—anything portable in the treasure-chamber. Lysenius had no good use for any pickings, and the Bamulas might need more than Scyra's gold to speed their way homeward. He would have to chance confrontation with any remaining mechanical or magickal defenses of the treasure-chamber, but he had taken greater risks with less need when he was far less skilled a thief.

Conan retrieved the purse and map and was crossing the chamber when he heard footsteps mounting the tunnel from below. These were human footsteps, and numerous, moving fast—mayhap the Bamulas, or perhaps Picts following in the wake of their shaman's creatures.

The Cimmerian slipped into the arch of the treasure-chamber's entrance and waited, then doused his lantern. Now he was all but invisible, unless one shone light almost squarely upon him.

The newcomers were carrying lanterns. Good. They would illuminate themselves well before they illuminated him. Then a quick rush, if they were Picts—

More footsteps. These were coming from the tunnel Conan had just followed. They were slower, fewer—and now the Cimmerian heard the click of claws on stone. *Chakan*, or whatever else they might be; the one thing they were not was human. Did Lysenius have creatures of his own conjuring at his service, to defend his strong-hold?

The oncoming men seemed to hear the others almost at the same moment as Conan did. He heard their foot-steps stop, then a whispered command to set the lan-terns down in front of them. Relief washed through the Cimmerian. The language was Bamula, and he could have sworn the voice was Govindue's.

Three *chakans* now slipped into view, one of them on all fours, sniffing the floor. From Scyra's description, that had to be the one trailing the Cimmerian. The oth-ers were to guard it while it trailed and help it to strike down the prey when they came upon it.

Conan resolved to alter their plans. There seemed to be far too many of these shaman's pets roaming about tonight. He intended that by dawn, there would be far fewer.

He bent carefully, without any betraying scrape of skin on stone or rattle of gear. He picked up a small stone between thumb and forefinger, then tossed it out onto the rubble-strewn floor.

The rattle seemed as loud as a war cry in a temple. It certainly drew the *chakans'* attention. Whuffling uncer-tainly, they stopped and looked about them. They had to be able to see the Bamulas' lanterns, but could they see the men beyond?

At least one of them did. With a cry that was part-scream, part-howl, it leapt toward the lanterns. It landed among them, knocking two over. Darkness re-doubled, as did sound, with Bamula war cries, Cimmer-ian war cries, and the bestial howls of the *chakans* all vying with one another.

The two remaining *chakans* sprang to join their com-rade, or so Conan judged as best he could by the scant light remaining. If that was so, then all three had their backs to him.

He leapt from his hiding place, landing amid fallen rocks and barely keeping his footing. A charred piece of wood cracked under him, but the sound was lost in the uproar and no *chakan* turned to face him.

That was fatal to one of the beasts almost at once. Knowing their strength, speed, and tenacity of life, Conan struck with two hands on his sword. The cord of the spine, the bone of the skull, the flesh of the *chakan's* neck all gave way together. The creature's high-peaked head lolled on its shoulders as its body lurched forward, bounced off its comrades, and fell to the floor. Two spears thrust from above into its back ended its last struggles, and the rank odor of its death filled the chamber.

"Don't close with them!" Conan shouted. "Form a hedge with half your spears and throw the others!" The Bamulas were no weaklings, but Conan doubted their power to come alive out of a *chakan's* unnatural grip.

For answer, someone threw a spear. It passed wide of both living *chakans* and nearly struck the Cimmerian. He snatched it up, ready to return it point-first to the fool who had thrown so wildly.

Or had it been wildly? He remembered those footprints on the bank where he fought the river-horse, and Kubwande's taste for intrigue. A "wildly thrown" spear in the darkness could give any man excuse should it slay a friend.

The next moment, the Bamulas brought down the second *chakan* with spears both thrown and thrust. Conan heard a warrior cry out in pain and fury, and then came the death-rattle of the *chakan*. The third *chakan* seemed bemused and astray in its wits; it

crouched on the floor and whimpered until Govindue
stepped forward and thrust it through the neck.

The young chief had withdrawn his spear and was
bending its point back into shape when Conan approached him. They pounded each other on the shoulders, then Conan led Govindue apart and whispered:

"A spear came near to taking me instead of the
chakan. Did you see who threw it?"

"Is that their name? We thought them apes. Are they
more?"

Conan told him of what he had learned from Scyra.
Govindue looked grave. "It is not good, to have two
kinds of evil magick against us."

"Tell me what I don't already know, or hold your
tongue."

"I know who threw the spear. Need I name him?"

"I have no wish to curse him. Kill him, if needs be,
but not curse him."

"Then you need no name. Such as he, I think curse
themselves from the day they are born."

"Likely as not." Conan raised his voice. "Ho, Bamulas! We have a treasure-room to loot. Take only what
you can carry easily. We must leave here swiftly and
keep up a good pace for some days."

"Why are we leaving Lysenius?" That was not
Bowenu, as Conan might have expected. He did not recognize the speaker in the darkness, but someone apparently did and spoke up:

"Scobun, do you want to share quarters with these?
Or serve anyone who commands them? Better to take
our chances with the Picts! A cleaner death, if no more."

"Yes," Conan said. He told briefly of Lysenius's
planned treachery. He spent no time explaining how he
had learned, although Kubwande did ask where the
crystal was.

"Where I intended it to be," Conan replied. "I judged rightly. It is woman's magick, and a good thing for us. Scyra will not make war on her father for us, but she has no love for treachery. What strengthens her works for us."

"Wise words," Govindue said. "Now . . . the treasure-room lies over there." He pointed with his spear. "Four at a time, and each four only while I count to a hundred. Anyone greedy or stealing from his comrades will not live long enough to fear Lysenius or the Picts!"

The young chief's voice was still a trifle too high-pitched to give him a real air of command, but he had everything else a captain might need. If luck and the gods spared him, Govindue would leave a mighty name behind him.

If, of course, he did not tonight leave his bones in Lysenius's caves.

The looting of the treasure-chamber went swiftly enough. Chests and bags alike had been sundered apart by the *chakans* and the magick defense against them. Gold and silver coins, some freshly minted Aquilonian crowns, others from realms long lost in the mists of time, jewels, massive necklaces, arms rings and ornaments, and finely decorated weapons, lay strewn wantonly about.

Conan kept a close watch on the men, partly to encourage them to pick the precious rather than the showy, and partly to prevent trickery. He had his sword drawn and even the thought of taking something from a comrade was hard to hold if one sensed those ice-blue eyes boring into the back of one's neck and seeming to read one's innermost thoughts.

The Cimmerian contented himself with a jeweled dagger, which he added to the purse of gold from Scyra.

The blade had never been of the best steel, and now showed signs of rust. The jewels might be worth a manor; the dagger itself was barely fit to cut salt meat in a starveling siege camp.

Everyone had a bulging pouch or bag when he left the treasure-chamber. No one seemed any the slower for his burden, but the day's march would test the Bamulas far more rigorously. Conan resolved that any man who fell behind from an overabundance of loot would have to divide half of his cache among more prudent comrades. If they also were fully burdened, the man would have to leave his baubles for the Picts and the wolves.

With this decision made, Conan formed his men up and led them down past their old quarters and out into the night. Dawn found them well on their way east, and as yet unpursued.

The Bamulas rejoiced at this, and seemed to regard their escape as a certainty. Conan was silent about his own doubts. They were a long way from the border, Lysenius might have resources not yet used or be letting them go for his own purposes, and the Picts would not be long in coming.

Even if they survived all these perils, the border might be closed to them. They had raided in the Marches, and it might well be that no amount of gold would make Bossonians forgive men who had marched with the Picts.

"They are gone! Gone! Gone!" Lysenius thundered.

Scyra hoped that he would not try to cast any spells until his mind was less troubled. Now, if he tried to warm a bowl of herb tea, he was likely as not to set his robe on fire.

She had seen this sort of thing happen before, and it had helped speed his way out of both Aquilonia and

Bossonia. In Aquilonia, men paying good gold and silver for spells unlawful even under the decadent Numedides brooked no failures or partial successes. In Bossonia, bungled spells betrayed Lysenius and his family to hard-handed neighbors who might otherwise have not learned who lived among them.

But a tiger who missed his leap three times out of four was no less dangerous to the man under the fourth leap.

"We must raise the Picts and be after the Cimmerian and his men," Lysenius groaned. "But what can I do to pay blood-price for the warriors who will die?"

From a brief look at the treasure-chamber, Scyra doubted that her father lacked gold for this purpose. Twenty Bamulas had wrought further havoc after the wardings slew the *chakans* and shattered the door, but they had by no means stripped the chamber bare.

But offering part of that gold would make the Picts wonder if there was more. Indeed, they might already have learned of it from the *chakans*. Neither god nor man nor magick could stand between Picts and that much gold.

Her father would escape as a beggar, if he escaped at all, with no gold, no magick not unlawful in any land they could hope to reach, nothing but her—if her marriage to a Pictish chief was not the price of his escape. There had to be some path out of this that would neither beggar her father nor slaughter Conan and his Bamulas.

If she could save Conan (she shivered at the memory of his lusty embrace) and leave the Bamulas to their fate—

No. Conan would refuse such a solution and die cursing her. His honor bound him to save those who had followed him through the world-walker and into a land

that must be as strange to them as the Black Kingdoms
would be to her ... else he would die with them.

But if she could save Conan's band without ruining
her father. ...

She stepped back and drew from her purse the Crystal of Thraz. Her father's eyes were fastened on the ceil-
ing when she did so, and he seemed to be talking to
some being there, or even in the solid rock beyond. It
took some moments before he lowered his gaze.

He started then, and let out a roar that nearly made
Scyra drop the crystal. She stepped back two more
paces, as he looked ready to snatch at it.

"No, Father. It was a gift from Conan. He took it from
the Bossonian caravan, then gave it to me."

"But ... you know what these can do?"

"Am I not your daughter?"

"Do not, for once, answer a question with a question,
Scyra. It is clever, but this is not the time for clever-
ness."

In that, Scyra thought, her father was very much mistaken. It was indeed a time for her to be clever beyond
her wont, or Conan was doomed.

"Wait, Father. I know what this is. I have ... I have
tested it, in small ways. Not great ones, but the small
ones have been enough to tell me that this one is
bonded to women and women only."

Lysenius frowned. Scyra hoped he was not trying to
remember the names of the spells that she might have
used. If he interrogated her even aloud, let alone reaching into her mind, betrayal was likely and disaster not
impossible.

"This is the truth?"

"By all that I know, yes."

"You cannot swear by more," Lysenius said. His

broad shoulders bowed for a moment under the weight of all his years and memories.

Scyra knew how many of those memories were of failure and loss, and wanted to hug her father as she had when she was a child. It had comforted him them; would it comfort him now?

Perhaps, and she would feel even worse a traitor than she did already. Her father might not scruple at selling her to the Picts to advance his schemes, but when she stood before him, he had not the heart to call her a liar. There remained in him more of the man he had been than she had thought.

Perhaps she could find a way entirely out of this land with Conan's help. Surely the Cimmerian knew the way to some land where she and her father could live out their days, on what they could take from the treasure-room and what she might earn with her healing skills. She also could appeal to that northern iron honor of his.

Again she fought the urge to embrace her father. He looked ready to weep, and she knew that if he began, she would join him. Amidst her tears, the truth would come out, and all that she feared might come to pass.

"Father, I have a plan."

"Do not put yourself in danger for it."

"We must not fear danger, if we are to avoid doom. We both know that Conan has no ghost-voice. We cannot hear his mind across the wilderness. But he can hear my ghost-voice if I fling it toward him through the Crystal of Thraz."

"That is potent magick."

"Then you must teach me what I do not know, and how to use it in safety. If I can speak to Conan, I can subtly guide his band toward the Cave of the Warrior. Meanwhile, we can follow them with a stout band of

Picts, enough to seize the Bamulas when they reach the cave. Conan alone has enough spirit in him to raise the statue. If we are able to sacrifice the whole band—"

"That was my very plan!" Lysenius exclaimed. He grinned down at his daughter. "Truly, you are my daughter of the spirit as well as of the body."

Scyra wanted to scream that she was anything but that. Instead, she went on. "We might well use the world-walker, to pass ahead of Conan's band."

Lysenius shook his head. "The Cave of the Warrior is hard upon the land of the Snakes. We would not last a day without more Owls ready to defend us than I could pass through the world-walker. I also doubt that very many Picts would pass through it even if I could send them. What they have seen of my magick already puts them in fear. The world-walker would drive them mad."

Lysenius drew himself straight. To his daughter, he appeared for a moment almost as kingly as Conan. Then he bent and kissed her on the forehead, letting his hands rest lightly on her shoulders. She stood entirely still, but her stomach churned.

"So be it. Do as you must, to guide Conan. I will reach out to the chiefs of the Owls and assemble the warriors. Shall I ask them to bring litters as well?"

"Unless you think we can match the pace of marching Pict warriors, yes," Scyra said with a wry smile. "No doubt, if I could do so, I would be worth more than ever as a bride for a chief. But I fear we cannot pretend that we are any sort of Pict."

Nor, in the end, even any sort of friend to them.

Fifteen

To Govindue, this land of the Picts would always seem more perilous than his homeland. This was not without reason either, as even Conan granted.

There were the nights so cold that even the strange, all-enveloping clothes made of the hides of furry beasts barely kept shivering at bay. There was the rocky ground, the streams that held no crocodiles but could rise to a flood after a swift rain. There were storms, as fierce as any in the jungles, if not as frequent. There were animals, not as numerous as those of the jungle, but in their own land every bit as dangerous—and with habits Govindue did not know.

Before and beyond all, there were the Picts. They had to be out there, Govindue knew, even though they had remained quite unseen and nearly unheard since the band left the caves of Lysenius. Any tree in the ex-

panse of sinister green he saw now from a low ridge
might hide a Pict. The forest ahead might hide enough
to swarm over the Bamulas and bring them down with
bare hands, if they were of a mind to capture them alive
for Lysenius or for their own purposes.

Govindue could not withhold a shudder at the
thought of what Pictish schemes might mean to cap-
tives. The Bamulas and their enemies were adept at
tests of a prisoner's endurance, but the Picts made them
seem like weak-willed children.

Conan scrambled up to the ridge beside Govindue
and shaded his eyes against the rising sun. They had
been on the march this day ever since all the sky one
could see overhead was a sullen gray. Now it promised
to be a fine day, in which they could make a good long
stride toward safety—or doom.

"You look uneasy, young chief," Conan said.

"How I look only speaks my thoughts," Govindue
said. "But I suppose a chief must keep such thoughts
from more than his mouth?"

"You do not need to ask, I think," Conan replied.
"Had I known half as much about leading when I was
your age, I might be a general or a prince today. Well,
the gods make our paths rough or smooth as it pleases
them, and we can only walk where they will us to. Although I see you seem used to walking paths in sandals,
or even in boots now."

Govindue laughed. "They will never feel natural. But
in this rock-fanged land, walking barefoot would feel
much worse, and that quickly."

"As Vuona discovered. Have her feet healed?"

Govindue felt the blood rush to his face. Conan gave
him a sidelong glance, and for a moment he feared his
chief was about to strike him.

"I saw you rubbing ointment on her feet and binding

them in strips of cloth. Was there more that I did not see that I should know about?"

"I have not bedded your woman, Amra," Govindue said stiffly.

"I am still *Conan* here in this band, in this land," the other said sharply. Then he grinned, to take the lash from his words.

"Your sense of honor would not allow it, I know. But is Vuona displeased at the idea?"

"You know her better than I do," Govindue said. "It is as well that her feet are sore, or I might not be able to outrun her."

"No, but you could give her a good long chase so that by the time she overtook you, she'd be too winded for bedsport."

Govindue's face remained hot, and the bigger man saw that he had embarrassed the young chief. "As long as Vuona makes no trouble among the men, I will not chain her. If she makes trouble, I will not chain her either . . . I will run her through. As for the future . . . when we know we'll not end as bones bleaching on a Pictish midden-heap, you might think of a first wife and do worse than Vuona. You know that she is daughter to one of the three highest chiefs of the Fish-Eaters?"

"I did not know."

"Never miss listening to a woman who's willing to talk. Half the trouble women cause is by silence, and Vuona will never have that fault. Others, no doubt, but you as a chief in the Dead Elephant Valley bound by marriage to a chief of the Fish-Eaters—"

"Yes, and since I am oath-bound to you, it could mean peace between you and the Fish-Eaters. Indeed, you might serve me by advancing my suit."

"Small chance of that. Her father, I judge, is the chief

whose headdress I skewered when he was trying to have his people kill me as a demon-lover."

"One can see that he might not love you, nor think well of any suit you brought. As you wish, Conan."

"You have not so much to learn as you think, young chief. Indeed, I've no desire to exchange fleeing the Picts for fleeing the Fish-Eaters."

"All who have followed you here would stand by you to the death."

"Yes, and to the death of a good many Fish-Eaters, which would make war between them and the Bamulas. A man finds enough wars in his path by chance, without going out and seeking more!"

Conan looked about him. "Now let's be down and off. The men should have finished at the stream, and these boulders might hide more than Picts."

Conan saw no signs of Picts on his way down the hill or in the trees around the pool where the Bamulas were filling their water bottles. The forest was not short of water, even in high summer, but Conan had warred in deserts that made Hell seem moist and temperate. He would never miss a chance to take on water, and if he and his band never had to stand off Picts on a waterless hill, so much the better.

Indeed, he was beginning to wonder if they might make their way clean out of the Pictish Wilderness without having to stand off any of the tribes. They were still some days from the Marches, and trails, blazed trees, and every so often a fallen feather or discarded moccasin, told of a Pictish presence.

No living Pict had showed so much as a feather-tip however, and even Picts were not such cunning trackers as to remain so completely invisible for so long from eyes as keen as the Cimmerian's. They had also missed more than one chance to slaughter the little band with small danger to themselves.

Conan had been using Scyra's map and his many years as woodsman and warrior to guide his people around the many dangerous passages. But only a god able to lift them into the sky could have taken them past all perils. Half a dozen times, Conan had felt the flesh of his back crawl with the anticipation of an arrow sinking into it, but no arrow ever came.

It was a mystery, and he did not like mysteries. Not in this land, where the Picts were deadly enough when they behaved in their common fashion.

He would have liked to ask Scyra for an answer, those times when she reached out and touched his mind with advice on the best way to go. The first time it had been at night, as he was drifting into sleep after a weary scramble across the worst stretch of hills on their way east. He had thought of Lysenius's magick and resolved to fall on his sword rather than let the sorcerer master him to the harm of his people.

But it had only been the sorcerer's daughter. Her thoughts came in her own voice, which he remembered well (and not only her cries of joy). Also, she offered as proof of who she was, memories that no one else could have had.

So he came to accept her advice, and more than once tried to send his thanks back, and more than thanks. No answer came, however. In time, the Cimmerian realized that this sending of thoughts might remain from her to him, unless he himself turned sorcerer—which was about as likely as his willingly becoming a eunuch!

Mayhap there was nothing sinister behind the lack of Picts. Scyra might well have been able to dissuade her father from unleashing the Owls. Now the fugitives were at, or even beyond, the land of the Owls, into land

disputed between the Wolves and the Snakes. The
Snakes at least were no friends to Lysenius, and the
Wolves might have too much on their hands fighting
the Snakes to fret over handfuls of curiously hued strangers wandering across their land.

Conan joined the column close to the rear, behind
Vuona. He walked beside her as the band left the clear-
ing and saw that she was casting sharp looks at
Kubwande.

"Has he been making trouble?" Conan almost said
"again," but did not care to discuss the stray spear in
the dark during the battle against the *chakans*.

"What would you have me say?" Vuona replied. "I
have no quarrel with him. Have you?"

"Not unless he is fool enough to find one before we
are out of the wilderness," Conan said shortly. He also
said it loudly enough for others besides Vuona to hear.
Kubwande might have friends who would serve his
schemes safely at home but could see wisdom until they
had left the Picts behind.

"He does not seem that big a fool," Vuona said. "Also,
I think you will be a bigger chief than he is."

"As the gods will," Conan said.

"Could they will us a safe place nearer than these
Marches?" Vuona asked, almost pettishly. Conan saw
that she winced sometimes as she walked, and that dark
stains showed on her foot-bindings.

"Not safe from the Picts," Conan said. "Sore feet are
better than a slit throat or a cracked skull. Besides, in
the Marches they have warm houses with soft furs on
the floor."

"Warm? How does anybody keep warm in this land?"

Conan did not say that if Vuona kept more of her
clothes about her and showed less of her lithe form, she
might stay warmer. Perhaps she would not be so good a

match for Govindue after all. The young chief deserved at the very least to know who was the father of the sons born to his wife.

"They build their huts of stone and heavy logs, and put fires in stone boxes inside."

"They must stifle!"

"Not in the winter."

"Winter?"

"A time much colder than this, when there is snow—frozen water—lying as deep as a man's height on the ground. All the streams freeze so that one can walk dryshod across them, and to be caught without shelter is death."

Vuona looked up at the sky with the face of one struggling not to cry out. Conan rested a hand lightly on her shoulder.

"No snow today, and not for many days. Do not fear."

"Who fears?" she said haughtily. Then, more softly, she added. "I do hope that we are out of this land before the *winter*."

"Woman, in that we think alike," Conan said.

The hoots the Owls used for signals on the march came back from the head of the line, passed Scyra's litter, and faded away to the rear. The bearers halted, and Scyra climbed out, disdaining the helping hands offered by several warriors.

Perhaps that was giving offense to those who meant well, but Scyra would believe in a well-meaning Pict when she saw the sun stand still in the sky. She also feared in her innermost heart that her flesh would creep and crawl away from a Pictish touch.

All along the trail from the caves, she had been troubled by nightmares in which Picts by the score made free with her body in ways that would have made a

Stygian turn away in disgust. Once she awoke so drenched with sweat that she had to quickly change her garments, lest her father suspect that she was fevered and try to cure her in ways that would betray her secret.

Scyra had small doubt that it was that secret that was unsettling her mind and tormenting her spirit, by night and sometimes by day. However, it had not yet kept her from learning the arts of the Crystal of Thraz, nor from reaching Conan with her messages of guidance.

Indeed, she had begun to suspect that if she had the time, she could make her lie the truth. She could bind the crystal, if not to women only, at least so tightly to herself that her father could not use it without risking its destruction. He would not chance that unless he became persuaded that she was lying to him—and it was still not in Lysenius to believe that the daughter who was all that remained to him of his dead wife would betray him and his plans.

And speaking of her father's plans—here came Sutharo, one of the five greatest war chiefs of the Owls. Lysenius had named him most often as Scyra's likely husband among the Picts, and it seemed to the young woman that the Pict had learned of this. Certainly his manner around her was that of one who wished her goodwill. She doubted that this grotesque parody of courtliness would last beyond the marriage circle and the dousing of the torches, but for the moment he was being as civil toward her as it was in a Pict to be toward an outland woman.

Sutharo wore leggings and a wolfskin cloak, as well as a breechclout of the finest deerskin, lavishly embroidered with colored shells and bits of bone. He carried bow and quiver with bronze-headed arrows, a spear likewise bronze-tipped and decorated with heron feathers, and in his belt a hatchet and a well-kept piece of loot from some battlefield, a Gunderman-style short-sword.

Halting before Scyra, he gave his best imitation of a bow. "I trust I find you well, gracious lady," he said. Like nearly all pure-blooded Picts, he spoke no Hyborian tongue, but there were similar modes of address in the Pictish speech used among chiefs or toward shamans. Scyra recognized that he was using both at once. Considering the common lot of Pictish women, this was near to a Hyborian kneeling at her feet.

"I am well. The journey is not hard, and the hope of victory at the end of it strengthens any warrior's spirit." She used the same mode of speech as Sutharo, remembering at the last moment that in Pictish there was no feminine form of the word "warrior."

"Yes. May it also strengthen your regard for one who leads warriors to that victory." At least that was one meaning of the Pictish word for regard. Another meaning was "lust."

Scyra doubted that if Sutharo conquered the whole world and laid it at her feet, she would feel either meaning of the word for him. But that particular truth would help no one and nothing, and she did not feel any of the qualms about lying to Sutharo that she felt in the matter of her father.

"My father and I have always held the warriors of the Owls in high regard. Your friendship strengthens us in all ways."

"That fills me with joy." The word for "joy," like the word for "regard," had other and less polite meanings. Scyra did not doubt that Sutharo was using several meanings at once. The common Pictish chief might not shine at the court in Tarantia, but the common Aquilonian courtier would likewise not find himself well-suited to the intrigues of a Pictish tribe—if he lived long enough to join in them at all.

Scyra walked up and down, stretching her cramped limbs, ready to give everything but the Crystal of Thraz for a hot bath. (Perhaps also for a bundle of scented herbs to stuff in her nostrils against the reek of a thousand Pictish warriors under a sun climbing toward the zenith.)

Instead, she turned her thoughts from the discomforts of her body and toward remembering where Conan had been when she last touched his mind. He no longer shied like a startled horse from that touch, and so far, her father had not to her knowledge listened to her speaking to Conan.

The Cimmerian might have no ghost-voice, but he had a very keen eye for what lay about him. No doubt his many battles and hunts—and yes, flights for his life—had sharpened his eyes and ears alike. Seeing a tree through Conan's eyes, Scyra could almost count the needles on a branch fifty paces above the ground.

She did not return to the litter to draw out her map, the twin of Conan's. The Picts had no knowledge of maps, and while they respected the arts of the white shaman and his daughter, they grew uneasy seeing them practiced openly.

Instead, she sat on the bole of a fallen oak, feeling the sponginess of the rotted wood, smelling the rich mold, hearing only birdsong and the *chirr* of an insect just over her head. The human world and all its assaults on her senses faded from her awareness, leaving only nature surrounding her mind as she composed herself to send her ghost-voice out to Conan. . . .

She returned from her mind's journey just in time to hear the hooting pass by again, from front to rear. Now it meant an end to the halt. The scouts had reported the way clear, the hunters had returned with any game unfortunate enough to encounter them, the water bags had been refilled, and the warriors who swore by the Owl were ready to march again.

So, Scyra had learned, were Conan and his people ready. Indeed, she could let them march the way they intended for the rest of the day. They were moving almost as she would have wished had she been marching with them and guiding their every turn.

After tonight they would need to bear farther to the south to come upon the cave in good time. They would also need protection against the Snakes, whose lands they approached.

The Snakes had been for some time at odds with the Wolves. It was short of open warfare, but most of their warriors would be facing the Wolves at the other end of the Snake lands. Some would still remain close to the cave—too many for twenty Bamulas, a Cimmerian, and a woman to meet successfully.

She could not trust her father to offer magickal protection. He would ask more questions than she could answer with believable lies, and her masquerade would be ended.

A vanguard of Owl warriors, going on ahead? Yes, and what was to keep them trustworthy? Even if they did no more than fight the Snakes—

Sutharo. If she gave him certain promises she had no intention of keeping, he might swear to bind his warriors to peace with Conan, and even with the Snakes, unless the other tribe attacked first. Snake and Owl were old enemies, but there was no declared war between them now, and the Snakes had the Wolves on their hands.

She would make promises, and pray that he did not ask her to keep those promises until after the battle. She

could make some excuse that would keep him away
from her; Picts had as many superstitions as any about
the business of men and women, and more than most.

Afterward, Sutharo's wrath would be something to
fear, but his writ could not run beyond the Pictish lands.
If she and her father lived, those lands would not see
them again.

Sixteen

Scyra's directions had kept Conan's band wandering along ridges and over hills for the best part of two days now. The Cimmerian had no difficulty in finding paths that kept the band concealed, but he was beginning to find it hard to believe that Scyra knew what she was doing.

She said that she wished the band to have ample warning of any attackers, so was sending them high, where the Snakes seldom roamed. The Picts were creatures of the forest, she said, and the Snakes more so than most. They were uneasy on bare rock, and those who kept to it might pass through Snake lands almost unhindered.

It was much in Conan's mind that high, cold, rocky land was enough hindrance to his Bamulas even without Snakes crawling out from under the boulders. One

213

night it grew so cold that Conan ordered a fire built, fearing detection less than he feared finding half his people in the morning frozen as hard as the rocks around them.

Perhaps it was too strong to say that Scyra did not know what she was doing. She knew Picts and the Pictish Wilderness. She did not know the Bamulas and what was needed to keep their trust—which was *not* leading them across bare slopes with nothing between them and the naked sky but clouds and perhaps a circling eagle!

Conan even tried once more to return Scyra's mind-message, but received as little reply as before. After that, he held his peace. If by some quirk of fate he did sprout a "ghost-voice" at this time, Lysenius would be as likely to hear it as his daughter. The border was still three days' unimpeded march away, and the spells of any sorcerer as potent as Lysenius could strike from an even farther distance.

It was toward evening at the end of the second day that Conan climbed a tree that rose higher than the nearest crest and offered better concealment. He came down with such a grim look on his naturally harsh countenance that only Vuona was bold enough to ask what he had seen.

"Picts," was all the Cimmerian would say.

"How close?" Govindue asked.

"Close enough that they could move between us and the border if they wished to."

"Then our task is to make sure they do not wish to," Bowenu said.

"How are you going to do that?" Kubwande snapped. "Cloud the minds of their chiefs with magick beer, flung across the hills to their camp by your powers?"

"Let Conan send a few of us in some direction the

others are not taking, to show ourselves to the Picts and then hide. A small band can hide easily, and while the Picts seek it in vain, the rest can be away to the border."

"My thanks, Bowenu," Conan said. "But you don't know the Picts. They can track a man if he leaves only two needles out of place on a trail. Also, they would surround a small band with a few warriors and send the rest on in search of the band's comrades. I honor your courage, and hope all will do so, but it would be wasted.

"We cross the border on our feet and together, or we lie down together. And if we lie down, it will be among enough dead Picts so that their tribe will be known as the Tribe of Widows and Orphans!"

They would have cheered him gladly then, even as "Conan," but he silenced them and sent out the guards and watering parties. Afterward he walked a little apart and was sitting on a rock when Govindue came up.

"It is now my turn to ask if you are troubled, Conan. I cannot offer as much help as you gave me, but what I can give is yours."

Conan looked at the young chief. Even the smallest lie would be a larger betrayal than he could manage.

"I saw the fire-smoke of two bands of Picts. One is the one I spoke of, doubtless Snakes. They will be looking for Wolves, and might stumble on us only by chance. The other is to the west, and closer. I would not say surely that they are on our trail. I wouldn't wager against it either."

"You think . . . has Scyra betrayed us?"

"Not to her father, I am certain. Otherwise, we'd have his spells splattering about us like hawk droppings. But neither Lysenius nor Scyra may be masters now. The Picts may have tortured our plans out of both, stuck their heads on poles in an Owl village, and set out after us to do the same."

"We shall sing a death-song for Scyra," Govindue vowed. "Even for her father, if you think his spirit would be calmed."

"I've known few sorcerers who could ever have a quiet spirit, no matter how many songs you sang for them. Save your breath to drink your beer, and leave Lysenius to the gods. They've more time than we mortals, or so the priests say."

Sutharo, son of Yagan, war chief of the Owls, waited with scant patience for his scout to descend the tree. It would have been swifter for the man to shout from on high, but this was not Owl land.

"Have you seen Snakes? Are they close?"

"Many Snakes. From the fires, I think more than three hands of hands. Not close. Not between us and the hill the white shaman says is the place."

"You have done well. You may drink first when next we find water."

"I thank the chief."

Sutharo hoped they would find water soon. He and the warriors with him had been traveling swiftly for two days now. They had not overtaken the demon-men and their giant chief. The demon-men seemed as swift as Owls, even on bad ground.

It would be worth all that his warriors endured if they came to the place in time to protect the demon-men from the Snakes. If they did, then the white shaman's daughter would lie in Sutharo's bed, and a son of such blood would surely be both war chief *and* shaman.

Such a son might rule over more than one tribe. His father's tomb would be a place all men would know, and in the aftertime, the father would sit by the fire of the highest gods.

It was as well that his warriors did not know that they

were bruising their feet and drying their throats to protect men they would afterward be killing. They might wonder at Sutharo's asking such a thing, and even speak doubt to his face.

Some might even challenge him. They would be fools to do so, in the land of the Snakes and where the white shaman might see the quarrel among the Owls. But there were always fools, even among the Owls. There were also those who would not follow a chief who had lied to them for no better reason than to fill his bed with Scyra.

Sutharo had long wished for another chance to fight the Snakes before he grew too old to lead the Owls in war. But he had begun to think that it was always better to fight as one's own chief, even if the reward for that was not Scyra.

Scyra's last message bid Conan bear to the south, around the end of a ridge he could see ahead. That would be all very well if the southern end was not the one closer to the Snakes. Going straight over the ridge would be possible only if he was alone. His eye for ground told him that the far side of the ridge was too steep for the Bamulas to face.

Very well, then. They would go *north*. It was time to see what disobeying Scyra would bring. If no harm, well and good. If it proved that she was right—well, a man could only die once.

If it drew the sorcerous wrath of Lysenius—again, a man could only die once. But Conan knew he would die with an easier mind if Scyra did not prove treacherous. He had been deceived by more women than some men ever knew in their lives, but he had also met his share of the other kind, and not only Belit. They were something he would regret leaving behind, if indeed his time was at hand.

He pointed his sword toward the north. "We go this way. Be more watchful than ever. Every step takes us deeper into Snake land."

"If the Snakes strike, they will feel that they have bitten stone!" Kubwande shouted. It was the most worthwhile thing he had said in some time.

Scyra cursed under her breath in the Pictish tongue, using words that her father would be astonished she knew. She cursed Conan, invoking parts of his body that would, again, astonish her father.

She did not curse the Crystal of Thraz, although she knew full well that without it, she would never have conceived her plan. As for attempting to put it into execution, sooner would she have tried to spy on a Pictish soul-changing, where a man's soul might enter a snake and a snake's the man.

But it seemed to her, as she sensed Conan swerving farther and farther from the right way, that perhaps the Crystal had made her too ambitious. She had tried to guide, and even to bind, a man who was no more made for that than was a tiger of the Vendhyan jungle, or a wolf of his own native forests. She had known Cimmerians only by their reputation before she met Conan. Now that she knew him, she did not wonder that Cimmeria remained fiercely independent and that Aquilonian intrusions to the north met bloody ends.

Her father stepped up behind her. She felt his breath on the back of her neck, and smelled the Pictish beer on it. Words of reproach almost reached her lips; she swallowed them.

"Conan goes on as you wish?"

"Not altogether. He circles the ridge widdershins."

"Ah. Can you send Sutharo's warriors after him?"

"Even if I could touch Sutharo's mind, I would not. He would call it witchcraft and fear me."

"Any man in his senses would fear you sometimes, Scyra. Just as they would your mother. In that way, there is almost too much of her in you."

Next, he would start rambling about her mother; then he would cry, and then he would drink more Pictish beer and fall asleep. She hoped he would not so unman himself that he could not cast a proper spell when they reached the cave.

No, she had come to hope that he would. If his magick deserted him at the last moment, he might never learn of her betrayal. She would not have to take the final steps of pitting her magick against his. If he could not complete his vengeance, might he not remember that there were other things in the world besides that?

Scyra squeezed her eyes shut and felt them stinging even so. It was hardly likely. Lysenius had lived for his vengeance for too many years to remember much of what life had been like before that.

Also, if his powers deserted him, he would be dead—swiftly if he was fortunate, slowly if he was not, and his daughter with him. It was near to madness already, her scheme to betray Picts while they were all about her. It was not wholly mad, only because she had hopes of concealing the betrayal long enough for her and her father to be beyond the reach of any Pict.

He would forgive her. The Picts would not. Nor would Conan, although if matters went awry, doubtless the Picts would put an end to him before he could take vengeance on her.

Life seemed to be one betrayal leading to another.

Scyra realized that she did not hold such a life as dear as she might have.

The Bamulas had learned the art of climbing hills as they had learned archery. A few of them were skilled. Most were better called "determined." Not much to Conan's surprise, Govindue was among the most adept at handling himself on hillsides. Rather more to the Cimmerian's surprise, Vuona was almost as light on her feet. He wondered if she was trying to flaunt her strength before someone, and if so, whether it was him or Govindue.

It happened that the young chief and the woman were the two closest to Conan when he led the band over the north end of the ridge. It wound off to the south, with the side before them bare and rocky, the side behind them thickly wooded. At the foot of the slope, more trees rose, firs and pines, making a sullen darkness that could have hidden enough Picts to sweep away a province, let alone a band of strangers in this land.

Conan went to ground and motioned those with him to do the same. They passed on the message, and no one allowed himself to stand boldly on the rocky spur, in plain sight from below and above alike.

The band had gone its own way, rather than the way Scyra bade them. Nothing had come amiss—yet. It would still take a better reason than defying Scyra to make Conan lead his people across the bare eastern slope of the ridge.

The Cimmerian had perhaps the time of two or three deep breaths to hold this thought. He had time to wave to those behind him, bidding them move to the north, within the tree line.

Then arrows hailed from the sky. They were numerous enough to warn their targets, but not to do grave hurt. Shooting eagerly, without closing the range, the Picts did not inflict so much as a flesh wound.

Conan knew that such good luck, or the gods' favor, would not last much longer. He also saw from the fall of the arrows that they were coming from the very trees where he had intended to lead his people.

This was not much to his liking. He thought briefly that perhaps Scyra had the right of it, and that he owed her an apology, if he lived to see her again. For a sorceress who had barely seen her twentieth year, she had a wise head on those round, freckled shoulders—

"Run!" he shouted, pointing down the slope toward the trees to the east.

"The Picts—?" somebody shouted.

"That way, and already shooting at long range. If we run, they'll have to run too, to keep us within bowshot. Shooting on the run makes poor practice. The best archers to the rear. If you find a good place to hide and see Picts in the open, give them a little present. But don't fall too far behind. We can't stop to let anyone catch up."

Running was something the Bamulas knew well. Even when their lack of skill on hillsides betrayed them and they went down, they rose again quickly. No one broke bones or sprained muscles, and men whose bruises and cuts left blood trails in the dust on their bodies ran as swiftly as before.

Conan remained in the middle, where he could see and speak to everyone alike, and also be ready to join the rearguard of archers. He bore a stout Bossonian longbow, with a good edge in range over anything Pictish, and a quiver of two dozen arrows, besides his other weapons. The Bossonian longbow seemed almost clumsy to one who had learned his archery on the subtle but powerful Turanian horsebow, but the Cimmerian despised no weapon that could kill a man.

If the Picts gave him any sort of a chance, he would add a good many of them to his escort from the world, even before drawing steel.

Conan had just seen Picts breaking into the open to the north and unslung his bow when Vuona let out a shriek as if the pits of the netherworld had opened at her feet. Without slowing, Conan turned his gaze toward the woman and saw that she had reason to cry out, for Picts were also sprouting from the trees ahead. Some had already nocked, and the first arrow from them fell almost at Vuona's feet. She dodged sharply to the left with a yelp of surprise.

Conan knew that if his people stopped moving, they would be shot down where they stood, and if they ran, they might be running from one danger into another. The only way to safety seemed to be along the slope, toward the south—toward the way Scyra had bidden them go.

Most certainly, Scyra had seen clearly. The Cimmerian vowed to swallow his pride and admit as much, if he ever saw the witch-girl again.

The gods' hands remained over the band as they ran south, some now staggering and lurching, but all remaining on their feet. Conan heard breath rasping like ill-kept bellows in the forge of a slovenly blacksmith, the kind his father would never have countenanced in their village. It was not his own breath yet, and he knew he had speed and endurance enough to leave his band behind.

He also knew he would do no such thing, Nor would the band abandon the first one who fell. They would form a circle around the fallen comrade and try to stay alive until nightfall. That was too far away to offer much hope, but nothing else offered any at all.

No, that might not be wholly true. Up the slope and ahead lay a shadowy recess that looked very much like the mouth of a cave. Around it, boulders were strewn in a pattern that did not look entirely natural, but that offered as a good a place as any to go to ground.

"That way!" Conan shouted, pointing with his free hand.

It took a few moments for everyone to see where he was pointing, more for everyone to turn. Those moments gave both bands of Picts time to close the distance. The Bamula archers and Conan nocked and shot. The range was long, but the Bamulas and the Cimmerian were shooting more downhill than not. Two Picts fell; two more halted. Most of the returning arrows dropped short, and none did great harm.

Vuona picked that moment to stumble, going down hard enough to furrow one leg on a sharp stone. She rose, bleeding, cursing, and weeping all at once. After a few steps, it became clear to Conan that she could not keep on her feet all the way to the boulders.

He slung his bow and made ready to snatch her up, but it was Govindue who reached the young woman first. He lifted her on his shoulder as if she had been no heavier than a basket of grain or he as strong as the Cimmerian, and ran the rest of the way up the slope with her. Conan was not the last man into the boulders, but he was well behind the young chief.

A final spatter of arrows clattered on the stones. Conan reached out from the recess to pick them up; they would need every weapon they could command. He had just gripped the last arrow when he heard a barely stifled scream from Vuona, and curses from the men.

Only Govindue seemed in command of himself. "Conan, I think you should see this."

The Cimmerian slipped past a boulder that seemed blackened by fire too hot for earthly flame and stared past the next two boulders. He had judged correctly: a cave lay beyond.

It was no longer shadowy, however. A stark blue witchlight glowed within, brightening even as he watched. Two steps closer and he could see that the light came from niches carved in the walls of the cave, which wound back into the hill out of sight.

Two more steps and the witchlight fell on his skin. He waited to see if any other spell came to life at human presence, or only the light. As he waited, he became aware of a murmur of doubtful voices among the Bamulas.

"Easy," he said without turning around. "This kind of light seldom does harm. If it's meant to, it would already have done so. Would you care to take your chances with the Picts on the open hillside?"

"We've Picts to the front and magick to the rear," Bowenu said dubiously. "How is that better?"

"We can retreat into the cave if the Picts, their arrows, or even their stink, grow too thick!" Conan said, hardening his voice. "One man can hold the mouth of a cave against fifty."

"That is true for the Picts as well," Kubwande said. Conan refrained from cursing him or laying him out with a well-placed fist. Instead, he shrugged.

"Only if we have to come out this way. I've never been in a cave yet that didn't have at least two ways out."

That seemed to soothe most, if not Kubwande. Conan saw no reason to say that the Picts might well know of any other ways out and guard them as well.

Sheltering in the cave might end his band's lives swiftly under the power of the magick there, and would likely only delay their end at the hands of the Picts. But Conan was no man to give any foe an easy death, and time and again, staying alive for moments, even for days, longer had turned the battle.

Seventeen

Scyra was as weary as if she had walked all the day, but she could not sleep—it was not because of her father's snores in the rear of the tent either, nor the reek of the scores of unwashed Picts sleeping upwind of the tent. Some of them were snoring too.

She had taken off no more than her boots, and it was easy to draw them back on silently. She considered bringing along bow and arrows as well as her dagger, but decided to leave them. She was an indifferent archer, and anything that made her look as if she wished to leave the camp might make the warriors suspicious. There were enough with unsettled minds already; she had no wish to see more.

The Owls were growing uneasy as their march took them closer to Snake and Wolf lands. The Snakes barely pretended friendship. The Wolf Picts had not fought the

Owls in some years, but if the Owls grew weak from a clash with the Snakes, the Wolves might be at their throats before the snows came.

Five hundred Picts were more than any except a major war chief could keep in order. The only such chief on this march was Sutharo, gone off ahead with his clansmen to ward Conan against the Snakes. Scyra found most of the warriors asleep, a few mounting a desultory guard, and the remainder of those awake crouched around a small fire, chanting quietly. Scyra hoped her father's guard-spells would at least wake him if any danger struck the camp.

She leaned against a tree and listened to the chanting until some of those on the outside of the circle noticed her. One called out a bawdy greeting, others laughed, and someone else asked her to step back that her shadow not fall on them.

She replied by gestures. If they were making war-magick, it was a man's rite. A woman's voice could ruin it as easily as a woman's shadow. As she turned and stepped away from the fire, someone called out his thanks.

She had not learned to love the Picts in the years of her exile in the wilderness. But she realized that she had largely ceased to hate them, after seeing them do all that other folk did. Or perhaps not all—their homeland was harsh, and she missed the sight of fat herds and bulging barns.

But something would be gone from her life when she could not wake to hear the drums and the cries of the hunting bands. Something would be gone from the world, too, when high roads pierced the wilderness, and the Picts who yet lived became docile farmers and shepherds.

Too late, she heard the twigs cracking to her left. She

had her dagger drawn and was whirling to thrust into the darkness when a hairy hand buffeted her across the temple. The blow flung her off her feet, striking her head a second blow against a tree. The world was suddenly fire-shot darkness whirling about her.

Another hand, vast, hairy, and inhumanly strong, gripped one ankle. With her free foot, she kicked savagely, and felt her foot strike rock-hard bone. Pain roared up her leg and burst in her skull like a thunderbolt.

She had lost her grip on her weapon and now scrabbled desperately for it. Her enemies were beyond her power, but she could still turn the dagger against herself. These—they had to be *chakans*—could be sent by no friend of herself, her father, or Conan. She would not be used—

A hairy foot sank into her stomach. Her head snapped back and struck a root. All her senses failed at once, and she swam down into blackness from which the fire slowly faded until there was only an infinity of nothingness all around her.

The Picts seemed to have no taboos about the cave or any fear of its magick. They crept so close that a few well-placed arrows were needed to kill the boldest and discourage the rest.

The Picts' boldness would have discouraged the Bamulus, but Conan urged them to look once more at their hopes rather than at their fears. "It could be that the Picts expect the magick here to end us. They also may expect us to find a way to use it against them, and want to end us first."

At least nobody was ready to call this nonsense to his face. In his own mind, Conan could only hope he was right—or at least that nothing more went amiss to prove him wrong. If the courage of the Bamulas snapped, their last hope would be gone, and only a final stand would remain to the Cimmerian and such as chose to make it with him.

That might be all that remained even now, but Conan remained convinced that every moment a man lived was another he was not dead. Dead, nothing changed; alive, who could say?

Meanwhile, there were wounds to be tended, the scanty food (hard biscuit and salt meat) handed around for a few mouthfuls apiece, and sentries to be posted. Conan wanted them both at the mouth of the cave and a little distance inside it, but did not press the matter. He sensed the unease of the Bamulas at being too far within the cave, and was not quite without unease himself. Also, posting sentries inside the cave would say plainly that he feared attack from there, besides dividing his scanty strength and keeping more men awake.

The sentries had barely taken their places when a hideous uproar of Pictish cries made all hope of sleep impossible. Conan stared out into the darkness, then crawled out, risking an encounter with lurking Picts in the hope of learning what might be going on.

He was ten paces beyond the boulders, all his senses sharpened by sheer willpower, when he sensed movement close to his left. He lay still, unable to judge the other's distance by sound. If the Pict was making any, it was lost in the uproar from downhill.

Then, in one moment, the Pict was leaping at Conan, and in the next, another shadow was leaping to meet the first. The Cimmerian rolled out from under the collision of the two Picts and sprang to his feet. He clutched a braid with one hand and a feathered headband with the other and slammed the two heads together. The Picts reeled but continued to struggle.

Conan shifted his grip to their greasy hair, tightened it, and slammed their heads together again.

This time he heard bone crack, and both men went limp in his grip. The Cimmerian dragged them like snared deer back to the boulders, then onward into the light.

The light resolved some of the mystery. One of the Picts bore the war paint, feathers, and tattoos of the Owls. The other, it was equally plain to see, was of the Snakes.

"Lysenius's friends the Owls have come to the hill," Conan said.

"You do not call them our friends," Kubwande said. It was not a question.

If it had been, it was not one Conan would have cared to answer. The best thing that could be said for the Owls coming to fight the Snakes was that by the time the fighting was done, there would be fewer Picts around the hill. Whoever won would be nursing wounds and gathering up dead, while Conan's band regained its strength in what had so far been the safety of the cave.

He wished they had no need to wait. In the confusion of a night battle between two ill-ordered bands, neither of them knowing the ground, a band five times the size of Conan's might slip through—if its captain and men had no scruples about abandoning comrades who could not march.

Four of the men and Vuona were past running, at least tonight. Conan would not lead anyone into certain death, least of all at the hands of Picts. He could not leave them, nor kill them with his own hands while any hope remained. That hope grew scanter by the hour, but it was not gone yet.

Angry with everything—including himself for following Vuona through the demon's gate, and the dawn for not coming sooner—Conan paced the cave like a caged lion. The blue witchlight brought a hue to his eyes that led some of the Bamulas to rites of aversion.

Once he thought he heard the grunting of some unnatural beast out of the dark hillside. Another time he was even more certain he heard running water from within the cave, where all had been silent before. He almost went in search of it, but saw that Kubwande was wakeful and Govindue and Vuona asleep, not yet in each other's arms but with their hands almost touching.

The Cimmerian would not leave that rattlejawed intriguer in command if he had to watch all night. Kubwande could not sell to the Picts anything that they would not buy, but his warcraft did not seem what it had been. Conan had brought his band too far to lose them one moment before fate required it of him!

It did not take half the night for Sutharo to count his warriors. It only seemed to. When he had finished counting, he was even less happy than when he had begun.

The Snakes had fought well, as they always did. They also knew the ground better than the Owls did, which had not been so the last three times Sutharo led his warriors against the Snakes. This time he had driven off the Snakes as before, but many Owls were dead or too hurt to fight.

Also, this was Snake land. If even one Snake warrior fled to the chiefs with word of the coming of the Owls, the Snakes would return in strength. Sutharo and his remaining warriors would be caught between the hammer of the fresh Snake warriors and the anvil of the hill above them.

In spite of this, Sutharo had no intention of leaving the hill before Lysenius came, and thus abandoning the

foreigners to the Snakes. He was a warrior of the Owls.
Also, he was a man to whom a beautiful woman (even
if not a Pict) had promised herself, if he kept his promise to her.

He only hoped that he would not lose too many more
warriors. Then he might seem unlucky, and he would be
much less of a chief by the time he and Scyra were mar-
ried, or perhaps not even alive at all.

Sutharo was sitting cross-legged on the trunk of a
fallen tree when he heard a *chakan* give its warning cry.
The hoots of sentries also came back to him. He rose
and walked into the forest, in the direction of the
chakan's signal.

There was not one *chakan* but three, and two of them
carried on a litter—

"Scyra?"

It was her, but she did not speak. He saw bruises and
smears of blood on her face, and her clothes had been
torn in several places.

The remaining *chakan* stepped forward and reached
for Sutharo. The chief drew back, then remembered
that shamans used these beasts not only to track enemies, but to bear messages. He forced himself to stand
waiting while the *chakan* rested a bristle-haired palm on
his forehead.

. A message flowed into Sutharo's mind, placed in the
chakan by Vurag Yan, chief shaman of the Owls, and
carried across the wilderness in such a way that
Lysenius could not learn it. Yan seemed angry, and as he
listened, Sutharo understood why, and even came to
share that anger.

The white shamans, father and daughter alike, were
abandoning the Picts. There would be no blood-sacrifice
of the Cimmerian Conan and the demon-men, nor even
of one of the Picts, to bring the statue to invincible life.

Scyra intended that she and her father should flee, deserting the Picts, leaving the Owls at war with the Snakes as well as with the demon-men.

The demon-men were few, but they might have powers Sutharo did not know of, and he did know that the Cimmerian was even more formidable than most of his folk.

"*So what is your command, Vurag Yan?*" Sutharo asked. He did not know if the *chakan* could send a message to the shaman as well as bear one from him, but he thought it best to discover that for himself.

After a moment, a reply passed through the *chakan* into Sutharo's mind: "*See that the blood-sacrifice is Conan and his band. With enough of such strong blood, even I can bring the statue to life and command it.*"

It was the first hint of modesty that Sutharo had ever heard in the shaman. He resisted laughter. He also considered the wisdom of bargaining, and decided that it was necessary, if not wise.

"*Scyra remains with me.*"

"*You still wish to wed her? Your sons will have tainted—*"

"*I will have more sons of purer blood than you ever will, you old woodsrat! I wish to command her father and Conan through holding her. Much they might do against me could put her in danger, as long as I hold her. Or can you protect me against Lysenius, Conan, and the Snakes all at once?*"

"*You are defiant and disobedient, Sutharo.*"

"*I lead the warriors who are here now, and whom you will need to finish your work. You need me as much as I need you, Vurag Yan.*"

The *chakan* moaned in outright pain; apparently the shaman's wrath at this reply hurt. Sutharo waited, but the night returned to silence, both within his mind and outside his body.

He looked up the hill. It would not be an easy matter, breaking into the cave against the Cimmerian and the demon-men. It would cost warriors' lives. Sutharo hoped it would not cost so many that the Snakes came and finished off those left before Vurag Yan or the warriors left behind could help him.

If it could be done, though . . . the praise-songs would be without end for the warrior who gave the Picts vengeance for their wrongs, and raised the Owls to the highest place among all the folk of the wilderness. Vurag Yan would no doubt try to seize all the glory himself, but there would be enough who knew about Sutharo to give him his share, too many for the shaman to silence.

He sent messengers to summon his underchiefs. They had best move swiftly, before the enemy had time to regain strength, or worse, to summon any magick from within the cave.

The captured Snake Pict was dead when Conan dragged him into the cave mouth. The Owl Pict was senseless and never awoke enough to speak. Before long, he too died. The Bamulas began to mutter among themselves, fearing the spirits of the dead might walk if the Picts' bodies remained among them.

After all that the band had survived on its journey thus far, Conan thought Pictish ghosts were hardly worth a child's concern. He did not say so, however. Instead, he nodded.

"Let us take them far back into the cave, so its magick will bind the ghosts."

"What if it makes them stronger?" Kubwande asked. To do him justice, he now seemed less calculating than half witless from fear. Conan did not altogether find fault in that—here they were close to treading on the shadows of the gods, or even of less friendly beings . . . as Conan had sworn to Belit he would not do.

But what a man did for himself was one thing, and what he was ready to do for those who had followed him so far and so bravely was another.

"If the magick of the cave was our enemy, it would have struck us down by now. It cannot be a friend to Pictish ghosts. But if you wish, someone can come with me to perform the Bamula spirit-binding on these Picts. It should at least give their spirits too much of a head-ache for them to come bothering us."

It was Bowenu who stepped forward, even before Govindue, about the last man Conan had expected to volunteer. This was as well. The two lesser chiefs could watch each other, and Bowenu could hardly be a danger to him. Each of the two lifted a body and set out down the tunnel into the hill.

The corridor ran level for some distance, perhaps fifty paces. Then it sloped gently downward, widening as it did. Conan thought he saw weathered reliefs of serpen-tine shapes on the walls, like decorations in a temple of Set, but not quite the same. Or mayhap they were just natural patterns in the rock and he was seeing what was not there. Too much magick and not enough wine for too long could set a man's fancies in a whirl.

At last they rounded a corner and reached a point where the tunnel both widened and rose into a domed chamber. The rock of the walls, a grayish-purple under the witchlight, was too smooth to be wholly natural, but quite undecorated. Dust lay thick, except for a circle about a spear-length wide in the middle of the chamber, which might have been swept and sponged only mo-ments before.

In the middle of the circle rose a statue. If it was life-size, its subject had been taller and broader even than the giant Cimmerian. It also seemed to have just been thoroughly and lovingly cleaned, and Conan saw a faint pattern of scales on the skin.

There was something vaguely reptilian about the eyes, and memory chilled Conan. Was this one of the legendary serpent-men of Valusia? So ancient they had fought with the Atlanteans, they had been gone even before the long-dead Empire of Acheron rose to wreak its black havoc. But some of their magick had survived; it was said to lie at the heart of the cult of Set, the Great Serpent.

Conan stepped closer, without venturing into the clean circle. Magick had to be alive here, to make that circle; he would not tempt fate. He walked around the statue, quieting his own cold doubts, and wishing that Bowenu would either command his quaking limbs or fall down in a faint. Ancient magick, like old predators, could scent fear, or so Conan's experience had led him to believe.

Was this a serpent-man? The scales and the eyes said yes. More spoke otherwise. The statue had the air of an aging mercenary, weary from long and thankless service in liege to succession of close-fisted masters, yet faithful to his trust and those who followed him. If this was a serpent-man, then there had been some virtue in at least one of that kind—or else a sculptor able to imagine it, which was far from the same thing. (Once, in Argos, Conan had sat for his portrait. When he saw what the painter had done, he threw the painting out the window and nearly hurled the painter after it.)

What unsettled Conan most was not what the statue showed. It was the statue's very existence. Had Scyra been treacherous all along, using her mind-touch to guide him and his band to the cave of the statue her father planned to reanimate? Reanimate as a champion of the Picts, by a blood-sacrifice of Conan and his band?

The thought made the cave seem even colder than the night outside, and the witchlight harsher. Conan felt the urge to step into the circle and push the statue from its base. If it toppled and shattered, all the spells at Lysenius's command could hardly bring it to life—

Conan leapt into the circle and threw his full weight against the statue. He might as well have flung himself against the walls of the cavern. Three times he tried to topple the image, three times he felt nothing unnatural but gained plenty of natural bruises and scrapes, and three times the statue did not so much as quiver.

"Conan," Bowenu said at last, "how long will you tempt the gods?"

"Until they're tired of being tempted and either strike me dead or topple this misshapen stone!" the Cimmerian growled. But he did not leap again. He still felt nothing amiss within the circle, but in the air around him he sensed power, great and old, leashed for now but dreadful if ever loosed.

He looked at the statue. It showed no trace of his efforts to topple it. The dust he had tracked into the circle lay where it had fallen—until suddenly it vanished, with a faint ruddy glow, so fleeting that Conan could have sworn he imagined it. Bowenu's wide eyes and trust in his own senses told him otherwise.

They left the dead Picts lying where they had set them down and returned the way they had come. "It will be a bold ghost that roams about under the eyes of that statue," Conan said.

They were only halfway along their return journey when Conan heard Pictish drums and war cries, then, louder and closer, angry Bamula voices. He and Bowenu looked at one another and broke into a run.

Lysenius thanked gods he had not worshipped in many years that the two spells he needed most this night could be cast without giving outward signs.

Outward signs of working magick would alert his Pictish guards. His reputation might daunt them, might hold their spears, arrows, and knives. It would do nothing for the *chakan* sent by Vurag Yan. He saw the creature sitting on its haunches on the other side of the fire, eyes glowing like the coals of the flames of the underworld. At a command from its master, it would be over the fire and its claws at his throat before he could take a deep breath.

The moment he could risk movement or speech, Lysenius resolved, he would put an end to that *chakan* and all others of its kind. Without his pets, the shaman would lose much of his power for mischief.

Lysenius gathered his thoughts, and this time his concentration on the statue in the cave did not slip away. "By the power of the Seven Waters and the Five Mountains, by Iblis, Mitra, Crom, and Set, by the Curse of the Unborn Phoenix—"

The incantation resounded in his mind as though his head had been a cave into which a herald cried messages. He kept his face carefully blank, a mask behind which all the magick in the world might have hidden, and his breathing regular. Even his hands lay in his lap, as motionless as the sleeping puppies he had once shown Scyra when she was a child of five.

In the corner of his mind not given over to magick, Lysenius prayed again. This time it was to no god in particular. It was only a wish that when this night's work was done, he might seem to his daughter as he once had. Not for long, but even a single day of his daughter's former love would be enough.

He could not ask more. Too much lay between them now, and regardless of that, she was a grown woman, no longer a maiden either, if her ghost-voice told the truth. (And had that been the Cimmerian's doing?)

But however much lay between them before this night, he now saw clearly. He might yet find a way to take his vengeance for his wife's death. Gentle as she had been, she deserved that at least. But he would no longer put Scyra in harm's way to gain it. He would take her out of danger first, then fight whatever battles might be needed when there was no longer risk of her being one of his enemies' victims.

Would that he could use the Crystal of Thraz! It would make easier, if not less perilous, this work of animating the statue by sheer will, without a blood-sacrifice.

Lysenius knew the gem was in the tent; he had touched it with his mind. He did not dare bring it out with the grip of that same mind. No outward signs could be allowed to warn the Picts that magick prowled the night.

Also, the Picts did not seem to know the uses of the Crystals of Thraz. Such uses were not in their magicks. The longer Lysenius kept the gem a secret, the better his hopes of using it to some purpose.

"By the fifth element, commanded by the gods for warriors, which is called *mud*. By Ishtar and Semiramis—"

Lysenius stirred enough to lick dry lips and take a deep breath. From far off, something had touched his mind. He opened himself to that touch, and recognized it. He thought a greeting.

In a distant cave in the land of the Snake Picts, a curiously wrought statue quivered on its plinth.

Eighteen

Conan's ears gave him no warning that the statue was on the march. The howling of the Picts drowned out all other sounds, including their own drums, the screams of their wounded and dying, and the war cries of the Bamulas.

So far, none of the Bamulas were down, and even those wounded in the running battle on the hillside were able to fight. It was not hard for a lame man to fight sitting down, and those with bows were making as good practice sitting as they might have done standing. Indeed, against the wall of flesh the Picts offered as they tried to cram themselves into the cave, a blind man could have made good practice.

Conan burst into the fight with a Cimmerian cry that sent echoes crashing about the cave and for a moment rose even above the Pictish howls. He flung his bow and quiver aside and snatched sword and dagger from his belt as he ran.

A Pict leapt over the first line of Bamulas, escaped being spitted on the spears of the second line, and stumbled into Conan. Conan brought his knee up and the Pict howled in a very different voice and doubled in the middle. A dagger-weighted Cimmerian fist crashed down on the back of the Pict's neck, snapping it as a mastiff would a rat.

Two more Picts who tried to follow the first died on Bamula spears and made the rock underfoot still more slippery with their blood. Conan braced himself as enough Picts surged forward to force the Bamulas of the first line back onto the second, and the second onto Conan. He held the two joined lines by sheer barbaric strength, arms stretched wide and sword and dagger outthrust.

"Hold there, you fools!" he roared. "Don't give them any more room to spread out! Force them to come to us a few at a time!"

Bowenu came up on one side of him, and Govindue joined him on the other. They also braced themselves and set their spears to work, darting the already-dripping iron points through gaps in the Bamulas ahead of them. With a sidelong glance, Conan saw Vuona backed against a wall. She had apparently speared one Pict in the belly and was unmistakably hamstringing a second. The Pict looked on her with stark horror, as if expecting her to begin on his manhood next.

The Picts at last gave way under the spears. Before the next attack surged forward, Conan moved up to the first line, then beyond it. Like a rock in rapids, he stood above the next onrush. In moments, his steel dripped red. He hewed, slashed, kicked, howled, and wove a circle of death around himself that snatched more than a

score of Picts from the next attack and strew them
across the floor. Some moaned until Vuona cut their
throats. A few dragged themselves toward the mouth of
the cave, where the archers had clear shots and finished
them.

From Conan to its mouth, the floor of the cave was
now packed with bodies and all but awash with blood.
Very little of the blood came from the defenders, a few
of whom had suffered minor wounds but whose fighting strength was undiminished. There would be no re-
trieving arrows beyond the cave mouth this time, but
this fight was not going to be won or lost by archery.

Indeed, it seemed to Conan unlikely that it was going
to be won by anything at the command of the Bamulas.
The Owls would surely lose so many warriors that in
their wrath, they would turn against Lysenius and
Scyra, and so avenge Conan and his band, but that
seemed about the best a man could hope for now.

It was then that Conan heard a grating sound from
within the cave, as of stone on stone. Then he noticed
that the witchlight had begun to flicker, as would a lantern in a strong wind.

The grating noise came again, louder. Conan looked
down the tunnel and saw a shadow creeping across one
wall. It had no shape he could name, or indeed wished
to name, but every time he heard the grating sound, the
shadow moved.

Then the grating gave way to a long, harsh squeal,
and something more solid than the shadow lurched into
Conan's sight. It staggered to the wall and leaned
against it for a moment, then drew itself upright again
and took another grating step.

The statue was walking toward them! It lurched like a
drunken pirate, but no pirate ever loomed so tall. Conan
saw that what he had taken for a scaly skin was more

likely a close-fitting, all-encompassing coat of mail. The face bore no more expression than before, and those eyes still seemed unnatural in any face asking to be called human.

Conan stood his ground. He really belonged in the rear now, facing the statue. Human flesh and steel wielded by a man might be as futile against the animated statue as it had been against the stationary one. Still, a good push ought to find any weakness in its balance—could the creation rise if it fell?

He saw the staring eyes of the Bamulas. Most of them were looking to their rear rather than to their front. If any of the dead Picts came back to life, they might have an easy victory over his band. The Picts outside might also be victorious if the Bamulas' courage finally broke and the men chose to take their chances with darkness and Picts rather than with this ponderous creation of sorcery.

The Bamulas would have to pass Conan if they ran, and he would not allow that. There were not many things worse than facing death by sorcery, but death at the hands of Picts was among them.

The statue came on. The eyes of the Bamulas could grow no wider. Some of the warriors dripped sweat, in spite of the coolness of the night and the cave. Govindue alone seemed to be keeping his eyes to the front and his spear in his hand.

One of the archers loosed an arrow. It was at such a range that neither the blind, the crippled, nor babes in arms could have missed the target. The arrow struck the statue on its chest—and the arrowhead vanished with a sharp crack and an eye-piercing globe of blue fire. The fire danced on the statue's chest for a moment, then vanished.

A sulphurous reek set everyone coughing and sneezing. The shaft of the arrow clattered to the floor, burned entirely away for a third of its length and charred for the rest. Smoke drifted up from it—until the statue's next step crushed the arrow into a dark smear on the stone.

Even the Cimmerian's courage did not keep him from shuddering at the thought of what would have happened to any man who had touched the statue with naked steel. It must be that steel warred with the magick in the animated image. What about bare hands?

That thought had hardly entered the Cimmerian's mind when a Bamula seemed to have the same idea. He ran forward, leaping as he reached the statue, arms outstretched, hands poised to grip the image's arm. Likely enough, he would try to catch the statue taking a step, off-balance, where even a little extra weight pulling in the wrong direction could topple a man—

The statue was not a man. It proved that all over again in the next moment. The Bamula leapt and gripped one arm. The arm rose, lifting the Bamula with it until the warrior dangled with his feet off the ground, like a child held by a parent's arm.

"Let loose, you cursed fool!" Conan bellowed.

His warning came too late. The statue brought its other arm around, too fast for even the Cimmerian's eye to follow. Its stone hand smashed into the Bamula's temple, and the man's skull cracked like an eggshell. Blood, brains, and pieces of bone showered the others.

The statue now gripped the man with both hands. Conan saw that the killing hand was smeared with red—but the red was disappearing as if the blood was soaking into the stone as fast as water into the sands of a desert. The other hand gripped so tightly that the fingertips vanished into the warrior's dark skin—but no blood flowed.

A moment later, Conan saw that the Bamula was *shrinking*, his skin wrinkling like a grape too long in the sun. As his comrades watched in gape-mouthed horror, the dead Bamula shriveled away until he was only a dried sack of skin dangling from the statue's hands.

And was it Conan's imagination, or did the statue seem a trifle larger, and was there a light in its eyes that had not been there before?

It was not his imagination, and indeed, it made sense—as much sense as sorcery or madness ever could, and this was both! The statue had been brought to life by some spell, most likely a conjuration by Lysenius, without a blood-sacrifice. That did not mean it could do without one forever. If no sacrifice was offered, it intended to take the blood itself.

At least the statue did not seem to be searching for prey at the moment. Another Bamula ran toward it and without a word from Conan, he darted under the reaching arms and rose to his full height behind the statue, unharmed. What he could do there seemed a mystery, if grappling barehanded was as futile as wielding weapons.

But it showed that they could pass the statue and leave it a clear path to the cave mouth, the hillside, and the waiting Picts. Likely, Lysenius had no more command of the statue than he had of the Snakes. Running free, the stone image would slaughter Picts and Hyborians with equal strength, feeding on each life it ended. It would have to be brought down sooner rather than later, and Conan's men could do their part.

Tonight, though, he'd lost to the statue the first of his Bamulas so far! He'd be cursed for a Stygian if he was going to lose more men, not when there were half the Picts in the wilderness for the statue's amusement. While it thus amused itself, he and his people were going to break free of the Picts and continue their journey south. Neither Scyra nor Lysenius would have anything to say about that!

The statue seemed too intent on making its way into the open air to spend any effort in seeking victims. One man actually blundered against it as he tried to duck under the arms, and the hand closed on his hair. The statue made no attempt to draw the man closer, however, nor did it bring the other arm around this time. The man cursed and clawed and ripped his hair from his scalp, but in the end, broke free.

Vuona went, three more men went, and then there was no one at all with Conan save the statue, so close he could almost have touched it with his dagger. He did no such thing; he gathered himself and, like a panther, leapt past it.

He landed rolling on his shoulders, and kicked out with his legs. Both feet slammed into the back of the statue's knees. The image quivered, pain stabbed through the Cimmerian, and the shock jarred him from his toes to the crown of his head. He rolled again and stood, testing first one foot, then the other, to see that they moved properly.

No hurt to him, save the sort of bruises that he could shrug off for now. None to the statue, either. As invulnerable and implacable as ever, it marched over the fallen Picts, pushing aside the low barricade the Bamulas had made of their enemy's bodies. Conan watched to see if it would soak up the blood, bones, and flesh of these Picts, but it only shoved the corpses aside or crushed them under its ponderous weight.

"Too long dead for it, I think," Govindue said. Conan started at the sound of a human voice, and realized that no one had spoken a word since his warning to the now-dead Bamula.

"Be ready to follow me out of the cave the moment that witling wizard's toy meets the Picts," the Cimmerian said. "While they're fighting it, we'll have a better chance to break free than we'll ever have again."

None of the Bamulas looked as if they thought the chance was very good, nor did Conan quarrel with them. But judging by the fear the statue put into him and the Bamulas, the Picts would be driven half-mad. That was no fit spirit for meeting a desperate foe at night—and Conan knew that he and the Bamulas would be desperate to the last degree.

The grating and scraping of the statue's footsteps was fading now as it climbed the boulders. It was almost beyond the witchlight, although Conan would have sworn that it had begun to glow with a light of its own. Soon it would be in the open, visible to the Picts.

"Be ready to run as you've never run before. We won't leave anyone alive, but we won't halt for any laggards, either."

Even the lame met his eyes and nodded. By Crom, this was fine company for one's last battle! If they'd been twenty thousand instead of fewer than twenty, he'd have been ready to clear the whole wilderness of Picts and present it as a gift to the Bossonians.

Lysenius could not have described in the words of any language known to men how he knew that the statue was animated but uncontrolled. Perhaps uncontrollable, at least from this camp, half a day's march from the cave. If so, certainly a menace to more folk than Picts—and even if a menace only to the Picts, that made Scyra no safer as long as Vurag Yan's *chakans* held her in the camp of the Owls. . . .

It was time to go where he was needed. He had never used the spell of the world-walker with so little preparation or so many witnesses. But then, he had never used it to take himself or anything else over such a short distance.

The dangers were two: his being detected while he was raising the spell, and his being followed through the world-walker by any of his guards. The first would catch him helpless; he could only do his best and pray.

As to the second—he much doubted that the statue had brought death to Conan, or indeed to most of the Bamulas as long as Conan was leading them. It occurred to Lysenius that if he wished a war chieftain to wed his daughter, the Cimmerian towered over any Pict—and not only in stature, either. If Conan's band was still alive and fighting-fit, any Picts who followed Lysenius through the world-walker would not live long once they came out at the cave end of the journey.

Lysenius assumed the posture of meditation, which seemed to arouse no suspicion among the Picts. They looked at him casually, then went back to their gambling. One left the circle briefly and returned with several gourds of beer. Its sour reek made Lysenius want to gag.

The names of gods seldom invoked, and never lawfully since the fall of the Empire of Acheron, swirled in his thoughts but did not pass his lips. Nor did any eyes but his see the world about him turn golden—until suddenly the golden spiral was so solid that no one could see Lysenius within it.

A Pict leapt frantically at the golden wall as his comrades flung spears and nocked arrows to bows. The Pict vanished with a cry strangled in mid-flight. As the echoes of his cry died, thunder boomed across the clearing, making the fire dance, the leaves quiver on the trees, and the mage's tent collapse.

Then darkness and silence both returned, leaving a

half-circle of gaping Picts staring at the place where Lysenius had been sitting.

In the confines of the cave, the thunderclap was deafening. Conan heard the Bamulas screaming with the pain in their ears, and he opened his mouth to ease his own. There was still no telling which way the thunder came from. For a moment, Conan feared that the statue had encountered magick, either Lysenius's or the Picts', and met its doom just when it was about to turn from menace to useful diversion.

Then footfalls, the clattering of metal on stone, and a Pictish war cry rose over the fading echoes of the thunderclap. Rose from *within* the cave, back toward the chamber of the statue. Conan snatched his sword from its scabbard and ran toward the chamber.

He had expected to see a whole band of Picts, sent by Lysenius to take his people in the rear. Instead, he saw only one Pict, and of all impossible visitors, Lysenius himself, grappling with the savage. The Pict had just drawn a rusty dagger to thrust into Lysenius's ribs when Conan ran him through.

"You can sheathe that sword," the sorcerer said with as much dignity as any man could contrive under such circumstances. He looked at the dying Pict and wiped a trickle of blood from his own upper lip. "I think only one of them followed me through—"

"I can sheathe that sword in you," Conan growled, "unless you talk fast. What are you doing here? Didn't your daughter's treachery—?"

"Scyra's—*what?*"

The bemusement in the man's voice was either real or consummate artistry. Conan kept his sword drawn but moved back a pace so that it no longer imminently menaced the sorcerer.

"Very well. If there is anything I need to know, best tell me now. That cursed statue has gone out of the cave and will be among the Picts—"

"Oh, gods! It is as I feared. It will not stop until Scyra is dead or the Picts holding her flee farther than we can pursue."

"Crom! I'm willing to listen to you if you talk sense. If you give me nothing but riddles—"

"Please. Let me speak."

The Cimmerian saw the effort it was taking the sorcerer to calm himself, and waited, as little as he liked the notion. He was no friend of sorcerers and seldom of anybody who could not offer a well-wielded sword at his side, but matters tonight might have gone beyond what swords could face. If Lysenius had turned his coat—

It seemed that he had, or at least had given over sacrificing his daughter to his lust for vengeance. It was hard to be sure, harder still to understand what he wished Conan to do. The Cimmerian's fingers itched to ram his sword into Lysenius so hard that the hilt rang against the sorcerer's ribs and the blade stuck far out from his back.

He resisted it. No woman deserved to end as a Pictish slave or sacrifice, even if she had betrayed him, ten times over if she had not. Moreover, Conan knew what chance his band had of winning free without more aid than the statue could give. It was somewhere between scanty and none at all.

Lysenius could hardly make matters worse, and might make them better.

"You've persuaded me," Conan said. "But my men and I will be watching both back and front. You hurl one thunderbolt, or whatever you wield, at us and you won't live to hurl a second."

"That is only just," Lysenius said. His empty voice made Conan wonder if the man was too shame-ridden to have about him what wits his sorcery had left. Sorcerers were a chancy lot, even when they called themselves your friend.

"So be it," Conan said. "Do as you think best, and I'll crawl out and see what our stone-headed friend is doing. Don't be surprised by anything you see me and my people do."

Lysenius managed a wintry smile. "I give you the same message."

Scyra regained her senses to see Sutharo standing over her. His face showed the fatigue of battle and no regard whatever for her. He was a Pictish chief among his warriors, and no care for a woman would enter his thoughts.

No word of what had happened passed his lips either, but Scyra could now listen with waking ears to the wagging tongues about her. The only ones who did not add to her knowledge were the *chakans*, being without speech that anyone except a shaman could understand.

Clearly, her father would be at the mercy of the Picts as long as she was a hostage. It did not matter if she ceased to be a hostage through escape or death; either way would end the Picts' hold over Lysenius.

Whether she escaped or died, however, she vowed one thing before any gods that might listen: Sutharo would not see another sunrise.

It was remarkable how that vow eased her mind. Bound to the litter as she was, she was still able to fall into a light sleep soon afterward.

She awoke to hear, all about her in the darkness, Pictish cries that held more terror than warlike spirit. Her first thought was that the Snakes had returned in such great force that the Owls were about to be overwhelmed. The idea of being slaughtered like a salmon, its brains beaten out on a flat rock, made her stomach heave.

She struggled, unnoticed by guards or *chakans*. Indeed, the *chakans* seemed to be nowhere in sight, although darkness and the forest could still hide menaces perilously close to her. She loosened one hand and one foot from the thongs binding her to the litter and contrived to turn her head to look uphill.

A blue glow poured from the mouth of the cave now, and against it loomed a towering black shape. For a moment she thought it was Conan himself, then saw that the shape moved too slowly and stiffly for any mortal flesh. The statue had come forth, however animated, seemingly with a will of its own and nothing commanding it.

The night suddenly seemed colder and darker than before, and the trees overhead ready to come to life and reach down branches like clawing hands, to pluck her from the litter, lift her high, and rend her apart like a rag doll in the hands of a willful child. . . .

Scyra bit her lip to hold back a cry of despair. She also began casting about in her mind for any spells that she could work, unaided by the Crystal of Thraz, herbs and simples, being spellclad, or by anything else except her own wits and memory.

Before this quest yielded consequences, the Picts had regained enough courage to approach the statue. Or at least one did. Scyra saw him close to the image, both figures dark against the blue glow from the cave. She saw the spear rise, and she could not tell whether in salute or challenge.

Then the statue moved. No longer heavily or slowly, but as swiftly as the Cimmerian himself might have done. One arm gripped the spearhead, and a globe of dazzling blue flame flashed, swallowing both spearhead and hand. The spear shaft burst into flames; the Pictish warrior howled and leapt back.

Not far enough. The statue's other arm gripped his free hand. The pict howled again, this time in mortal agony. The statue jerked him off his feet, holding him kicking frantically. His silhouette began to change, twist, shrink. Scyra watched in horror and awe as the Pictish warrior was drained to a limp sack of skin, then tossed away like a fruit sucked dry.

Horror and awe were also in the cries of the Picts. They drew back, and began hurling spears and shooting arrows from what they doubtless hoped would be a safe distance. Blue sparks flashed all over the statue as the spearheads and arrowheads immolated themselves, and a cloud of reeking smoke began to spread about the figure.

The image took no harm, though, and neither retreated nor advanced. Instead, it suddenly raised both arms, and blue sparks as long as lightning-bolts sprayed from both hands. Its aim was not perfect; some of the sparks left only smoking patches on the hillside.

Others caught fleeing Picts. A blue glow spread around them as they stopped, limbs writhing in convulsion, mouths opened in screams that reached Scyra's ears even through the crackling of the sparks. It was as if each Pict was being burned in a fierce flame at his own stake.

Then the sparks died and only smoke spreading out in a noisome cloud remained. Smoke, and a charred *thing* on the ground.

Scyra had found her spell now. If she could reach out with her mind as she had done to Conan, and if the Picts had not looted her tent—

There. The mind-touch she had sent across the miles had gripped the Crystal of Thraz. She kept her touch exquisitely delicate; this was as difficult as milking adders for their venom to make certain potions mentioned only in scrolls forbidden (and indeed, seldom found) outside Stygia.

Her concentration on the Crystal of Thraz was so complete that she did not notice dark shadowy figures creeping down the slope to either side of the statue.

Conan led his rescue party down the slope in silence, although the statue's thunderbolts broke the darkness more often than he cared for. None came his way. Now he could only hope that the statue's increasing power would draw the whole attention of the Picts, without driving them into panic-flight.

That was what he dreaded, next only to treachery by Lysenius. He had too few men to pursue Scyra and her *chakans* through the nighted forest, even if those few were united. As they were now, they would be divided between his rescue party and those who remained behind to guard Lysenius from wandering Picts, and the Bamulas from Lysenius's treachery.

The Bamulas had learned the art of moving as silently on rocky slopes as in their native jungles. No coughs and hardly a single rattling pebble betrayed the rescue party as it crept downhill. They could have made far more noise and still gone unnoticed amid the thunder of the statue's magick and the cries of the Picts.

Beyond the circle of death cleared by the statue, darkness fell again, and Conan's night-sight returned. He saw a single figure standing beside a tree, and behind it, shadows that did not look altogether human. Was it a fancy of the night and the magick, or was there something lying amid those inhuman shadows?

He would start with the standing figure. At least it seemed human and, from the headdress, a chief. Behead a Pictish war-band by killing the chief, after the band had already been shaken by magick, and one had a good chance of driving the foe into flight.

With hands and whispers, Conan guided the Bamulas with him to the left. There the ground offered more concealment, almost up to the very feet of the standing chief.

Unfortunately, a good number of Picts had also sought the same concealment. Conan found himself at arm's length from a crouching Pict. As he drew back, his hand came down on a twig. In the brief silence, the crack reached the Pict's ears.

He sprang to his feet and the Cimmerian did the same. Conan's dagger swung in a deadly arc, ending in the Pict's chest. Blood and breath sprayed from the man's mouth in silence, and he fell without a cry. But he had a comrade, and that one not only rose but cried out, before a Bamula spear silenced him forever.

Instantly, the slope seemed to grow Picts the way a cave grows mushrooms. All of them seemed to have both wits and weapons with which to meet human foes, and all were between Conan and the chief.

A Cimmerian war yell halted some of the Picts as abruptly as if they had been impaled. Before they could advance again, Conan had seen the thinnest part of their line. He charged it, sword and dagger reflecting unearthly blueness as the statue continued its work. The Bamulas streamed behind and to either side of him, shouting their own war cries and wielding blunted and blood-encrusted spears with the strength of madmen.

The Picts' brief flowering of courage withered. Conan knocked two down by the sheer weight of his massive frame striking at the run. He trampled them underfoot, thrust left with his dagger and slashed right at two more Picts with his sword. The dagger sank between ribs, the sword crippled an arm and laid open a skull. The Pict with the crippled arm died in the next moment as Vuona, of all people, cracked his skull with a Pictish war club.

"What are you doing here?" Conan snarled.

"This is my last chance to be a warrior."

"Or anything else, if the Picts rally while we stand here wagging our tongues!" Conan muttered. The woman seemed unperturbed, and a moment later a swirl of Picts drove between them and both had more important matters on hand.

A Bamula was down, and from the wounds Conan could see, not likely to rise again. But four Picts lay dead around the warrior and a fifth was reeling about with a lamed leg, until Conan's sword cured the man's limp and his every other earthly ill.

Now nothing stood between Conan and the chief. The two men saw this at the same moment—and the chief turned. Conan was up with him in a moment, ready to not only kill the chief, but also to disgrace him forever in the eyes of his warriors and gods by giving him a death-wound in the back.

The chief turned again at the last moment and thrust at Conan with a Gunderman short-sword. The Cimmerian needed to be as nimble as a deer to escape the thrust. By then he was too close to the man to wield a sword, and his dagger was in his other hand.

Conan's fist drove into the chief's face, the sword-hilt weighting the blow like a cestus. The Pict's head snapped back, and his second thrust was wild. It gouged skin over Conan's ribs; he felt blood trickle. He was already moving as the chief drew his sword back for yet another thrust.

This time Conan whirled, dagger in his left hand. The point drove into the Pict's throat, and the third attempt on the Cimmerian's life ended in a gurgle. The short-sword clanged on the rocks, a Pict dove for it, and Conan kicked the man in the face hard enough to snap his neck.

Then no merely human foes menaced the Cimmerian. In front, three *chakans* stood between him and Scyra, bound to a litter. Behind him raged the thunderbolts of the statue, and in the cave, Lysenius was at work.

Even *chakans* might have quailed at the Cimmerian's war cry. It drew the Bamulas still on their feet to their chief, and in a compact mass like a clenched fist, Conan's rescue party advanced toward Scyra.

Nineteen

Lysenius knew what had to be done, likewise how to do it, as soon as Scyra was no longer among the Picts. The only thing he did not know was the price he would have to pay. He did not expect to know that until the moment of payment, which was more commonly the case in sorcery than any sorcerer ever cared to think about.

Now he could only command his mind, fearing that Scyra might already be dead and he would not know it. Surely she would have sent him some final message?

If she had understood what he was trying to do, perhaps. If she had not, or if she had died too swiftly for any spell. . . . And Conan had no ghost-voice from which the truth might be learned another way—

Lysenius groaned. Outside, the statue's thunderbolts seemed to echo that groan.

* * *

Scyra now had both hands and one foot loose enough to be able to free them in a moment. Perhaps not fast enough to escape the *chakans* if they had warning, but with magick, darkness, and enemies all about, their slow wits might not perceive her movements.

She clutched the Crystal of Thraz in one free hand. So far, no one had seen it, let alone suspected its nature, but that could change at any moment. She lay still, commanding her breath to be silent and her muscles to end their futile quivering. Fear was in her, more than she had ever felt before, but also a sense of her own power, which allowed her to control the fear.

Picts no longer stood between her and the hillside, but she had no eyes for the statue. All her attention was on the gigantic living figure storming forward, cutting down Sutharo (she did not dare curse Conan for taking away that pleasure) and striding ahead.

Two of the *chakans* bent to raise the litter. Scyra made ready to jerk hands and foot from the thongs and do battle with the aid of the Crystal when, suddenly, the two bending *chakans* halted. All seemed to be listening to a silent voice.

Then two *chakans* advanced on Conan as the third *chakan* bent, snapping the thongs about Scyra's wrists and ankles as if they were spiderwebs. Fear and hope warred in her, as she understood. Vurag Yan had summoned the *chakans*, two to do battle and a third to carry her off. If she struck at the *chakans* while their minds were linked to the shaman's—

The thought summoned the strength to move. She rolled toward the *chakan* and slapped the hand holding the Crystal of Thraz against one hairy arm. At the same moment, she summoned all the strength of will she had ever dreamed of possessing into putting a single message into the *chakan's* mind.

DEATH.

The *chakan* howled and reared upright. It flung up its hands and threw back its head, still howling, unseeing eyes aimed at the stars. Blood started from its mouth, eyes, and ears, and it began to tremble in all its limbs.

Then its hair began to smolder, and stinking, greasy smoke poured from its limbs and body. It staggered, fell, pushed itself up onto hands and knees and spewed blood. The smoke grew thicker, and Scyra saw hair curling and frizzing to ashes that blew away on a wind that seemed to come from within the *chakan*. The stench grew until she turned her head away and gagged, all but ready to spew herself.

With a final gurgle, the *chakan* fell facedown and lay still. Smoke continued to curl up from the corpse as Conan knelt beside the litter and drew Scyra to her feet. She allowed her head to rest against his massive chest, savoring the pleasure of no longer being alone, but careful to keep the hand with the crystal well away from the Cimmerian's body.

She stepped back from him and saw the other two *chakans* lying dead, their corpses sprouting arrows and spears in profusion. A Bamula lay among them, his head at an impossible angle to his shoulders and one arm torn from its socket.

"I . . . thank you."

"Thank your father, too," Conan told her.

"My—"

"He's doing some wizardly business with that cursed statue. He'll do more once you're no longer among the Picts." He gripped her hand, then recoiled as his fingers touched the Crystal of Thraz.

"Pardon," she said. "It . . . I think it is awake now."

"What are you using it for, besides ill-wishing *chakans*?"

"I was ill-wishing their master, the shaman Vurag Yan. I do not know if the wish reached him through the *chakan*."

Carefully not touching the crystal this time, Conan lifted her onto one shoulder. "Tell me more later, when we've no Picts within stabbing distance."

"You asked."

"So I did, and that's never wise to do with a witch, when you may not like the answer!"

The next moment he was running up the slope, with the surviving Bamulas laboring hard to keep up with his hillman's pace.

Conan carried Scyra all the way to the boulders, then set her on her feet and went to cover the rearguard. This was easy enough, as no Pict dared pass to either side of the statue to approach the cave. A few bold archers were shooting, but making wretched practice against the dazzling thunderbolts from the image.

The reek of sweat joined that of the sulphur and charred flesh as the Bamulas arrived. Conan had just counted the last man in when a new outburst of Pictish war cries split the night.

"Do they never give up?" Vuona asked, trying to put an arm around him. Conan noticed that she had the other arm around Govindue, who was not protesting.

"Not easily," the Cimmerian said and gently removed the woman's arm. "Best we three not all stand together. Even arrows can find such an easy target, and they may not have emptied their quivers of spells."

From what Scyra said, the Picts had little magick left in them, at least for tonight. But from the cries, it sounded as if they had so many fresh warriors that they hardly needed the aid of spells.

Scyra came out and listened to the cries. "The Snakes

have come again, in strength. They are not attacking, though. I think . . . there. Listen."

Conan heard a peculiar, irregular beat, five or six drums all sounding together. The cries faded, leaving the drums to rule the night, along with the thunderbolts from the statue.

"That is the call to a parley," Scyra said. "I think the Snakes will offer the Owls safe passage from the land, in return for an alliance against us."

Conan spat. "That for Pictish intrigues. Will they be fit to stand against us and the statue both?"

Scyra said nothing, only stood closer to the Cimmerian. By the light of the thunderbolts, however, he read the answer in her face.

"Crom! The next time a woman runs through a wizard's door, I'll let him slam it behind her!" He looked down at Scyra. "I hope your father realizes that he's our best hope now."

"What the gods allow him to do will be done."

"Then let's hope they're feeling generous toward both him and us tonight!"

To Scyra, Lysenius seemed to have cast no spells during her absence, except perhaps one on himself. She did not care for the vacant eyes and the slack lips. But with what wits her father had left, he gathered to greet her. His embrace was hearty, though she could feel the chill in his flesh and the trembling in his arms and hands.

"I intend to free us of the Picts," Lysenius said. "With the help of the Crystal of Thraz—"

"I myself must use it if it is to help us," Scyra said.

"Is that still the truth?"

"It was not the truth the first time I said it," she replied. She could not meet her father's eyes. "Now I believe it to be the truth. If you try to bond with it, you may die, and surely your spell will not take effect."

"Why am I not surprised, Scyra, that you lied to me for my own good?" her father asked.

"Perhaps because it was not the first time I did so, although never before in so great a matter," Scyra answered. She raised her eyes, and her heart lifted at the wry smile on her father's face.

"If I cannot use the crystal, then I must find some other means of commanding the statue. For that, I need blood. A warrior's blood, above all."

Conan frowned. It made him look not merely menacing, but terrible. Scyra put a hand on her father's arm, lest he make matters worse by flinching away from the grim Cimmerian giant.

"Why don't you come right out and ask for my blood?" Conan said in a surprisingly even voice. "I thought the statue had already taken enough for itself."

"Not the blood of a man without a ghost-voice," Lysenius said. "I must ask, and pray that you will not shed my blood in reply. It will do you no harm, save by chance."

"Sorcery seems a pretty chancy business, and I've yet to meet wizard or witch who wouldn't lie to advance themselves. Scyra, what say you?"

"I have no truth-sense."

"I didn't ask that. You know your father better than I."

"Yes, Scyra. Speak freely."

"In your place, Conan, I would give the blood."

He nodded, and Scyra knew that the nod was as good as a solemn oath from a lesser man. "How much?"

Lysenius drew a small silver dagger. "Enough to cover the blade of this knife, but it must be from a fresh cut."

"Hack away, Scyra," Conan said. "But be quick about

it. The Picts may gossip all night. They may also attack before we're done with this witchery."

Scyra drew her own dagger, tested the edge on her thumb, then drew a line down the Cimmerian's arm, over bruises, small cuts already clotted over, and half a score of old scars. This man, she realized, had seen more war and battle than any two men twice his age.

The blood welled out, of a normal human color. Somehow, she had been expecting it to be green, or sparkling like certain Nemedian wines, or otherwise apart from nature.

Between offering his blood for a sorcerer's tricks and taking his chances with the Picts, Conan would have preferred to be drinking the cheapest wine in the lowest tavern in Aghrapur. Lacking that choice, and his people likewise, he chose to aid the sorcerer. Three of his men had died already tonight. If the Owls and Snakes made common cause against him, he would be lucky to escape the wilderness with three yet living.

Smeared thin, enough blood to cover the dagger was no great loss. He'd lost as much several times in his youth when his beard began to sprout and his mastery of the art of shaving was yet uncertain.

But giving your true name or anything from your body to some sorcerers gave them ultimate power over you. Power that Lysenius might not gain, and if he did, might not use—but who could be sure?

Conan was sure of one thing. He could slay both Lysenius and his daughter before they could unman him or the Bamulas. If wizardry offered a worse death than death among the Picts, he would choose the Latter.

The thud of Pictish drums floated into the cave. Bowenu came back to report that the Picts had neither fled nor advanced. They seemed in great strength at the foot of the hill and in the forest around it.

"Excellent," Lysenius said. "The more that are on hand, the fewer to impede your passage afterward."

Bowenu looked from Lysenius to Conan, then made to Conan the Bamula gesture of inquiring about madness. Conan shrugged and returned the Bamula gesture for ignorance. This did not seem to raise Bowenu's spirits.

Scyra was trying not to smile at the exchange. Conan shot her a sour look. "What's so funny, woman?"

"Yes, indeed," Lysenius said. "Dignity, please, Scyra. It honors those about to die."

Conan did not ask who those might be. He would know soon enough.

It did not improve his temper to be sitting and waiting while sorcerers who called themselves his friends finished the battle. He wanted to have a hand in the final victory himself, and with Pictish blood on his sword instead of his own on a sorcerer's dagger.

But what a captain wanted for himself had to give way to what those who followed him needed. That was a lesson he had learned in the rude school of the battlefield, as well as from more civilized teachers—Belit not least among them. He could sit and wait without anger now—but not yet with pleasure.

It seemed for a long while that nothing had happened, natural or magickal, except for louder drumming from the Picts. Conan did not much like that; it now sounded less like a parley than like whipping up the courage of warriors for a desperate charge. The thunderbolts still crashed and sizzled, and the witchfire still glowed, but the statue was not all-conquering. Enough Picts past it and—

The air in the cave turned a familiar golden hue and

began to swirl toward the cave mouth as if a giant were sucking it out. Conan went with the golden wind because he had no choice. His strength was as a child's against that wind.

He fetched up hard against a boulder, and for a moment he feared the wind would reach down behind the stone and pluck him out, to carry him onward to the hillside. Instead, he sat with his back braced against the rock, snatching at ankles and wrists as the Bamulas struggled past. One by one he pulled them from the wind, or they found their own niches, or on some outcropping they took a death-grip that the wind could not break.

Conan did not dare move to look at what was happening beyond. He saw the golden light swamp the blue of the witchfire, so that even the blazing thunderbolts from the statue were lost in the new light. The whole mouth of the cave now seemed the mouth of a giant's forge, whose fire burned stark gold.

Everyone in the cave knew the moment when the golden wind reached the Picts. None could have imagined that such screams could come from human throats, even Picts', and there were hundreds of men screaming at once. It seemed to Conan that the wind might be rending the warriors limb from limb, or disemboweling them, or crushing them slowly under massive weights—but they would not have been screaming so had they been crushed.

How long the screaming went on, Conan could never afterward say. In time, the golden wind ceased to blow and darkness returned to the mouth of the cave. It was a deeper darkness than before, and the statue had fallen silent. As cautiously as a cat sneaking past fierce watchdogs, Conan crawled farther out into the boulders, then onto the hillside.

It was the hour of false dawn. When he regained his night-sight, he saw a hillside bare of living Picts. The statue's prey still lay there, now cold ashes, and scattered weapons showed where living Picts had been before they departed.

Departed, along with a good part of the forest at the foot of the hill. The ground there was churned as if by a giant plow, and Conan's eyes made out gaping holes, that looked as if trees two men thick and a hundred years old had been plucked from the ground like carrots.

If Owls or Snakes remained alive, they were either running or, if very hardy, lying in wait on the new edge of the forest. Conan doubted the second. *He* would not have huddled beside that nightmare of churned ground for the wealth of a kingdom. Besides, if they were there, they were out of bowshot of the cave mouth. The statue remained, now lifeless to all appearances, but it would be a bold Pict who dared approach it tonight.

Conan left Govindue to watch the hill and went back inside the cave. It had been long since he'd heard a sound from Lysenius or Scyra. He no longer feared treachery. Instead he feared that they might not be alive to receive his thanks. He and the Bamulas owed to Lysenius their best chance of seeing another sunrise.

Lysenius coughed again. Scyra moistened a clean rag with the last of the water and wiped the fresh blood from his lips.

"It . . . does no . . . good, Scyra. I asked . . . too much of this old body."

"You aren't old, Father."

"It's . . . too late for lies," Lysenius said. His gaze shifted, and Scyra saw a shadow fall on the cave floor. Conan stepped up beside her, then knelt.

"Our thanks, Lysenius. What did you do with the Picts?"

"Oh ... took them with ... the world-walker. More power than ever before. Everyone out there ... gone."

"You must not talk, Father."

"I ... suppose not. Be ... be wiser than I have been."

They waited for Lysenius to speak more, but those were his last words. After a while, Scyra closed his eyelids and crossed his hands—hideously burned where his rings had melted from the power of the spell—across his chest.

"Scyra, gather whatever you need to take and be ready to move out. We can chant for your father or do whatever other rites he needs when we're beyond reach of the Picts."

"They will not come here soon, Conan." She stood up and leaned against him. His arms went around her with unexpected gentleness, which was her great need now.

"But they will come," she went on, speaking half to herself and half into the Cimmerian's chest. "You will not win free of the wilderness on foot. Not with Vuona and the wounded."

"Perhaps not, but the sooner we begin, the better the odds. Come, Scyra. I wouldn't care to waste your father's death."

"Nor would I. But I know better how that may be avoided." She felt him stiffen. "No trust in sorcerers even now, Conan?"

"It's been a long night, woman. Whatever you wish, say it quickly."

"I can command the world-walker. With the Crystal of Thraz, I can send you back to the Black Kingdoms. You need hardly walk a step."

"Nor did those Picts, and where are they?"

"Scattered the world over, all too far to ever see their

homeland again. But that was my father's intent. I intend to see you safely home!"

"The Black Kingdoms—never mind. I must ask the Bamulas. They have more at stake than I do."

"Ask, while I make ready."

Conan was never sure afterward if the Bamulas had come to trust Scyra or if they were so desperate to be done with the Pictish Wilderness that they would have mounted dragons bound for the moon to be out of it. Certainly none, even Kubwande, protested strongly against walking once more through the demon's gate.

"Remember, hold on to me but make your minds blank," Conan said. "Scyra says she can send us anywhere that one of us pictures in our mind. I intend to picture the bank of the Afui—"

"As long as it's the bank," Bowenu said. "I've no wish to swim among the crocodiles."

"I've no wish to repeat myself," Conan said. "Hold your tongue. I will picture the bank of the Afui, and the world-walker should take us there. Anyone who pictures something else may end up there himself, or he may end up nowhere ... or he may kill us all. So think of nothing, not even the beer you'll drink when we get home, and we may just—"

The harsh grating sound of rock against rock filled the air. Something loomed up in the mouth of the cave. Then a shadow stretched out across the blue-lit floor as the statue walked into sight.

"Crom!"

The statue walked slowly, like a man drunk, weary, or sick almost to death. It was blackened, and even burned in places, from the power it had wielded and the blood it had drunk. It also had a new face—the one Conan saw in any mirror.

As one man, he and the Bamulas stood aside as the statue lumbered past and into the cave. It ignored them, and likewise Scyra, who came hurrying out. She stood beside the Cimmerian, who was scowling down at her. He had just noticed that the walls of the cave now showed carvings unmistakably in the Stygian style.

"That—it was not my doing," Scyra said. "The statue and you—your spirit gave you a bond—"

"I am bonded by Stygian magick to that slab of rock?"

"That slab of rock is the image of a mighty warrior of times past. Why should it not bond to the spirit of a mighty warrior of today?"

Conan saw no reason why it should not, and did not suspect Scyra of flattering him. He also saw no reason why, the decision made to depart, any of those here should wait longer on the edge of unleashed magick. Unleashed, and clearly not altogether under Scyra's control.

"You're coming with us—" he began. Her eyes halted him even before her lips formed words.

"I must remain behind here, to cast the spell properly and command it until you are safely passed. If I do otherwise, it could go as much awry as when my father cast it."

"Can you follow us, or at least take yourself to safety?"

"When I have made this cave and my father's body safe, I will think about it."

"Stubborn woman!" He wanted to use harsher terms, but knew they would not move her.

"I think you do not fear such."

The Cimmerian laughed. "Likely enough. I'd not miss Belit half as much if she'd been some docile lap-kitten." He kissed her soundly. "Remember that you're wasted in a wilderness, Scyra, and get yourself out of it as soon as you can."

"As soon as I can—that I swear."

Scyra was as good as her word. The golden wind swirled about them, the cave vanished, and before anyone who remembered the Picts could cry out in fear, they were stumbling along the riverbank they had left. Thunder died away, the dizziness faded, and Conan's band looked about them and saw that they were all present.

All, that is, except for Kubwande. They searched up and down the riverbank until men from the village came and nearly ran away again, thinking they were seeing ghosts. Conan's people proved that they were indeed real and pressed the newcomers into the search parties.

They searched until sunset, when the villagers led them back and filled empty stomachs with porridge, roasted yams, and beer. They asked no payment and were given none; the band had sworn itself to silence about their treasure until they were closer to home.

It was then that Bowenu came over to Conan and made a confession. "Kubwande, I think, had the notion of going back to the chiefs of the Bamulas before the rest of us. At least he said he was going to put in his mind the picture of their Great Hall."

"The fool!" Conan swore. "Scyra told me, and I told all of you—"

"Ah, but Kubwande always thought he was wiser than other men. He wanted me to go with him, and put himself ahead of me in the line. But at the last moment, I stepped forward, so that he was last. Wherever he has gone, he has gone alone."

Bowenu poured himself more beer and wandered off.

After a moment, Vuona rose gracefully and followed him. Govindue watched her go.

"Perhaps I do not want her as a wife after all."

"Perhaps you don't," Conan said. "Perhaps you too need more beer."

Govindue drank, but his eyes were old in his young face. "Do you think we will ever see Kubwande again?"

"No, nor Scyra. She—curse it, one of the few witches who's honest enough to pay for her mistakes, and it had to be her!" Although she had probably not begrudged the price, with her father dead. Conan had seldom seen more acceptance of death in anyone's eyes than he had seen with his last look into Scyra's.

"Honesty in women is like a strong will," Govindue said. He stared as solemnly as a temple image at the smoke swirling in the hut. "It lets them do wonders."

"The only wonder I care about right now is more beer!"

"I will have some more brought," Govindue said solemnly. "But there is a price."

"What?"

"You must allow us to call you by the name of Amra."

Conan looked into the smoke. Belit was becoming a fond, warm memory rather than a pain he felt every day. The name no longer felt strange, and these folk meant its use as an honor.

"As you like."

Govindue wasted no time. He leapt to his feet, snatched a gourd of beer from a girl, and raised it high.

"Hear me, warriors who followed Conan! Tonight and afterward, we name him—*Amra*! *Ohbe* Amra!"

"*Ohbe* Amra!" The other warriors took up the chant, then the villagers, first those inside the hut, then those outside, until the jungle night seemed to throb with it.

Conan looked into the smoke and saw a dark-haired woman welcoming an auburn-haired one into the shadows. He wondered what Belit would tell Scyra, not that he would ever have much chance of knowing ... and here was good beer going to waste!

"Ohbe."

Epilogue

The Pictish Wilderness, many years later:

We listened to Vasilios's tale right through to the end, in a silence broken only by the beat of the rain outside. The last Pictish drums were stilled; the drummers were most likely sheltering from the rain, as much as one wished to believe they had departed.

"How certain is it that the warrior leading the demon-men was Conan?" someone asked. I thought it was Sarabos, but the Black Dragon was sitting as silent as the statue.

Vasilios shrugged. "My mother said that some of the Picts who saw him survived the casting of the demon's gate. A few lived long enough to fight again at Velitrium, and recognized the Aquilonian general."

It would be a very few. Apart from wars, the life of a

Pict had always been harsh and short, perhaps more so since Aquilonia had begun pushing hard through the Marches into the wilderness. Also, memories could play tricks on anyone, Hyborian, Stygian, or Pict.

But it made a good story.

It was not the only story we listened to during the two days we spent in the cave. There was little to do except keep watch for a Pictish attack that never came and search the cave as far as a rope and our scant supply of torches would allow. We found water just beyond the chamber of the statue, so we had little need and less curiosity to know about what might lie beyond in the bowels of the hill.

We were more curious about how soon help would come. Doubtless our company would send for reinforcements when the watering party did not return; we prayed that they would not try to rescue us unaided and fall prey to the Picts.

It was well on into the afternoon of the second day when we heard the Picts drumming again. Then the drums faded, bird and animal calls rose as warriors passed messages back and forth, and the sentries said they could see Picts moving about in the fringes of the trees. (If the story was true, the second growth must have come back thick and fast after the virgin timber was magicked away.)

All this might have heralded an attack, and taboos be cursed, but those with more experience in wilderness fighting said it sounded like the Picts were assembling the warriors for a march. Certainly the noise died away soon enough, and as the silence drew on, the sentries reported that the Picts were gone.

I had just come out to see this for myself when the silence ended in Bossonian war horns. Three times more they sounded, each time closer. Then half a dozen scouts in their green tunics and trousers scampered out of the trees and raced up the hill to us.

We were saved. With our company and those who had joined it, three hundred men were on the way, a force much larger than the Picts usually cared to face at this time of year. We would need to move on swiftly, and there was no more time for investigating the cave, no matter how many torches our rescuers brought, but that was a small loss.

Not so small was the mystery of how the commander at Fort Nyaro—who had sent our rescuers—had heard we needed rescuing. Scouts, sergeants, and captains all said the same thing: a messenger had come in reporting our party beseiged by the Picts at a place he so carefully described that a child could have found it.

No one, however, had actually seen the messenger. A few said they had seen a man who might have been he, but no two descriptions of the man agreed. Also, all did agree that the message had come during the first night of heavy rain—the very evening we found the cave!

A bird could hardly have flown in that rain. Even if it had, it could scarcely have traveled so fast. Nothing on legs—and above all, nothing human—could have carried a message to Fort Nyaro in a single hour.

After a while, I came to realize that I was raising more questions than receiving answers. I was already uneasy; it seemed futile to make others so. I left gathering the wounded and the remaining supplies for the march to the sergeants and walked back to the statue.

Sarabos was already there, sitting cross-legged on the floor, looking at nothing in particular. I stood beside him, and before either of us found words, Vasilios joined us.

"Ah . . . I thought you might be here, Captains. I was hearing of the messenger who wasn't."

"I think the less said about that, the better," I admonished him.

"Well, sir, it's a cat out of the bag and not to be put back in without more trouble than it's worth."

"Judge trouble after I see how much I can make for loose tongues," I said. I wanted to be alone, but Sarabos raised a hand.

"Let him speak his mind."

One did not argue with a Black Dragon of Sarabos's blood, as much as I wished it. "Speak, then, Vasilios, but briefly."

"Oh, it's nothing long. Just that I'm sure I'm not the only one who knows who Captain Sarabos's father is. Others might know, and I didn't want to get their hopes up. I wasn't any too sure myself about that part of the story."

"Which part?" I snapped. "Something you left out?"

"Aye. The story goes that the statue—the statue will come to help when the warrior's blood-kin need it."

I looked at the statue. It showed no signs of having moved a hair'sbreadth, let alone being fully animated. No charred Pictish corpses lay about the cave.

But would it show any traces if all it had done was to send a message that Conan's son Sarabos needed rescuing? That was help, in any sense of the word that gods or men might use.

"I stand by what I said before: the less this is noised about, the better," I said.

"True," Sarabos agreed, rising. "The priests of Mitra are grown rigid and fusty in recent years, not liking magickal mysteries. They might ask us to either cast the statue down or bring it out of the wilderness to one of their temples."

The statue had to weigh as much as two or three warhorses. The idea of hauling that deadweight through the Pictish Wilderness was too appalling to contemplate. I thought impious thoughts about the priesthood of Mitra.

"Except—what if the Picts learn to command it?" I asked.

"If it is bonded to a certain blood, that blood alone commands itself. It and the other children of my—of that blood. And that includes Conan the Second, a good steward of what he inherited, but one who may need some help to hold it."

We looked at one another and at the statue, standing there as we were in the darkness broken only by Sarabos's single candle and my torch. Perhaps it was only a trick of that uncertain light, but I thought I saw that the statue's face had changed its expression. Before, it had shown a grim mask to the world. Now I could have sworn it wore a wry smile, not unlike one so often seen on the face of Sarabos's father-who-could-not-be-named.

That was enough for me. "I repeat, let there be silence about this. It is our duty to the House of Conan."

"Our duty," the others intoned, almost keeping their faces blank. We turned and walked away from the statue, out of the chamber, and up the tunnel to the fading daylight of the outer cave.

TOR
BOOKS The Best in Fantasy

LORD OF CHAOS • Robert Jordan
Book Six of *The Wheel of Time*. "For those who like to keep themselves in a fantasy world, it's hard to beat the complex, detailed world created here....A great read."—*Locus*

WIZARD'S FIRST RULE • Terry Goodkind
"A wonderfully creative, seamless, and stirring epic fantasy debut."—*Kirkus Reviews*

SPEAR OF HEAVEN • Judith Tarr
"The kind of accomplished fantasy—featuring sound characterization, superior world-building, and more than competent prose—that has won Tarr a large audience."—*Booklist*

MEMORY AND DREAM • Charles de Lint
A major novel of art, magic, and transformation, by the modern master of urban fantasy.

NEVERNEVER • Will Shetterly
The sequel to *Elsewhere*. "With a single book, Will Shetterly has redrawn the boundaries of young adult fantasy. This is a remarkable work."—*Bruce Coville*

TALES FROM THE GREAT TURTLE • Edited by Piers Anthony and Richard Gilliam
"A tribute to the wealth of pre-Columbian history and lore."—*Library Journal*